A VISION OF MURDER

Also by
Will Overby

The Novelist

Moon Shadow

Devil's Catacombs

The Island

The Killing Vision

The Human Condition:
Short Fiction and Poetry

Drum

August

A VISION OF MURDER

WILL OVERBY

OWENSBORO, KENTUCKY
2018

WEDNESDAY, OCTOBER 1

2:35 PM

ADDIE RICHARDSON SAT on the worn wooden planks of the front porch, staring out across the weed-choked yard to the gray asphalt lane and the stand of woods beyond that was just beginning to turn a shade of dull green and thought, *Life is shit.*

On the light breeze, which was still hot for this time of year, she caught the sour odor wafting from the garage, the smell that meant Billy Ray was cooking in there and was not to be disturbed. She wondered how far the smell drifted, if any of the neighbors down the road ever noticed it, but she figured they were too far away. It was the whole reason Billy Ray had rented this place way out in the middle of Bumfuck in the first place.

Behind her through the screen door the television

blared an episode of South Park, and she knew Rico and Selena were no doubt sprawled on the sofa in front of it, crashed out from tweaking all night on one of Billy Ray's cookies. She had heard them through the thin walls of the bedroom, grunting and moaning for hours while Billy Ray lay beside her snoring away. She'd had enough of them. Selena never helped in the kitchen, and Addie was tired of dodging Rico's lusty glances and his fumbling hands when Billy Ray wasn't around. Billy Ray was ready for them to go as well, but right now he needed Rico's connections over in Springfield. "Just a few more weeks," Billy Ray whispered to her yesterday afternoon when they were out of earshot. "Once I get in good with the jugglers in town I'll tell him and Selena to hit the road. I promise. They'll be gone before the baby comes."

He kissed her then, his tongue slimy against hers and tasting of cigarettes, and she pulled away as sickness rose in her throat. She hadn't thrown up in weeks, not since she'd passed the first trimester, and she wondered if the sudden nausea had more to do with Billy Ray than with the pregnancy.

She rested her hands atop her swollen belly. The baby had been active earlier, rolling and kicking the way he did sometimes. Her little soccer star, she called him. He was quiet now. Resting she supposed, gathering energy for his next round of practice. She wondered what would happen after the baby was born. Billy Ray said they would get married, that he wanted his son to have a real family, not some make-believe shit, but Addie couldn't help thinking he was saying it more for her sake than the baby's. It was hard imagining Billy Ray settling down, especially now that he was poised to make some real money with those dealers in the city. But the thought of going on this way forever, dodging cops and living hand to mouth, made her feel hollow, as if she were poised precariously over a bottomless pit.

Precarious. That was one of those words she remembered from senior English class. Back when she wrote poetry and had delusions of going to college and making something of herself. Before Billy Ray pulled her back down to earth and grounded her with the lead shoes of empty promises of romance and adventure. Before his teeth turned yellow and soft, when his skin was still creamy and unblemished. Before he was cooking the shit in the garage and telling her they'd have enough money soon to blow off this place and head down to Florida where the real action was.

She'd been listening to this crap for almost two years now. Had moved out with him right after graduation to a little dump of a trailer just on the outskirts of Cedar Hill when he actually had a real job at the toy factory. Defended him to her parents when he got fired for testing positive for marijuana in a random drug test. Followed him out here to the country and tried to overlook his growing paranoia and possessiveness.

But now, maybe it was time to break away. She could go back to her parents' in town. Stay there at least until the baby was born. It would give her a chance to clear her head, and maybe then she would know what she needed to do. Her mother had already offered to help with the baby, and she knew her dad would be happy to have her home. And there wouldn't be the possibility of the baby being harmed by all these stupid chemicals around the house.

She needed to go to town today anyway. Maybe she would stop by and see her mother. And maybe she would feel her out on the subject. If there was a chance Addie might move back home, she was sure they would welcome her back with relief. Her dad had never liked Billy Ray, even though he had no idea what Billy Ray was really doing these days. It was almost as if Daddy had seen through Billy Ray's shell to the lifeless soul underneath from the beginning, something Addie had been too close to comprehend. Mom and Daddy would know what she needed to do, especially if she told them the truth. The last thing they would want was their grandchild being raised in a crack house. Billy Ray might cause a fuss at first, but she figured he would soon tire of it and go back to concentrating on getting in good with the folks in Springfield. And if there was a God, maybe Billy Ray would soon be out of the picture anyway, either in jail or in the ground.

Filled now with a sudden sense of purpose and re-lief, she stood and stretched. The sky was a deep blue, almost violet, and devoid of clouds. An endless, perfect dome. It was a great day for a drive, and it would be good to get away from here and consider the possibilities that now appeared in front of her. Maybe she had a real future after all. And maybe Billy Ray wasn't part of it.

Inside, Rico and Selena lay on the couch, wrapped around each other but keeping their gaze on the television. On the coffee table was a bag of weed and some rolling papers and an ashtray full of cigarette butts and ashes. The room reeked of pot and stale sweat. "I'm going into town," Addie told them.

"Pick up some Doritos," Rico said, not looking at her. "And some Cokes. The *real* stuff not that off brand you usually get."

Addie frowned at him. "Sure." She left them and made her way down the hall to the room she shared with Billy Ray. The bed was in disarray, and she thought briefly about straightening it up but dismissed the idea. She might not even sleep here tonight if the conversation with her mother went well. She might only come back here to pack up her clothes then leave for good. There was nothing else worth taking, nothing she couldn't replace. She stepped into her flip flops and grabbed her purse off the closet doorknob. In her wallet she'd managed to hide fifty dollars from Billy Ray, and she hoped to use that on things for the baby. It might not go far on new stuff, but if she was lucky she might be able to snag some first-rate used things from Goodwill.

She pulled the keys from her bag and swept through

the living room, not giving Rico and Selena another glance, and emerged back into the early autumn afternoon. The air now smelled of pine and the rich earth of the forest floor across the road. Maybe Billy Ray was finished for the day.

She approached the side door of the garage and knocked lightly on the foil-covered window. "Billy Ray?" She eased the door open with a creak and the pungent odor assaulted her like a slap. She covered her nose and mouth with her hand. "Billy?"

Billy Ray was sitting in a metal folding chair, his back to her. His blond hair looked dry and stiff as straw. He was bent over, tending to something on the floor. He half-turned toward her. "Don't come in here! You know you're not supposed to come in here while I'm working!"

She took an automatic step back. "I'm sorry. I'm going into town and wondered if you needed anything."

"I don't need nothing," he said. "Close that door."

She backed out of the garage and latched the door. Fuck him, anyway. He was making this easier all the time.

The Jeep Cherokee started on the second try, and as she pulled out onto the narrow lane she couldn't help but feel she was heading toward something fresh and new, not just an excursion into town. The radio was tuned to that country station that Billy Ray liked, and Addie turned the dial until she picked up the hard rock station in Springfield, the one that played the edgy stuff that Billy Ray said sounded like chainsaws cutting through rocks. She made the turn onto the highway at the end of the road and headed toward Cedar Hill, cranking up the radio volume as she did so. Today wasn't going to be about Billy Ray.

In town she stopped at the Goodwill first and sorted through the selection of baby boy clothes. There were lots of cute things, many of them looking as if they'd never been worn. She picked up a onesie with appliqued frogs, but then put it back on the shelf. It was only a few weeks before he would arrive and he would need something warmer. In the end she chose two pairs of footie pajamas and a package of tiny socks, but she couldn't resist the short-sleeved T-shirt with Cookie Monster on it. Maybe he would be big enough for it by the spring.

Back in the Jeep, she headed down the strip toward the residential section of town, and on a whim she whipped into the Hardee's and splurged on a cheeseburger and fries, then sat in the parking lot wolfing them down. She hadn't had anything that didn't come out of a can in a long time, and the salty fries were like heaven. Apparently the baby thought so, too, because he started turning flips inside her. "Calm down, little man," she said, rubbing a hand over her belly. "Mommy plays her cards right, you'll be eating good all the time."

She sank back into the seat and popped the last bite of the cheeseburger into her mouth. Across the parking lot in the strip mall was a tiny boutique she hadn't noticed before today. *Baby & Me*. It looked prohibitively expensive, but what the heck. Maybe they had a clearance rack.

She took a glance at herself in the rearview mirror and climbed out of the Cherokee. She was halfway across the lot before she remembered she hadn't locked it. She aimed the fob and squeezed the button, but nothing happened. The batteries must be dead. Whatever. There was nothing of value in the Jeep anyway except a pair of Billy Ray's hunting boots. And he was so wrapped up in cooking meth she doubted he would want them anytime soon.

She pushed through the shop door with the tinkling of a bell. The place was fresh and meticulous and smelled of vanilla, and Addie was suddenly aware of her own raggedy cutoffs and faded T-shirt, and she wondered if she smelled like Billy Ray's garage. Shelves of bright tiny clothing and shoes stretched along the walls, and farther back she spotted a lone rack with a "Sale" sign. She headed for it.

An older woman, probably in her late forties, looked up from where she sat behind the sales counter. "If I can help you find anything, let me know." She wore reading glasses and held a paperback in her lap.

"Thanks," Addie said. "You been here long? I don't remember seeing this place before."

The woman closed her paperback and set it in the counter. "We've only been open about a month." She smiled and slipped off her glasses. "When are you due?"

Addie instinctively placed a hand across her stomach. "Really soon. Halloween."

"Know what you're having?"

Addie smiled. "Boy."

"Your first?"

Addie nodded. "I'm scared to death."

The woman smiled, stepping around the counter. "Well, I've got three boys, and I can tell you the scary part is when they reach their teenage years." She held out her hand. "Carol."

Addie shook the woman's hand. "Addie." She looked around. "You have a nice place here."

"Thanks," Carol said. "Always been a dream of mine. And now that the youngest has started college, I've got the time to devote to it."

Addie sorted through the clothing on the sale rack. There was a powder blue suit with a yellow bunny on the jacket lapel. It would be perfect for Easter. She looked at the price tag and tried to keep her eyes from bugging. Even on sale it was too much. Besides, she didn't even know if it would fit him by then. She tried to hide her disappointment as she hung it back. "So many cute little things," she said.

"I love babies," Carol said, scrunching her face. Addie half-expected her to let out a squeal. "Is your husband excited?"

Addie looked back at the clothes. "I'm not married.

My boyfriend. . . I guess he's excited."

Carol covered her mouth. "I'm sorry. I've got to learn to stop assuming everyone is married."

Addie laughed. "It's all right."

"Different times now," Carol said.

Addie took one last glance at the little blue suit and gave Carol a quick smile as she headed back toward the front door. "Well, thanks for letting me look around."

"My pleasure," Carol said. "Come again."

Outside, the sun was bright and intoxicating, and Addie wished she'd remembered her sunglasses. If she wasn't careful the light would give her a migraine.

She had just stepped off the curb toward the Jeep when she heard a small whimper coming from behind her. She turned and glanced up and down the walkway in front of the line of shops. Way at the other end of the strip mall a young woman and a little girl were heading into Kmart, but there was no one closer. She turned back toward the parking lot and heard it again. Louder this time, but still only a whisper. "Help me."

The voice had come from a shadowy corridor running between two shops on the strip, a narrow alley that opened up to the back of the shopping center and an isolated parking lot beyond. Addy took a step down the passageway. "Hello?"

"Help."

Was that a woman? Or a man? Or a child?

Addie moved farther down the corridor. "Are you hurt?"

The voice had gone silent. Addie strained her ears but she could only hear the traffic from the roadway and the hum of the building's HVAC system.

She reached the end of the passage and glanced at the cars in the lot. This must be where the shopping center's employees parked. Beyond the vehicles were two rusting dumpsters set next to a small grove of Bradford pears. "Hello?"

Nothing. Had she imagined it? She pulled her phone from her purse. Maybe she should call the police.

She had just keyed in 9-1-1 when something slipped over her head and around her neck. The phone clattered to the pavement. She grabbed her throat. A cord. Tightening. She couldn't breathe. Her fingers dug at the cord. She was vaguely aware of someone behind her, could feel arms straining as the cord became tighter and tighter.

She kicked her leg back, and her heel connected with something solid and fleshy. A startled breath burst from her attacker. She kicked again, and this time she missed. Circles of light erupted in her vision.

All her thoughts narrowed to one primal, panicked focus – to breathe. *To breathe. To breathe!*

And then everything went dark.

THURSDAY, OCTOBER 2

5:25 PM

JOEL WHEELED THE TRUCK into the drive behind
Dana's Corolla and shut off the ignition, listening
to the tick of the engine as it cooled. God, it was
good to get home. After a full day of stringing cable,
listening to customers complaining about disconnects,
and putting up with his brother Wade's bullshit about
his latest conquest, he was looking forward to kicking
back in the recliner with a cold beer and just relaxing in
front of the tube.

Outside the air was hot and stagnant in the late afternoon sun, and the leaves on the maple in the front yard
were just beginning to yellow. He brushed his boot over
the grass next to the concrete driveway. The yard would
need mowing this weekend, and it had to be done be-

fore the forecasted rain moved in Sunday – a real gulley-washer they were saying.

Dana emerged from the screen door, drying her hands on a dish towel. "'Bout time you got home. I was starting to worry." She tucked a strand of blond hair behind her ear. "I made some spaghetti."

"Had some last-minute paperwork to get out of the way," Joel said, trudging toward the front steps. "Then Wade wanted me to run him by the liquor store before I dropped him off."

He looked at her standing there on the porch, marveling at how beautiful she was with her light hair and porcelain skin. Even more so now that her belly was round with his child. It just didn't seem possible that only two years ago he was a lonely, pathetic bachelor with nothing but an empty old farmhouse waiting for him at the end of the day. Now here he was with a wife, a daughter on the way, and a nice home in the suburbs. Life just didn't get much better.

Dana stood at the edge of the porch, and Joel stopped on the second step so they were closer in height, so his considerable frame didn't overpower her slighter one. He leaned forward and kissed her lips, and she wrapped her arms around his shoulders and pulled him close. "Hi," she said.

"Hey," he said. He could sense the colors of her day coming through with her touch – a rich symphony of her third grade students and fragments of conversations with other teachers and a general feeling of contentment. "Good day?"

She nodded. "Better now."

He rested a hand on her stomach. "How's Sofia?"

"Not as active as yesterday, thank God. I thought she was going to puncture my bladder last night."

He found it odd but not totally surprising that he could sense nothing of the baby's thoughts, even when he and Dana lay in bed with their bare stomachs touching and he could share the kick and fluid movement of little feet. He wondered if Dana's skin somehow acted as a barrier to filter out his impressions from the baby or, more likely, whether right now his little girl was simply an empty slate with no memories or fears or thoughts other than being warm and comfortable. And he also wondered, as they both had as soon as they discovered Dana was pregnant, if the baby would share their abilities. But at least if she did, she would have two loving parents to guide her through the discovery. She wouldn't be left alone and fearful as Joel had been.

He bent down and pressed his cheek against Dana's abdomen. "Daddy's home," he said, and he something – a foot or a fist – streaked across his jaw.

"Well, now you've done it," Dana said. "You've gone and woke the baby."

"Sorry." He leaned up and kissed her again. "Let's go in. I'm starving."

* * *

When he and Dana had decided to marry, Joel knew he wanted to get rid of the old home place where so much bad history lay. It was not only corrupted by the abuse he and his brother Wade had endured growing up there, but it also served as a reminder of that horrible evening two years ago when he and Dana had almost lost their lives to the psychopath who'd managed to outwit every law official in the state. It was not a happy place, and certainly not a home in which he wanted to raise a family. Likewise, Wade had no affinity for the house, and they'd placed it in the hands of a realtor. It sold within a month, and with his share of the proceeds, Joel put a nice down payment on the modest brick ranch on Acorn Lane in the Oak Ridge subdivision. It was good place to make a new start, to begin a life so far removed from his old one that he had become a different person. And he'd not realized until after moving out of his mother's house how deeply the ingrained memories had kept him flattened and inert through the years. Coming to the house in Oak Ridge had been like opening the windows to the fresh spring breeze after wintering in a dark cellar. He felt lighter. Unburdened. And clean. There was no menace here, no evil lurking within the woodwork. Whoever lived here before had a contented life full of love and happiness. One step through the front door and he knew it immediately. This was the atmosphere he wanted Sofia to grow up in. Especially if she inherited her parents' gifts. He didn't want her haunted by the past.

Compared to him, Dana had grown up in a fanta-syland, raised by two loving parents in a middle-class neighborhood in town. The fact that Frank and Bonnie were sensitives themselves was beside the point. Dana never knew the hell of avoiding a raving, drunken step-father, the burden of watching a mother wilt over the years like a delicate blossom cut off and left in the blaz-ing sun. She never knew the pain of being tossed across a room like a rag doll or the panic of having to hide stained underwear after a wet dream to avoid being humiliated. Never knew the relief of having that lunatic finally obliterated in a collision with a train. Yet in spite of their different upbringing, Dana also sensed the peace and calm embodied within this house; moreover, she understood its importance to Joel and how much he needed this sanctuary, even if it wasn't in one of the more established neighborhoods near the heart of town where she dreamed of living. She had put that desire on hold for the moment – for him – and when he focused on that thought it made him physically ache with love for her.

She forked out the spaghetti on a plate and held it out to him. "Your homemade sauce?" he said, taking it from her.

"Of course. No canned stuff in this house."

He grabbed a beer from the refrigerator and plopped down at the table. "Well, I never know when you might decide to get lazy." He grinned at her and she stuck her tongue out at him. He twisted the top off the beer and took a long sip. "Remember the first night you were going to cook spaghetti for me?"

She frowned, filling her own plate with noodles. "How could I forget?"

Joel twirled the pasta around his fork, remembering the bag of groceries hitting the floor, the cans of tomatoes rolling across the linoleum. The arm of that maniac wrapped around Dana's neck as he pulled her out the screen door. . .

Dana set her plate on the table and settled into her chair. "Let's don't talk about that now. Let's just enjoy our dinner."

He gave her a smile. "Sorry. I can't help but think about it sometimes." He stuck a forkful of spaghetti into his mouth and savored the taste.

She reached across the table and dabbed his face with her napkin. "You've got sauce in your goatee, Mr. Roberts."

"Thanks." He tore off a piece of garlic bread and popped it into his mouth. "I asked today about taking that week when the baby comes. Betsy said as long as there's no emergency it should be fine."

Dana shook her head. "What kind of emergency could the cable company have? A flood of customers needing HBO? Somebody can't watch the pay-per-view wrestling match?"

Joel shrugged. "I guess if somebody got sick or something. I don't know. She just said if something happened I might get called in." He looked at her. "I'm not going to worry about it. Nothing's gonna happen."

"Well," Dana said, mopping at her spaghetti sauce with her bread, "Mom will be here to help, too, so if you do get called in, it won't be a big deal."

"It'll be big to me," Joel told her. "I want to spend as much time as possible with my girls."

She grinned at him. "Aw, that's so sweet. You're such a goof." She took a bite off the slice of bread. "How were things with Wade today?"

"Oh, you know Wade. I got to hear all about what he's planning to do with his new girlfriend this weekend. Apparently he's rented a houseboat over at the lake." He stopped and shoveled a forkful of spaghetti into his mouth, and his face flushed as he remembered Wade saying he was going to "fuck her on every available surface." There were some things about his brother that Dana just didn't need to hear.

"We should do that sometime," Dana said. "Sounds like fun."

"I don't know the first thing about navigating a boat."

"So we just stay moored up in the harbor," she said, reaching out and running a finger along the back of his hand. "Who says we have to go anywhere?"

Her touch was an electric current through his skin, and a smile played on his lips. "We should probably wait 'til after the baby comes."

"Some weekend when Mom and Dad can keep her and we can be on our own."

"Yeah."

She grinned at him and went back to cutting up her noodles with her fork. "Don't forget I've got a doctor's appointment tomorrow. Not many more of those before the big day."

Joel frowned. "I wish you'd reminded me earlier so I could have asked off to go with you."

"It's not a big deal," Dana said. "They'll just check my blood and listen to Sofia's heartbeat. It's all routine."

He was amazed at how calm she had been through the pregnancy. When they first found out, Joel had been elated. Then terrified of the looming responsibility. Then afraid something would go wrong. He still worried about Dana – after all, she was so petite, and her swollen belly was almost half as big as the rest of her. He had gone to the first several appointments with her, and after being reassured by the doctor that Dana was healthy and more than capable of bringing forth a child, he had relaxed a bit. Still, he wasn't sure about this whole parenting thing, and he worried constantly whether he was competent to be a good dad. But then his brother had done it, and even as dysfunctional as Wade's household had been, Joel's nephew had still turned out okay. At least so far.

Dana looked at him, knowing what was going through his head. "Don't worry so much, Joel. Everything's going to be fine."

* * *

They spent the evening relaxing in the living room, Joel sprawled in the recliner nursing a beer and staring at the television and Dana curled on the sofa as best she could, lost in a book about the first year of a baby's life. He watched her – marveling at her light hair, the tiny freckles sprinkled across the bridge of her nose, the delicate fingers as they turned the pages – and wondering as usual if Sofia would possess those traits of Dana's that Joel found so mesmerizing. He hoped she would be slender and petite like Dana and not large and ungainly like himself. They had an image of her from the ultrasound, and though it was fuzzy and small, it was clear enough to see her high cheekbones and full lips. Clear enough to see that she was perfect.

Sometimes when he awoke early and couldn't go back to sleep, he wandered down the hallway to the nursery and turned on the nightlight that threw a scattering of stars across the walls and ceiling of the room. He sat in the rocker and wondered about the daughter that would soon occupy this space. This is where she would sleep and play and dream. Where she would come to find solace. Where she would one day have slumber parties with friends, and they would giggle all night and whisper about boys. Where she would cry over her first heartbreak. Where she would imagine her future. Where she would do her homework and maybe struggle with math or history. And always, he saw himself here with her, laughing with her, crying with her. Sharing everything with her. The thoughts of her brought joy and terror and peace all at once. Sometimes he slept, sitting there in the rocker, and dreamed of her, of chasing after her while she giggled and squealed, but he could never quite reach her, could never quite see her face. And when he would wake, frustrated and disappointed, he would remember that he would be gazing upon her in just a few short weeks, and a thrill would shoot through him.

And now, he continued to watch Dana, wondering if she felt these same things, knowing that surely she did, and unable to put into words all that flowed through him. So he said, stupidly, "Whatcha thinking about?"

She looked up at him and smiled. "Thinking about how this time next year we'll be looking for a Halloween costume for a little girl."

He rubbed a thumb across the label on his beer bottle. "I'm seeing a princess."

She looked back at her book. "Maybe."

"You don't sound too enthused."

"It's a year away, Joel. She's got to get here first."

He laughed. "You're right." He reached over and grabbed her toes, fondling them through her socks but feeling nothing from her. He had noticed lately that he wasn't picking up sensations from her as clearly as he used to. Where once he experienced images and emotions as sharp and vivid as if they were happening to himself, they now came to him muddy and fleetingly as though remnants of half-remembered dreams. He wondered if the pregnancy had something to do with that and whether it would change once the baby came.

Once they were settled in bed and Dana was propped on the pillows she was sleeping on these days, Joel turned on the television and leaned against the headboard to catch the news. And the news was gruesome. A body found in a dumpster behind a strip mall here in Cedar Hill. A young woman, almost nine months pregnant, the baby ripped from her womb and nowhere to be found. No suspects and very few clues. He switched off the television and sat staring at the blank screen.

Beside him, Dana whispered, "Oh, God, that's terrible." She looked at him. "How could anyone do such a thing?"

He shook his head. "I don't know." He took her hand, feeling her concern and trying to conceal his own horror from her. "They'll catch whoever did it. Surely somebody saw something, knows something."

But deep within simmered doubt, as if he'd been standing in a hot shower and the water had suddenly turned ice cold. He squeezed Dana's hand, felt her churning fear and projected his own reassurance back at her.

She intertwined her fingers with his and gave him a quick kiss on the lips. "I know what you're trying to do." She smiled. "I'm all right. It was just a shock, that's all."

"I don't like you to be upset."

"I'm not upset." She reached over and turned out her lamp. "Go to sleep."

He rolled over against her and cradled her belly with his arm. "Good night, girls," he whispered. And in moments he was drifting away, chasing his daughter through a field of yellow daisies and butterflies.

* * *

10:35 PM

Dana lay awake, staring at the ceiling and listening to Joel snore beside her. It amazed her how quickly he could fall asleep. One moment he would be talking to her in a lucid conversation, and the next he would be completely out of it, sometimes drifting off mid-sentence. She envied the ease with which sleep over-took him, especially these days when she just could not get comfortable in any position. She sighed and careful-ly lifted Joel's heavy arm from around her abdomen, then remained frozen as he rolled away from her, mum-bling something before settling back into his rhythmic snoring. She slid out of the bed and made her way through the dark toward the hallway, cringing as the floorboards creaked and popped.

The past few weeks she had barely slept because of the pain in her back, a fact she had managed so far to keep from Joel. Instead, she spent most nights either on the sofa watching old movies and infomercials or sitting in Sofia's room, always careful to sneak back to bed before Joel awoke. She knew Joel sometimes sat in the nursery early in the mornings, too; she had found him dozing in the rocker a time or two, sitting there in his underwear, and once he had been holding a stuffed yellow bear. But so far he'd managed to sleep through her bouts of insomnia, and she hoped that would continue. He would just worry about her, and she didn't need any more of that right now.

She stood in the hall, trying to decide whether to head to the couch, to the kitchen for a glass of milk, or to Sofia's room. She opted for the couch, where she could at least stretch out and get comfortable. Maybe if she left the television off she might miraculously get some sleep. She paused just inside the living room and adjusted the thermostat. The house was stifling. The autumn had so far been extraordinarily warm, and the unusual heat was making her miserable. When she heard the air kick on, she shuffled on into the room and collapsed on the sofa, hoping the movement wouldn't give Sofia a bout of hiccups.

She lay on her side, feeling the pain subside, and closed her eyes. Even this far from the bedroom she could hear Joel snoring, and she smiled to herself. She wondered sometimes whether Joel would keep Sofia awake when she arrived. Dana herself was accustomed to it, although it had been a hard adjustment the first few months of their marriage. But then there had been many adjustments during that time, not the least was learning to live with someone other than her parents.

When she had first seen Joel at the group meeting that hot summer two years ago, she never pictured herself falling in love with him. He was such a big guy, not particularly attractive, and introverted, too, which she first took for arrogance. But as she worked to draw him out of his shell, his shyness gradually dropped away, and she began to find his quiet nature endearing. And she discovered a desire within her that went far beyond the physical. Here was a man who liked her for who she was, from whom she didn't have to hide her peculiar abilities for fear of scaring him off. A genuinely good guy who understood the pain of growing up "different." A man she was comfortable with and whose company she truly enjoyed. Her parents felt the same, especially her father, who prided himself on being an excellent judge of character and had never thought of any guy as being worthy of his little girl. But after the encounter with that madman when Joel saved her life, her father took her aside and told her, "Dana, you need to marry him." And so she did. She knew she would never find anyone like him again, and this was one chance she was not going to give up.

When she first discovered she was pregnant, she had been surprised. Her and Joel's size difference meant that sometimes their lovemaking was a little unconventional; positions conducive to baby-making tended to be uncomfortable for both of them. She was also a little disappointed; after all, she and Joel had only been married a few months. They'd not even had time to settle in together yet. Neither of them seemed ready for parenthood. And she wondered if physically her body was even capable of carrying a child. She'd always been tiny, and the idea of a baby growing inside her was terrifying, not to mention the thought of childbirth.

It was this combination of feelings that had led her to keep the pregnancy secret from Joel for two weeks while she sorted things out in her head. Two weeks in which she agonized over possibilities and choices. Two weeks in which she carefully guarded her thoughts from Joel lest a stray touch bare the truth before she was ready to disclose it to him. Finally, she told him over dinner one night, and he was ecstatic. He immediately began clearing out the room that would be the nursery, and he constantly babbled about things they would do as a family once the baby arrived. His joy had been infectious, and Dana's earlier fears were swept away and forgotten.

Not that it had been the first time she had kept her thoughts from him. Living with a sensitive who could see into her thoughts with a touch of his hand had made her cautious. Much different from growing up with parents who could only receive impressions from objects and places, as she herself could. Back at home she'd only had to hide physical things – notes from a boy, a pair of daisy earrings she'd lifted from that little shop in the mall – items that were easily concealed or hidden in plain view among the clutter of her room. But hiding thoughts meant she'd had to build a fortress in her mind that walled off certain thoughts or memories, things she forced herself to forget and keep out of sight from wandering eyes. She'd been overwhelmed with guilt at first; after all, how could you build a marriage on trust while you were hiding aspects of your life? But in the end she decided she wasn't deceiving Joel so much as protecting him from knowledge that would only burden and sadden him. She was doing it out of love. And that's what a marriage was all about, right?

Her parents, Frank and Bonnie, were over the moon about her pregnancy. Dana remembered how her mother had gushed about baby clothes and toys and outfitting the nursery. "We'll buy all the furniture for you," she said, "and your father will put it all together. You and Joel won't have to do a thing." Dana had thanked them profusely, but inwardly she groaned. Bonnie had always been a hoverer, and Dana cringed at the thought of her mother trying to oversee everything from Sofia's wardrobe to her diet. Not that Frank was much better; he'd apparently already started a college fund. And when Dana expressed her frustrations to Joel, he always countered with, "Stop being so hard on them. It's their first grandchild. Of course they're going to be excited."

Everyone was excited except Dana. While she was no longer afraid of the physical aspects of childbirth, she dreaded parenthood. Dreaded more sleepless nights and unending weariness. Dreaded losing her own identity to becoming nothing more than Sofia's mother and Joel's wife. She was just coming into her own as Mrs. Roberts, whom all the third graders adored and the other elementary teachers envied. It just wasn't fair. And yet, even as she burned with defiance, she was at the same time racked with overwhelming guilt. How could she, Dana Marie West Roberts, who so loved kids and teaching not be excited at the impending birth of her own child? She had talked to her OB/GYN, Dr. Connolly, about these feelings, and as a mother herself, Dr. Connolly assured Dana that this reaction was not abnormal. "Your hormones are working double-overtime," she told her. "You're naturally going to feel emotional during this time, and it's understandable that some of it will come out as resentment and guilt." But Dana wasn't so sure. And so she hid these fears from Joel, hoping that the front she projected as an excited mother-to-be was convincing, hoping that by pretending to be overjoyed she could make it so.

And now she stroked her belly as tears welled up in her eyes. "I'm sorry, baby," she whispered. "I wish you had a mom that wasn't so crazy."

FRIDAY, OCTOBER 3

11:45 AM

LIEUTENANT MIKE HALLORAN sat at his computer, clicking through the crime scene photos of the Richardson girl's murder and wishing to God he had a cigarette. What the hell had happened to Cedar Hill in the past couple of years? How had a quiet little college town become such an epicenter for depravity and violence? How had the previous decade of stray dog reports and occasional shoplifting and party noise complaints given way to kidnapping and murders and disappearances? This was not what he had signed up for. Not at all. And even after that nasty business two years ago, he'd hoped he'd seen the worst of his career. Now that was looking tame compared to this.

His partner Greg Brooks stuck his head in the door. "How's it going?"

Halloran clicked out of the photos and leaned back in his chair. "Nothing new. How'd it go with the boyfriend?"

Brooks slipped into the worn chair opposite Halloran's desk. "'Bout the same. I'm confident he doesn't know anything."

Halloran nodded and reached over for his coffee cup. The contents were cold, but he took a sip anyway. "Yeah, that's a dead end."

Billy Ray Fields was devastated, and not just because his meth lab had been busted. When Halloran and Brooks had first questioned him, he'd barely been coherent. He blamed himself for letting Addie go to town on her own, for arguing with her just before she left, for running his operation all that time while she begged him to stop. He pleaded for news of the baby – asking them repeatedly whether it was possible his son could survive being cut out his mother's womb and for how long. Yes, Halloran had assured him, it was possible. Addie Richardson's pregnancy was almost full-term, and with the appropriate care there was no reason to doubt the baby might still be alive somewhere. And with that sense of hope, Billy Ray had opened up about his meth operation, including his plans to get in with the people over in Springfield. A few disclosed names and the cops in Springfield had busted a drug ring operating throughout the city. Billy Ray's loyalty apparently had its limits.

The two housemates had been little help. Rico Garcia was taken in for possession and an outstanding warrant from Jefferson County, Missouri, for failure to appear; Selena Ramirez was arrested for obstruction of justice when she barricaded herself in the bathroom and tried to flush a bag of weed down the toilet. These were petty crimes; Garcia had been extradited back to Missouri and Ramirez sent to minimum security lockup, but they would both be back on the street next week. And while they acknowledged there had been no real friendship between them and Addie Richardson, neither had any motive or opportunity to murder her.

"It's *all* looking like a dead end," Brooks said, frowning. "What do you think about Billy Ray Fields' drug connections?"

"I don't know," Halloran said. "What reason would they have? They all stood a chance of making some bucks off him."

There was a lot that bothered Halloran, even more so than the child abductions and murders two years ago. Those had been horrific and sad, orchestrated by one sick fuck that knew how to manipulate the system. The Richardson girl's killing was just barbaric, almost animalistic, as if committed out of extreme rage. It made Halloran's skin crawl.

The call had come in around five o'clock from Carol O'Dowd, the owner of a small boutique in the North Plaza strip mall. She was hysterical. She'd taken the day's garbage out back and found Addie Richardson sprawled in the dumpster, her abdomen splayed open.

The girl had been in the shop not two hours before and now she was dead, carved up like a side of beef and left to rot with the garbage. Carol O'Dowd had seen nothing out of the ordinary, but she was convinced Addie Richardson had been attacked by Satan worshippers; she'd heard about this kind of thing in big cities, and now maybe it had come to Cedar Hill, and what were the police going to do about it? It had taken quite a while to calm her down, and before they left she had already been wondering aloud if this would be bad for business.

As it turned out, no one else had seen anything out of the ordinary, either. A check with the strip mall's owner revealed that although the parcel was outfitted with security cameras, none had actually worked since they'd been vandalized back in the late summer. He'd been meaning to replace them, but he'd been preoccupied with more pressing things, and his budget was tight these days anyway, and surely Halloran and Brooks understood how it was. They did indeed, but they left him with a suggestion that he get his cameras in working order as soon as possible.

On a fluke, Halloran spent some time researching satanic rituals, especially ones involving babies and children, and what he'd found sickened him but did nothing to convince him the Richardson girl's killing was anything other than a homicide. He hoped the O'Dowd woman didn't stir up some kind of mass hysteria by continuing to spout her unfounded beliefs. All the department needed was a crowd of villagers with torches and pitchforks demanding a witch hunt.

Brooks arched his back and cracked his neck. "I was just going out for something to eat. You want to join me?"

Halloran glanced at his computer screen. He was hoping to get the last of his notes on the case written up before lunch, but right now he thought if he had to spend another minute looking at the monitor he'd rip his eyes out of their sockets. "Sure. Let me grab my jacket."

* * *

Brooks drove them down to Grace's Diner on Harper's Lake Road, and Halloran was relieved to see the place was fairly quiet. Being just outside of town, Grace's was never overwhelmed by the lunchtime crowds the way other Cedar Hill restaurants were, which made it a good choice whenever Brooks and Halloran needed to clear their heads and get away from official business. Grace and Charlie Johnson had renovated the old place about a year ago, and while daytime crowds were light, the restaurant's proximity to the city park gave it heavy crowds during the evenings and weekends during the summer when Little League and softball games were going on.

Grace herself seated them and laid out laminated menus, then returned with their usual drinks – a water for Brooks and a Diet Coke for Halloran. "Bad business about that poor girl," she said, setting down the glasses and tossing paper-wrapped straws on the table. "I don't envy you guys having to deal with that kind of thing. I can't see how you sleep at night, seeing stuff like that all the time."

"Who says we sleep?" Halloran told her with a wink. "Besides, I'm sure you do your fair share of dreaming about flipping burgers."

She laughed. "You don't know the half of it. I usually have nightmares about the place being full and I'm the only one here and I'm trying to cook and wait tables and do it all."

"That's a stress dream, Grace," Brooks said. "You stressed?"

She blew out a breath. "You don't know stress 'til you've run a business with your spouse." She took their orders and grabbed up the menus, then hesitated a moment, her gaze fixed on Halloran. "You don't think this is anything like what we had two years ago, do you?"

"I don't think so," he said, and he saw her visibly relax before she walked away from them. He looked across the table at Brooks. "Of course, even if it was, I couldn't tell her."

Brooks gave a humorless chuckle and tore the paper off his straw. "So you got any plans for the weekend?"

"Not really," Halloran said. Truth was he never bothered making plans anymore. With no love interest in his life, no family, and the crazy hours he sometimes put in, it was pointless.

"I'm taking the boat over to the lake tomorrow," Brooks said. "Thought I might get in a little fishing before the weather starts getting cool. You want to come?"

Halloran took a sip of his Coke. "Yeah, I might do that." He and Brooks hadn't had a day out on the lake since early summer. Halloran holed up in his apartment most weekends with nothing but his cat and a bottle of beer for company, and he was feeling restless. "Your family coming along?"

Brooks shook his head. "Diane's taking Carly over to Springfield for a day of shopping. It'll just be you and me."

"That sounds fine."

Halloran enjoyed being with Brooks. He'd always liked working with him when Brooks was still a beat cop. He'd never been mouthy and full of himself like many of the young guys. He always followed orders, always completed his reports, always showed up for duty. Halloran had requested Chief Pettus consider him for promotion to the investigations unit two years ago, and now Brooks and Halloran were partners. It was a good fit. Brooks was thorough and methodical, but he always allowed himself to be accessible, and that was important when you were dealing with people in high-stress situations. It was an important trait in a partner, too, as Halloran had learned the hard way.

The two of them hung out often, and Halloran had

lost count of the number of times he'd been a dinner guest at the Brooks house. Greg and Diane always went out of their way to make him feel welcome, whether it was at their house, on their boat, or, once, along for a weekend trip to Kings Island. "You're like the big brother Greg never had," Diane told him in confidence during that excursion. "Someone he can ride roller coasters with, go fishing with, and just generally cut loose with. He's changed since he started working with you. He's *happier*. He's like he was when we first started dating." Halloran didn't know how to respond to that, but he was grateful to at least have some friends again.

"You know," Brooks said after Grace served their burgers and fries, "there's a girl who works with Diane at the credit union." He looked at Halloran. "She's single. Widowed."

Halloran blew out a breath. "Oh, don't get started on that again." The last thing he needed was a woman complicating his life.

"Her name's Kelly Worsham," Brooks went on. "She's thirty-eight and she's got a twelve-year-old son."

Halloran squeezed a puddle of ketchup on his plate and met Brooks' gaze. "You serious? What would I do with a kid?"

"I'm not telling you to marry her. I just thought you might want to meet her. Diane said something about having the two of you over for dinner one night."

Brooks took a bite of his burger. "She's pretty," he said, his mouth full.

"You've seen her?"

Brooks nodded and wiped his mouth with a paper napkin. "Met her at the employee picnic the credit union threw a couple of weeks ago."

"I don't know." Halloran poked a fry into his mouth, then froze. "Wait. You didn't tell her about me, did you?"

Brooks grinned. "I might have."

Halloran swallowed his fry. "You sneaky bastard. What did you say?"

"That you were a jaded cop that was hard up for a woman."

"You better be lying."

Brooks stirred his ketchup with a long, skinny fry. "I am. Diane did most of the talking. She said you were a nice guy."

"Did she say how good-looking I am?"

Brooks looked at the ceiling. "I think the word she used was 'rugged.'" He laughed and Halloran couldn't help joining in. "She did say you were more handsome without your porn 'stache."

Halloran's fingers went instinctively to his upper lip. He was still trying to get used to the feel of the bare skin. He'd had his mustache since college, but when he started noticing all the gray hairs he decided it was time to get rid of it. Shaving it off had been like losing some essential part of himself, but he had to admit he now looked about ten years younger. "So what does Kelly look like?"

"Blonde. Snaggle-toothed. Has a wooden leg, so she kind of drags it when she walks." Brooks covered his mouth, trying to hide his grin. "She has a great personality."

Halloran shook his head. "You prick. Be serious."

"All right, all right," Brooks said, and took a bite of his cheeseburger. "I told you, she's pretty. And tall, probably close to your height. And she really does have a good personality. You two would really hit it off."

Halloran took a sip of his Coke. "I'll think about it."

"Well," Brooks said, "don't think about it too long. Somebody'll snatch her up pretty quick."

"Don't push it," Halloran told him."

Brooks held up his hands. "Ain't nobody pushing nobody. I'm just sayin', bro'."

Halloran threw a fry at him.

* * *

2:40 PM

Joel watched Wade descend the tower with agonizing slowness. The local channel feeds were full of noise, and the two of them had been sent to check it out. Wade was still about twenty feet up when Joel called out to him. "See anything?"

"Not a fucking thing," Wade said. His eyes were invisible behind his dark shades, but Joel could feel them boring in to him. "Antennas and lines look okay. That goddamned demodulator must be bad, just like I thought."

Joel squinted up at Wade. "Even if they overnight us a new one, it'll be Monday before we get it. Be a lot of people bitching. That Kansas City-San Francisco game is Sunday. Betsy won't be happy about that. She's liable to make us drive to St. Louis and pick one up from Corporate." Betsy was the general manager of the local Cable-Com office and a tough broad. And while a lot of people would call her "business savvy," most everyone who had worked under her just called her a bitch. But all of those people were gone. Cutbacks at the corporate level had led to staff reductions at the office here in Cedar Hill, and now Joel and Wade were the only two installers left at the local office. Counting Betsy and Rhonda the front desk clerk, only four people remained at Cable-Com here in Cedar Hill, which meant anything outside the office was left to Wade and Joel.

"Betsy can just fuck herself," Wade said. "I got plans this weekend and I ain't going to St. Louis."

"Relax, man," Joel said. "I was just kidding."

Wade dropped the last few feet to the ground. "Well, it wouldn't surprise me." He pulled off his white hardhat and locked it into the compartment on the side of the truck. "Sure as hell ain't anybody else to do it."

"Tell you what," Joel said, watching Wade step out of his safety harness, "if she does, I'll volunteer."

Wade ran a hand through his sweaty dark hair. Though closely-cropped, it had begun to curl in the humidity. "I can't let you do that. What if Dana needs you?"

Joel shrugged. "Just a thought."

Wade shook his head as he stowed away the harness. "Not a very good one. Besides, Betsy ain't gonna ask us to do that. She won't pay for the gas."

Joel snickered, opening the door to the truck. "You're right, she won't."

Wade hung back, pulling a pack of cigarettes from his shirt pocket. "Gimme a minute," he said. "Let me smoke one before we get back." Company policy didn't allow for smoking in the truck, and Wade took a chance to grab a cigarette whenever he could.

"You really ought to give those up," Joel told him. He shut the door and rested his elbows on the truck's hood.

Wade lit his cigarette and blew a plume of smoke at him. "Yeah, I know, they'll kill me and blah, blah, blah. Don't forget you smoked your share of 'em back in the day."

"Yeah, and I quit, too," Joel said.

Wade leaned back against the truck, facing the woods that spread across the slope down from the tower. From here the top floors of the Cedar Hill College dorm were just visible over the tree line across the valley. "Marla called me last night."

The sound of his brother's ex-wife's name sent a jolt

through Joel like electricity. Again he saw flashing lights and heard the wail of sirens, felt the terror of watching Dana being dragged out the screen door – everything about that horrible summer. "What the hell did she want?"

Wade shrugged. "Fuck if I know. I heard 'Collect call from the Department of Women's Corrections' and I hung up."

"Maybe she wanted to talk to Derek."

Wade blew out a breath. "Well, he wasn't home, and I'm sure he's got nothing to say to her anyway."

"She's still his mother."

"Like that matters a damn."

"When was the last time you talked to her?"

Wade took a drag off the cigarette, then blew the smoke through his nostrils. "Over a year ago. I told her then I never wanted to hear from her again." He un-clipped the sunglasses from his shirt and perched them across his face. "Did I ever tell you about that letter she sent Derek when he graduated?"

"No"

Wade shook his head. "Bunch of sentimental shit. Telling him what a good kid he was, how she still loved him, how she knew he could probably never forgive her for what she did. . . Just a bunch of bullshit. He threw it away, never responded to her. So you'd think she'd just give up and not contact us again."

"Maybe she needed something."

"Well, I need a million bucks, too, but that ain't

gonna happen."

Joel could understand Wade's anger. Marla had deceived them all. And while in some sick sense she was probably justified in what she did, no one would ever feel sympathy for her again. Right now she was rotting away in a women's prison upstate, and would be for at least the next twenty years. Time enough for all of them to get on with their lives. Maybe even time enough to heal from all of it. He decided to change the subject. As much as he didn't want to hear about Wade's sex life, it had to be better than dwelling on that dark period in all their lives. "So, looking forward to the weekend, I guess. What's your girlfriend's name again?"

Wade took a drag off the cigarette and Joel caught a hint of a grin. "Parker. I've told you a million times."

"Sorry, man. She's not *my* girlfriend. Besides, you go through 'em like bottled water. I can't keep up."

Wade laughed. "That's 'cause you're an old married man, now. You'll really be pitiful when that baby gets here, big guy."

Joel smiled. "Yeah, so you keep telling me."

Wade looked back out over the view. "You know, being a dad is really something special. I think you'll make a good one."

A pang stabbed at Joel's chest. "Thanks, man, I appreciate that. It's scary, though, you know?"

"I know."

"I keep thinking, what if I screw up?"

Wade looked at him. "Everybody's afraid of that,

and don't think it hasn't crossed *my* mind a time or two. I've made my share of mistakes."

"Derek's a good kid."

"Yeah, in spite of everything that happened."

"You've done the best you could."

Wade grunted and sucked on his cigarette. "Oh, bullshit, Joel. I could've done better. A *lot* better. I partied way too much. I know I wasn't the best dad. Marla and me were just kids ourselves when Derek was born. Hell, I was only seventeen. I didn't know anything about responsibility or raising kids. But you and Dana are different. You're grown-ups." He glanced away. "You're not gonna screw it up, Joel. You're way too smart."

Joel studied him, unable to see Wade's eyes behind his sunglasses. Wiry and good-looking and charming and sometimes an asshole, and so much an opposite of Joel that it seemed impossible they had come from the same parents. But Wade was still his brother, and somehow these few words of encouragement touched him to his core. "Thank you."

Wade dropped his cigarette butt and ground it into the dirt with his heel. "Well, now that we've got the sappy bullshit out of the way, let's get the fuck out of here." He pulled open the door to the truck. "And don't drive too fast, I don't want to get back to the office until it's time to go home."

Joel shook his head and laughed. Wade couldn't be sentimental for very long.

* * *

11:25 PM

Dana sat at the kitchen table with a half-drunk glass of milk in front of her. She'd been startled awake by a burning cramp that radiated throughout her abdomen, tightening her belly and giving her a wave of nausea. She climbed out of bed and stood frozen in the darkness until the feeling passed. Now roused from sleep, she'd made her way to the kitchen and had been sitting here for half an hour, waiting for but not feeling any further spasms. Braxton-Hicks contractions. The first time she'd felt them at thirty weeks she'd made Joel drive her to the hospital, certain she was going into early labor. But now she'd learned to ride them out. They always occurred in the middle of the night, usually when her back wasn't hurting and she had just drifted into a good sleep. If it wasn't one thing, it was something else. Either her back or her uterus was going to make certain she never slept again.

"Whatcha doing?"

She turned to see Joel standing in the doorway pulling on a T-shirt, his dark hair ruffled and his eyes half-closed. "Couldn't sleep," she said. "You scared me. I didn't hear you get up."

He smiled. "Yeah, pretty fly for a fat guy, huh?" He opened the refrigerator and pulled out the gallon jug of milk. "Mind if I join you?"

"Sure."

He poured a glass and sank into the chair opposite her. "You feel all right?"

She nodded. "Braxton-Hicks. It's nothing."

He reached over and took her hand and she steeled her thoughts against him. "Did you talk to the doctor today about not sleeping?"

She looked at him. "No. And how long have you known I wasn't sleeping well?"

He smiled crookedly and took a sip of milk. "About a month. I didn't say anything 'cause I figured you were going to tell me about it but you never did."

"I didn't want to worry you." She sighed. "I guess I should have known I couldn't keep things from that psychic brain of yours."

He frowned. "Actually, you've become pretty good at that," he said, and she immediately felt a stab of guilt. "But when you don't sleep well, I don't either. I wake up and you're not in the bed and I get concerned. But usually I can hear you watching TV in the living room and I can go on back to sleep."

She stared at her milk. "Sorry. I always try to be quiet when I get up at night."

"You are," he said. "But the bed just feels weird without you in it. It's like, even if I'm asleep I know you're not there and it wakes me up."

She pulled her hand away. "I said I was sorry," she said, then immediately wished she'd stayed quiet.

Joel's eyes narrowed. "Don't get mad. I wasn't

complaining."

"I know," Dana said. "I didn't mean to snap at you." She leaned back in her chair. "I'll just be so glad when the baby gets here. I'm so damned tired of being pregnant."

Joel looked at her squarely. "You know, I don't you to take this the wrong way, but. . . "

"But what?"

He broke his gaze and stared at the table. "I feel like you're keeping something from me. I know it's hard to. . . to live with someone like me. And you know I try to stay out of your private thoughts as best I can."

"Yeah, I know that."

"And you know how hard it was for me to learn to control what I sense. But ever since you got pregnant you've been. . . distant. Cold."

She knew he was right, that she'd been a fool to think he wouldn't notice she had shielded herself from him. But when they first became involved and she learned of his abilities, she knew she didn't want him knowing every time she wiped her ass. Joel understood there were certain boundaries, specific areas of her brain where he wasn't allowed, and he claimed he had mastered the ability to stay out of there. So far she had believed him. But now she wondered if he ever caught a glimpse through the wall into her safe zone, if now he was feeling her out to see what she would tell him. But nothing she ever sensed from him gave any indication he was ever dishonest with her. The impressions she picked up off his clothes, his watch, his wallet – all of it pointed to one fact: that he loved her. And the idea that he knew she was hiding something deep down and that it hurt him was almost too much to bear. She took hold of his hand. It was big and soft like the rest of him, and she pulled it to her lips and kissed it. "This is the moment that if I wasn't pregnant I would tell you to shut up and come back to bed and we'd make love."

He laughed. "So since you *are* pregnant, what are you going to tell me?"

"To shut up and let's find an old scary movie to watch in bed until we go back to sleep."

"Honeymoon's over, huh?"

She patted her belly. "At least 'til our little girl decides to make her appearance." She looked at him, at his scruffy goatee and his round face and his sleepy brown eyes, and knew she would do whatever it took to keep him happy. And if that included hiding one shameful secret in the deepest, darkest parts of her, then so be it. "Drink your milk, Mr. Roberts, it'll help you sleep."

SATURDAY, OCTOBER 4

12:40 PM

I WANT TO STOP UP HERE for some stuff before we get to the lake," Brooks said to Halloran, pointing at a tiny convenience store just up ahead. He slowed the truck and eased off the road onto the gravel lot. Brooks always stopped here for supplies; everything was higher in Harper's Lake and the streets there were narrow and congested. Halloran watched through the rear glass as the twenty-foot bass boat and trailer shuddered as they made the transition off the pavement. Brooks was a pro at handling the beast; Halloran knew he probably couldn't back it in a straight line himself if his life depended on it, and he'd seen Brooks maneuver it into some pretty tight spots. "I'll get the beer today," Brooks said.

"I can get it," Halloran told him. "It's the least I can

do."

"Nothing doing. But you can pick us out some snacks." He opened his door and looked back at Halloran. "I like Doritos and Slim Jims."

Halloran emerged from the stuffy cold air of the truck into the sticky heat. The sun blazed more like July than October, and beads of perspiration popped out on his forehead almost immediately. If it were as hot on the water as in this parking lot, all the sunscreen he'd slathered on his arms and legs would be sweated off in no time. He swung his sunglasses to the top of his head and followed Brooks into the store.

He'd just made a beeline for the snack aisle when a man and a woman slipped through the door behind him. They were hugged up together, giggling, and it took him a second glance to place the man as Wade Roberts. Halloran had interrogated his share of suspects over the years, most of them long forgotten. But the memories of Roberts's case along with his brother's ties to the other events of that horrible summer were still vivid and sharp. Halloran tried to glance away, hoping Roberts wouldn't spot him, but the other man was just whipping off his shades and they locked glances. Halloran nodded. "Mr. Roberts."

Roberts's smile faded and his expression became guarded. "How're you doing. . . ?"

Halloran could tell he was reaching for his name. "Halloran," he said, "Mike Halloran." He extended his hand and the other man shook it. "I'm good, and you?"

"Doing well," Roberts said. The blonde hanging off his arm was younger than Halloran had first thought. And prettier. Roberts tilted his head toward her. "We're headed over to the lake. Rented a houseboat for the weekend."

"Yeah, we're going for the day ourselves."

"That your boat outside? It's beautiful."

Halloran shook his head. "Co-worker's." He craned his neck. "He's in here somewhere buying us some beer." He looked back at Roberts. "How's your brother?"

"Fine. You know he and his wife are gonna have a kid?"

"No, I didn't."

"Any time now. She's about to pop."

"Tell him I said congratulations."

"Will do." Roberts and the blonde headed toward the rear of the store.

Halloran grabbed two bags of Doritos and a package of Oreos, then spotted Brooks and followed him to the cash register. He nodded at the case of Budweiser in Brooks' hands. "Just one?"

"We'll have to pace ourselves," Brooks said. "Who was that you were talking to?"

"Remember the Marla Roberts case two years ago? That's her husband. *Ex*-husband I guess now."

Brooks peered over the shelves in Roberts's general direction. "Oh, yeah? Looks like he's doing pretty well for himself."

Halloran grunted in agreement. "Oh, I almost forgot," he said. He pulled a couple of Slim Jims out of the rack in front of the register. "Don't want you to go hungry."

* * *

The lake was hot, crowded, and loud. Everyone was trying to squeeze in one more weekend of fun on the water before the weather turned cool. Halloran and Brooks had been in the boat all of twenty minutes when the water patrol boarded a pontoon fifty yards away and hauled away the driver in handcuffs. Boating while intoxicated no doubt. Halloran didn't envy these officers out here on the lake; watching for drunk drivers was bad enough on land, let alone on the water, and he was grateful he was no longer on the streets.

Brooks peeled off his T-shirt, and his body was well-muscled and bronzed from all the time spent on the boat. Halloran considered taking his shirt off, but then he thought of his scrawny white body and the paunch that hung over his belt and he decided against it; no sense in frightening the children. "You care if I smoke?"

"Suit yourself," Brooks told him. "Your lungs, not mine."

"I've been dying since we left Cedar Hill." He dug the pack out of his shirt pocket and lipped a cigarette, then lit it and closed his eyes as the nicotine flowed through his lungs. He'd just blown out the first plume of smoke when his cell rang, and he recognized the number of the medical examiner's office. "Hey, Scotty, what's up?"

Carl Scott harrumphed on the other end. "Just finished up the Richardson girl's autopsy report."

"Hang on," Halloran said. "I'm on the boat with Greg. Let me put you on speaker." Brooks moved closer with keen interest. "It's Scotty," Halloran mouthed, then punched the speakerphone button. "So what's the cause of death?"

"Strangulation. A rope – probably nylon – consistent with the size of a standard clothesline you can pick up at Walmart or any other discount store. A granny knot caught her just at the center of her throat. Perp knew what they were doing. And they were strong. There's some damage to the deeper tissues in the neck and throat."

"Jesus." Halloran rubbed his eyes. The sun glaring off the water was suddenly nauseating. "What about the baby?"

"Well, whoever did it has had some medical training. It was an almost perfect C-section, and I'd bet dollars to doughnuts that infant is still alive."

Brooks leaned in. "So you think the perp was a *doctor*?"

"Can't say," Scotty said. "But it's someone with experience. Could be a skilled nurse."

Halloran chewed his lip and thumped the ash off his

cigarette over the railing. Across the water a small houseboat drifted toward the shallows. He could see two people at the stern of the boat. Wade Roberts and the blonde. Roberts stood behind her, his arms encircling her waist. One hand reached for her breast and she slapped it away playfully. "Anything else?" Halloran asked. "Do we at least know the sex of the person who attacked her?"

"Got some scrapings from beneath the victim's fingernails. Looks like she scratched the hell out of somebody. Skin and a couple of blond hairs. I'll send the scrapings over to the big lab in Springfield, they'll run us a DNA profile, but you won't have that for a couple of weeks. In the meantime, you can be on the lookout for somebody with some pretty nasty claw marks on their arms. But no. I can't do much with skin here. If I had blood. . . maybe. The only thing I can say with accuracy is that the hairs came from a Caucasian person."

Halloran took a deep breath. "Any signs of sexual assault?"

"No. I'd say they were only after one thing and they took it with 'em."

Halloran disconnected the call and sat looking out over the lake, at the boats bobbing complacently in the water, at the lone skier zipping over the surface farther out. He glanced back at the houseboat. Roberts and the blonde were gone, and Halloran wondered if they had gone inside for an afternoon delight.

Brooks slid into the white vinyl seat beside him. "Billy Ray Fields has blond hair," he said, pulling a can of beer from the cooler, "but I didn't see any scratches on him anywhere, did you?"

Halloran shook his head and took a drag off the cigarette. "No. And he doesn't strike me as the kind to have any medical knowledge."

Brooks grunted and took a sip of his beer. "Or any other knowledge, for that matter."

Halloran grabbed his phone and punched in the station's number.

"Who you calling in such a hurry?"

Halloran looked at Brooks. "We need to get the word out to every hospital and medical facility to be on the lookout for a male newborn. Someone will see him. That baby will need medical care somewhere."

* * *

3:15 PM

Joel leaned back on his elbows in the grass and gazed up into the deep blue sky. Beside him, Dana lay on her back on a blanket, lightly dozing. Her soft snores mingled with the birdsong in the trees, and Joel thought there couldn't be a more pleasant harmony on earth.

Tomorrow was supposed to be cold and rainy, and they were planning on making the trip to Springfield for the monthly group meeting of sensitives. But today they had come out here to Riverside Park to take in one last day of warm sun. Joel dragged a reluctant Dana out of the house where she was piled up on the couch under a quilt pretending to read while he pretended to watch Auburn football from the recliner. Autumn was coming, Joel reasoned with her, and soon they would be cooped up in the house for the winter with a crying baby. They needed to enjoy the weather while they could. At last she relented, and once they were here he could tell she was glad they'd come.

A woman with a boy and girl, who both looked under five years old, smiled at them from the toddler playground. Joel tried to visualize a few years down the road, bringing Sofia here and letting her run around the mulch-covered area, and all he could think of was scraped knees and mashed fingers and bruised shins. He would hover around her, keeping his hands out to catch her if she so much as stumbled. And Dana would call him silly and tell him he was being overprotective. And they would have a good laugh and leave the park and go have ice cream. But for now he could only imagine it, and it seemed a million years from now.

Dana gave a loud snort and jerked awake. "Oh, sorry, I didn't mean to doze off."

He smiled at her. "You're fine."

"This hard ground feels so good to my back."

"Maybe you should try sleeping out in the yard tonight."

"Har, har." She struggled to sit up, and Joel took her

hands and pulled her upright. "Thanks."

"You don't have to do that, you know."

"What's that?"

He smiled crookedly at her. "Brace yourself for a mental attack every time I touch you."

She blew out a breath and looked away toward the mother and her kids at the playground. "Sorry. It's just a reflex."

"You're giving me a complex."

"Let's not talk about this now."

Irritation burned in his chest. "Then when do you want to talk about it? Because you can't keep shutting me out. I know you're keeping something from me. And I don't care what it is. It's not going to change how I feel about you."

One tear, fat and round, streaked down her face. "It might."

"It won't."

Dana swiped the tear off her cheek and looked at him. "If I tell you, you've got to promise me. . ."

"What?"

"Promise that you won't stop loving me."

Joel looked at her, incredulous. "I could *never* stop loving you." He reached for her hand, but she stopped him.

"No," she said. "If I tell you, I'm going to tell with words. I don't want you to. . . *see*. Not yet." More tears spilled down her face and this time she didn't bother to wipe them away.

Now the burning in his chest turned to dread. "My God, baby, it can't be that bad. Just tell me."

Dana took a deep breath and kept her gaze on the playground across the broad expanse of grass. "When I first found out I was pregnant. . . "

"What?" He was resisting the urge to grab her shoulders and shake her. She was making this as dramatic as those TV shows that broke away to a commercial right at the big reveal.

"When I first found out, I panicked. I suspected for a couple of weeks, so I bought a home pregnancy test and it was positive. I didn't know what to do. I wasn't ready to tell you about it yet. I even bagged up the test and threw it away in the trash at school so you wouldn't see."

"I don't understand. *Why?*"

"Because I was terrified. I had all this crap going through my head. What if I turned out to be a horrible mother? What if something happened between us and we split up? What if my body couldn't physically handle pregnancy and childbirth?"

"Why didn't you just talk to me about it?"

She shook her head. "You don't get it. I couldn't talk to *anybody* about it. Not even my mother. I just needed to sort everything out in my head." She looked at him. "That's when I looked into. . . options."

"What kind of options?" He suddenly didn't like the direction this conversation was headed.

"I went to the women's clinic on the other side of

town. I wanted to talk to someone besides Dr. Connolly. Someone who didn't know me and wouldn't judge me. I wanted to find out everything. I talked to them about natural childbirth and C-sections. And I even talked about. . . " She looked away. "Termination."

Joel's heart sank. "You talked to them about an *abortion?*"

Dana wiped her eyes on the sleeve of her shirt. "I was *scared*, Joel. I didn't know because of my size whether I'd even be able to carry a child to term, let alone deliver one."

"And you would have gone ahead without talking to me about it first?"

She turned to him quickly. "Of course not! I wouldn't have done *anything* without you knowing. I would *never* go behind your back like that." She grabbed his hand and sat staring at the ground, tears continuing to spill down her cheeks.

Joel watched her for a moment, waiting for her to say more, and when she remained silent, he felt a sudden urge to laugh. "Is. . . is that it?" And when she nodded, he *did* laugh. "That's what you've been hiding from me all this time? The fact that you talked to a doctor about an abortion?"

"I didn't just talk about it," she said, "I considered it."

"But you didn't do it."

"When the doctor told me there shouldn't be a problem with a full-term pregnancy it wasn't an option anymore. That's when I came home and told you I was pregnant."

Joel shook his head. "But why hide that from me?"

"You were so excited over the baby. I didn't know what you would think of me, that I was being selfish, that I was a murderer. . . it wasn't anything we'd ever discussed. I just figured it would be best if you never found out about it."

He pulled her close and kissed the top of her head. "I can't believe you thought you had to keep that from me. That you couldn't talk about it with me." He pulled back and looked into her eyes. "I can understand being scared. I get it. But don't think that it changes how I feel about you. I love you, Dana. Nothing can ever change that."

Fresh tears slid down her face. "I'm still scared," she said.

"I know."

She pulled away from him. "Sometimes I'm worried because I feel like I should be more excited than I am. That I'm gonna be a lousy mother because when it comes right down to it, I just don't feel ready for a baby. I see all these other pregnant women and they look great, and they seem so sophisticated and wise and happy. And I just feel like a big lump. My back hurts and my feet hurt and I can't ever get comfortable and I just freaking *hate* being pregnant."

She collapsed against him, sobbing. And as he held her close, as she nestled her face into his chest, he realized that at some point the wall she had built up inside herself had vanished.

* * *

9:45 PM

The baby was sleeping.

She adjusted the IV line around his tiny body and loosened the blanket a bit. He had been dozing most of the day, only waking when he needed to be fed or changed. Earlier, after she had fed him and given him a clean diaper, he lay quietly, watching her with his round blue eyes, his tongue darting in and out of his mouth like a snake's, his arms and legs twitching with involuntary muscle movements. She cooed at him and sang softly until his eyelids drooped and he fell into a peaceful slumber.

Wednesday evening had been touch and go, and she had worried he might not make it through the night. But he was a tough little thing, and by Thursday afternoon his skin was already pink and healthy. He had cried very little, even when she'd inserted the IV needle into the back of his tiny hand. His heartbeat was strong and steady, as the incessant beeping of the monitor proved, and his breathing was normal. Much of the equipment in the room would probably not even be used. Unless there was some kind of emergency. And she didn't want to think about that.

Kris took one last look at him and dimmed the lights, then stepped out into the hallway. She needed a cup of hot tea.

She made her way to the kitchen, passing through the living room where an old Jimmy Stewart movie was playing. The sound was off, and the captions scrolled across the actors' faces as if the words were the real stars of the show and the images were only an afterthought. The past few days she'd become quite intimate with the TCM channel – the wonderful old Technicolor musicals and the screwy 1930s comedies, the old tearjerkers and overblown epic dramas. She loved them all, and they hearkened back to when she was little, spending drowsy Sunday afternoons with her grandmother and watching old movies through the haze of the old woman's cigarette smoke. She remembered lying on the braided rug and watching Jane Russell and Marilyn Monroe sing and dance their way through *Gentlemen Prefer Blondes*, and the impossibly vivid colors of that otherworldly land of Hollywood while the late summer sun poured through the thin living room drapes and she and Grandma Hettie snacked on over-salted popcorn and bitter Diet Rites. How even now those old movies brought back that taste of salt, the scent of Grandma Hettie's sachet powder mixed with the smoke from the Kools she puffed relentlessly, the claustrophobic closeness of that house that was both suffocating and comforting.

She missed those old days and that last summer before Grandma Hettie got sick. It was the last time she'd really been free. Because after that her own mother left town, unable to deal with Grandma Hettie's illness and the responsibility, and the next three years were spent caring for her grandmother alone in that dark back bedroom where the old lady withered and died. She'd watched Grandma Hettie shrivel like a rotting apple and braved the sickroom stench of urine and rot and feces and vowed that when Grandma Hettie was gone, she would never spend another minute around sickness and death. That she would get out of that stupid little town and flee to Hollywood's Technicolor glory to dance. To sing. To *act*. To be Famous. And Rich.

But as she watched Grandma Hettie in her final weeks, she began to understand something about herself. There was beauty and fulfillment in caring for people. She was doing a part to ease Grandma Hettie's suffering, to bring a sense of dignity to her death. And after her grandmother was gone, the lure of Hollywood's lights dimmed to a mere fading ember. Nursing was now calling her, and she traded in her dreams of designer gowns for the practicality of nursing scrubs.

Through grants and what little Grandma Hettie had saved up for her, she was able to put herself through nursing school, and it wasn't long before she found her calling as a neonatal nurse. Or so she thought. For several years she attended births, cared for the newborns, nursed the preemies through the first few delicate weeks, and sent the babes home with their happy families. She watched the new moms and dads bond with their newborns, felt their joy and grieved with them when things didn't go as planned. But inside of her was a hollow ache. She knew she would never be able to experience these events for herself. And the shared happiness of birth and new life gradually morphed into bitterness. While she became apathetic to the young pretty new married mothers and their handsome husbands, she hated the unwed teenage girls who came through her unit. Some were starry-eyed and stupid about their futures with boyfriends who would bolt at the first opportunity, some were resentful and bitter about the lives they had now created for themselves whether through accident or sheer negligence. They were hussies, all of them. Never understanding the value of what they carried inside them, not knowing the *importance* of the new life incubating inside them. Not appreciating the *responsibility* of caring for an infant. And when she finally broke one day and called a thirteen-year-old African American girl a "fucking whore" to her face in the presence of the girl's mother, that was the end of her job at Lake County Medical Center.

Fortunately, there was an immediate opening at Four Oaks Hospice, and though the majority of her career had been spent in the maternity ward, the director, a handsome dark-bearded man by the name of Nicholas Larkins, took an interest in her during her initial interview and hired her on the spot.

At first it had been wonderful. She loved her patients

at Four Oaks Hospice Center and they loved her. Trusted her. She became intimate with the families, and many times they wanted her present as they said final goodbyes.

But then came the trouble with Nicholas. The constant flirting. The furtive "accidental" brushes of his long fingers against her buttocks. The persistent invitations to dinner. And finally, when she relented to a date and found herself in his bed, the explosion when he discovered she couldn't bear children and the threat of firing her. But he couldn't do that without exposing the fact he had dallied with an employee and his own position would be at risk. In the end the matter was dropped and the two of them went their separate ways. Eventually he left Four Oaks and she never saw him again.

As the years went by, it became harder and harder to let go of the people she grew to care for. Whereas earlier she had opened up to her patients and willingly met their needs – most times going beyond her job duties – she realized she would need to distance herself. The pain of losing these people was too great, especially the older women who brought back so many memories of Grandma Hettie. "You get too close, Kris," a fellow nurse told her once during a smoke break. "We're just here to ease their suffering, not become their friends."

At the time she thought the words callous and horrible, but as time went on she started to understand the wisdom of that thinking. And eventually she was able to turn her feelings off. To see it as just a job. But when that happened, the resentment began to build. The hatred of bedpans and shit-stained sheets, the choking odor of urine and vomit. Of rot. Always the rot. As if death itself lived in the hospice center and emitted its stench from deep within the bowels of the building.

Then a new patient came to the center. Mr. Felix Manley. She would never forget the name. Slightly pudgy with a quick wit and twinkling blue eyes when he first came to Four Oaks with colon cancer, he quickly wasted away during the next four weeks until he was only skin stretched tightly over brittle bones with his gaze clouded and his mouth unable to do anything except drool. One evening she was making her final rounds and entered Mr. Manley's room to the stink of shit. He had filled his diaper and he would need to be washed and changed. It had been a long, exhausting day. She'd barely slept the night before, and when she'd arrived at the center she'd been informed there would be no pay raises for the next year. Budget cuts, they said. And tonight they were short-staffed; she would have to take on extra duties. And when she found Mr. Manley wallowing in his own mess, it was too much. She sat down in the chair next to his bed and cried while he gazed uncomprehendingly at the flickering television on the wall. And suddenly, she hated him. Hated the sight of his stupid, glazed expression and the putrid stench of shit and death that hung around him and every other patient in this godforsaken place.

She remembered the rage flowing through her like

fire in her veins, and she felt as if she were watching a movie or some episode of one of those cop shows. She saw her hands pull the pillow from beneath Mr. Manley's head and press it onto his face. He didn't even blink.

It took much longer than she expected, even though the old man barely struggled. A full five minutes of holding the pillow down with all her strength. And when at last Mr. Manley's breathing stopped, she was covered in sweat. She removed the pillow, closed his sightless eyes, and sat back down in the chair to look at him. She was surprised at the complete lack of guilt she felt. In a way she had freed him. He was no longer suffering. And though his mouth still lolled open and a string of spittle dangled from his lower lip, she thought she could detect an expression of peace. She placed the pillow back under his head, checked his pulse to verify he was gone, and then went to the nurse's station to report the death.

After Mr. Manley it was easier to end them. Many times she did it while they were sleeping, and they never woke. Only one ever fought her, Mrs. Simpson, who seemed to use the very last of her Alzheimer's-ridden brain to comprehend what was happening to her. But no one ever questioned the deaths. They were, after all, in a hospice center where people came to die. There was never an autopsy, never an inquest. Never an eyebrow raised, even though all the deaths occurred during her shift. It was, it seemed, what she was meant to do.

And then she met Maria Furtado, an immigrant from Portugal whose mother was a patient at Four Oaks. The petite dark-haired woman had taken a liking to her, had confided things to her. Had offered her a job. An opportunity. A way to use her earlier prenatal skills and save lives instead of watching them end. A way to right certain wrongs. And more importantly, she knew or at least suspected what Kris had been up to.

Intrigued, Kris had slept on the offer for weeks, even kept in touch after Maria's mother died. And when the hospice center finally announced it was closing due to the continued budget cuts, the decision came quickly and easily. Yes, Maria said, of course the offer was still open, and Maria would herself pay all relocation expenses. (What exactly Maria did to afford all this she didn't ask.) And yes, Maria assured her, what they were planning to do was for the best.

And now she sipped her tea at the kitchen table. The only light came from a dim fluorescent fixture above the sink, and the shadows in the corners of the room seemed to reach toward her the longer she sat. The nights here bothered her. Not because she had a fear of the darkness, but Maria had told her she must remain vigilant. Certain people would not understand what they were trying to accomplish and the importance of God's work. And just as she felt what she had been doing at Four Oaks was ultimately good, she knew what she was doing here was just as vital. But she tried to remain watchful for signs they had drawn attention to themselves. Especially during the night. Maria said this place was safe. It was the reason she had chosen a nondescript house in a nondescript neighborhood in a nondescript town. Maria said she had taken care of everything. Maria said as long as her instructions were followed no harm would come to either of them or to any of the children.

Because there were going to be more.

SUNDAY, OCTOBER 5

8:25 AM

HALLORAN CAME AWAKE SLOWLY from a dream about Kelly Worsham. At least who his mind told him was Kelly Worsham, since he had no idea what she really looked like. A blonde, long legs wrapped around his waist as he thrust reflexively into her. He rolled over onto his back, his erection tenting the sheet, and stared at the ceiling. Even with the curtains closed, the room was darker than usual, and he remembered it was supposed to rain all day.

As much as he railed on Brooks for trying to fix him up, he had to admit the thought of being with a woman again was both exciting and comforting. Comforting, because it would be nice to actually have someone to do things with – dinner, movies, TV. Companionship. Someone he could spend time with and not feel like he was intruding the way he did with Brooks and his family. Exciting, because, well. . . sex. It had been a long time since he'd been with a woman. Any woman. Way before all that trouble two years ago. In fact, he hadn't even been on a date since he'd made lieutenant, let alone had a relationship. Unless he counted the fondness for his right hand.

Mel hopped up on the bed beside him and settled down, staring at him with intense green eyes. "Hey, you stupid cat," Halloran said. He stroked the brown tabby behind the ears and Mel began purring immediately, pressing his face against Halloran's fingers. "Maybe I should just get neutered like you," Halloran told the cat. "Then I wouldn't have to think about women."

Thunder rumbled outside, and Halloran burrowed down into the covers. It was a good day for sleeping in, except most of the time anymore he didn't sleep well. A combination of stress and getting older, his doctor told him during his last checkup. "And the smoking doesn't help," he'd told Halloran, giving him a crooked grin.

Well, fuck that. He reached out into the cold from beneath the sheet and grabbed his cigarettes and lighter off the bedside table. He lit his first smoke of the day and groped for his cell. There was a text from someone. He squinted at the screen but couldn't read it. He was going to need glasses soon. He finally brought the message into focus and saw that it was from Brooks.

Diane says dinner mon nite. Us u and Kelly. Lasonya. 6 pm work for u?

Shit.

He lay back on the bed and stared at the motionless ceiling fan, sucking on the cigarette and blowing the smoke toward the inert blades. The rain had come, and he could hear it pattering against the window behind the bed. This was one of those days it would be nice to wake up next to another warm body. To snuggle and kiss and make slow passionate love while the rain drummed on the roof and the thunder rolled. Then nap and wake later to do it again. Then share a steamy shower and have a late breakfast. Then cuddle on the couch and watch an old movie. A lazy, sensual Sunday. It sounded like heaven.

Well, he had to start somewhere. He picked the phone up and tapped out, *Make it 7 and I'll be there*. He hit "send" before he could change his mind, and took a drag off the cigarette. He hoped he wouldn't regret this.

The phone dinged with a response from Brooks: *K*.

He threw back the sheets and sat in his boxers on the edge of the bed, shivering, the cigarette still dangling from his lips. He'd ended up wriggling out of his shirt yesterday on the lake – damn Brooks and his tanned muscles – and wound up with a nasty sunburn. Now his arms and back stung like fire in spite of the chill in the house. Luckily he'd kept his cap on, so his cheeks only showed a slight ruddiness that almost made him look handsome. Almost.

He stepped into the pair of jeans he'd let drop to the floor last night and pulled on a sweatshirt. It was an old one from college, one that hadn't been laundered very many times so the fleece inside was still soft and cottony and easy on his burned skin. Maybe he'd try to get somewhere today to pick up some aloe vera lotion. If he could even find it this time of year. Who the hell got a sunburn in October?

Mel followed him to the kitchen and hopped up on the counter, watching patiently while Halloran started the coffee, and rubbed his face against the edge of the cabinet. "Yeah, I know you want something," Halloran told him, pulling out a package of treats and pitching one to the cat. "We all want something." He took a drag off his cigarette and padded to the front door of the apartment to grab the Sunday paper from the hallway.

He spread the paper out on the table and finished his smoke while looking over the headlines. Blessedly, the Clark girl's murder no longer warranted a front-page story. He wondered if the plea for information that went out to the area hospitals had resulted in any calls, but figured if anything had turned up someone would have let him know. He leafed through the rest of the paper, then folded it and tossed it aside. Nothing good in there. Nothing worth reading or looking at.

He stubbed out his cigarette and reached for his phone. He should have done this earlier, but he hated to feel like a stalker. He opened Facebook and searched for Kelly Worsham. A seemingly endless list of faces popped up on his screen. He scrolled through them, wondering whether he would even know if he was looking at the right profile. But one caught his eye. And he had two mutual friends with her. He tapped on it.

Kelly Worsham. Employed at Lake County Credit Union. From Cedar Hill. Studied at Vanderbilt University. Mutual friends, Greg and Diane Brooks. He clicked on her profile picture.

Greg was right. She *was* pretty. Shoulder-length blonde hair, eyes so blue they were nearly luminous, and a smile that curved upward on one side that made her appear she was privy to some hilarious secret. She had a nice face. An honest face. He liked that face. He scrolled down the page and opened her pictures. There was a photo of her with a young boy. They were dressed up and standing outside a brick house, as if they were on their way to dinner or church. Nice looking kid. Dark, longish hair, eyes so brown they were nearly black. A thin pinkish scar trailed down his olive skin from behind his ear and disappeared beneath the collar of his green polo. The caption said *Trevor & me on Mother's Day* ♥♥♥.

Farther down was a picture of the boy by himself. He was seated in a Mexican restaurant with a giant serving of fried ice cream, wearing an oversize black sombrero and giving a toothy grin. *Trevor's 12th birthday dinner at Señor Don Gato's.* Again Halloran's gaze was drawn to the scar on the boy's neck. What could have happened to cause such a thing?

Below was a photo of Kelly and Trevor in front of a Christmas tree. Trevor looked quite a bit younger, and when Halloran looked he saw the picture had been posted almost three years ago. No scar.

What had happened to Trevor Worsham in the past three years that would have left such an angry, permanent mark on his skin?

Mel leaped up onto the table and plopped down onto the newspaper. Halloran gave him a scratch behind the ears. "Stupid cat." Mel pressed his eyes closed and rubbed against Halloran's fingers. "You think someone that pretty is going to be attracted to a crusty old son-of-a-bitch like me?" Mel purred in reply, then stepped closer and rubbed his face against Halloran's stubbled cheek. Halloran ran his fingertips along Mel's spine, feeling the cat arch upward to his touch. "Yeah, you're right," he said. "What have I got to lose?"

* * *

12:50 PM

"We got everything?" Joel said, throwing the Corolla into gear and easing out of the drive.

"I think so," Dana said. "I hope the apples in that pie got good and done." She glanced at the back seat where the pie she'd baked for the meeting sat in its carrier.

Joel reached over and patted her leg – lightly so as

not to intrude on her thoughts – but he still stifled the sting as he felt her flinch. After their conversation yesterday, he didn't think she was still holding back. Maybe it was force of habit from guarding herself for so long; but maybe there was still more she hadn't told him. He didn't want to ponder that possibility. After all, he'd felt the tension ease out of her yesterday. Had actually *seen* it dissipate like a vapor. If there was something else, he wasn't sure he wanted to know what it was. Ever.

The drive to Springfield was dark, and the approaching cold front created a wispy fog that shrouded the trees in the low spots along the interstate. The colors of fall hadn't blossomed fully, yet the foliage had the lighter yellowish hue it always presented just before the leaves began to turn in earnest, and the woods were dotted here and there with the vibrant red of sumac. There was a sense of beauty in the way the hollows and tree lines hid in the mist, although the darkness of the day gave Joel a sense of foreboding. He wasn't sure whether it was the claustrophobic atmosphere of the low slate-colored clouds or the sense that Dana was being evasive. In any event, he remained quiet and so did she, and only the music from the 'nineties channel on the radio kept him from going insane.

The rain hit about ten miles outside of Springfield, light drops at first, then a downpour that the Corolla's worn wipers couldn't keep up with. Joel lost sight of the lines on the pavement, and when it didn't seem that the storm would let up, he switched on the emergency flashers and pulled off onto the shoulder to wait out the torrent.

Dana said nothing as they sat and listened to the rain pound the roof of the car. She stared straight ahead at the water washing down the windshield, her fingers tapping slightly to the beat of the Cranberries' "Linger."

"I never could understand half the words to this song," Joel said. "I think it's her accent. Aren't they British or something?"

"Irish," Dana whispered, not looking at him.

He leaned closer. "What?"

"Irish," she repeated, this time meeting his gaze. "The Cranberries are Irish."

He held her stare. "What's wrong?" he asked. And when she looked away without answering, he said, "Have I done something?"

She turned to him abruptly. "No! God, no." She put her hand to her forehead. "I'm just tired. You know I haven't been sleeping well. And after our talk yesterday, I still worry about what you think about me."

He took her hand and she squeezed back. "I love you," he said. "I told you last night everything's going to be all right. And no, I don't think any less of you for being scared and considering options. Especially considering your concerns." He raised her hand to his lips and kissed it. "But. . . "

She looked at him. "What?

He traced his fingertip across her palm. "You're still holding back. You say you're okay, but I can tell. Something's eating you."

Dana took a deep breath. "I'm just worried. About this whole birthing process. About being a mother. About the baby after she gets here. I'm terrified something will happen." A large tear spilled over and ran down her cheek. "I'm just not sure I'm ready for this."

Joel reached over and pulled her to him, held her as she sobbed silently. "It's going to be all right. Everything's going to be all right. I promise you." He kissed the top of her head, inhaling the scent of her hair. "You're just. . . emotional right now. The doctor told you it would be like this sometimes."

"I suppose."

He hugged her tighter. "We'll be okay. You'll be okay." He drew back and looked at her. "Sofia will be okay."

She pressed her head against his chest and nodded.

But he knew there was still more she wasn't saying. And as the rain continued to beat on the Corolla's roof, he wondered how much longer she was going to keep it from him.

* * *

1:55 PM

Truthfully, in spite of what Joel said, Dana wasn't sure that everything *would* be all right. Since laying her soul bare the previous afternoon, something had nagged at her. Had gnawed at her thoughts all through the night and chased away her sleep, like a wolf hiding in the shadows, just out of sight and ready to leap and rip out her throat. She had thought telling Joel about visiting the women's clinic would make the feeling go away, that confessing what she'd done would eradicate the guilt she'd carried all these months. And that poor Joel's blind loyalty and forgiveness could make it all better.

But it hadn't.

Something loomed over the horizon, something dark and horrible that had nothing to do with her fears of parenting or childbirth. It was something bigger. Something she wasn't sure Joel could protect her – *them* – from. All her life she'd gleaned her preternatural knowledge from objects. From the impressions left behind. From the *past.* This was different. She didn't know where the idea of danger was coming from, but it was in the future. Lying in wait for them. And the worst part was not knowing what it was.

Joel pulled into the lot behind St. Thomas Church beside Frank and Bonnie's blue Caravan. The rain had lulled to intermittent drops, but the clouds still hung low and black. "Well, your mom and dad made it," he said.

"Yeah." She wasn't sure she was in the mood to be with her parents today, not with the dread hanging over her. She took a deep breath, trying to calm the jittery electricity coursing through her. "Will you get the pie?" She pushed open the door and hauled herself out of the bucket seat, careful to avoid the puddle just at her feet. It was getting harder and harder to maneuver her massive self out of this little car. When the baby came, maybe she and Joel could swing trading the Corolla in for a minivan. Getting Sofia in and out of a little sedan sounded like a nightmare.

Inside the activity center, people clustered together in their usual groups, everyone catching up before the meeting started. Dana spotted Frank and Bonnie chatting with Father Michael and she ambled toward them. Bonnie caught her gaze and waved. Dana plastered a smile on her face and headed into the fray. "Hey, everybody."

Frank turned and caught her up in his beefy arms and kissed the top of her head. "How are you, pumpkin?"

"Tired," she said.

Bonnie gave her a quick hug. "I was worried about you two. We're almost ready to start."

"Got caught in a big shower," Dana said. "We had to pull over for a bit." She gave Father Michael a nod. "Father."

Father Michael reached out and squeezed her hand.

"Good to see you, Dana." She noticed he was trying, but failing, to keep his gaze from her belly. "How are you feeling these days?"

"Okay," she said. "Ready to stop being pregnant." The others laughed, and she forced herself to smile.

"How many more weeks?"

"I'm due on the twenty-ninth."

"Not much longer then." Father Michael looked at her with his piercing blue eyes. "You seem troubled."

She felt an immediate stab of guilt, though she wasn't sure why. "Just tired," she said. "I'm not sleeping well."

"I had so much trouble sleeping when I was pregnant with Dana," Bonnie said to the priest. "Didn't I, Frank?"

Her father was looking at her, too, an expression of concern etched on his rugged features. He turned abruptly to Bonnie. "What, hon?"

"I said I had trouble sleeping when I was pregnant," Bonnie said, and huffed in feigned exasperation. She shook her head at Father Michael. "I guess after thirty years together he's finally started to tune me out." She rambled on about pregnancy and hormones to the priest, who only seemed to be half-listening.

Frank took Dana by the elbow and steered her away from her mother and Father Michael. "You don't look well, pumpkin."

"I'm tired, Daddy."

"You look pale."

"I'm all right, Daddy. I was just at the doctor's on Friday. Everything is normal."

He gave her elbow a squeeze. "I just worry. It's what daddies do. Joel will tell you one day."

She nodded, then looked about the room for Joel. She spotted him near the dessert table talking with Joseph. The elderly man was speaking animatedly to Joel, and Joel's eyes were narrowed, as if he were trying hard to comprehend the conversation. Joseph, who she remembered, had the gift of foresight. She felt a momentary rush of panic, wondering what they could be discussing and if it had anything to do with her sense of dread.

She didn't have long to think about it, because Deb was clanging a fork against a glass. "Okay, everyone, let's get seated and come to order." She was wearing a light turquoise dress that was a perfect complement to her dark skin and lithe figure, and Dana wondered if after Sofia came, she herself would ever look that elegant and thin again, whether she would ever fit into modest sophisticated clothes. Or if she would be doomed to spend the rest of her life in stretchy cotton knit pants and baggy T-shirts. The thought of that made her tear up, and she hid her face quickly so that no one could see.

She settled into a metal folding chair beside Bonnie, and Joel slid in next to her. She glanced at him and caught a slight note of concern in his eyes. He gave her a quick smile, but it wasn't enough to reassure her.

"What's wrong?" she whispered.

He shook his head, staring toward the front of the room where Deb was setting up at the podium. "Nothing."

"What were you and Joseph talking about?"

He cut his eyes at her, then quickly away. "Nothing really. The baby. When she's due, stuff like that."

Dana turned her attention toward Deb, forcing herself to focus on the bright turquoise of that dress. Because she knew Joel was lying. And if she let herself think about it she was going to cry. And if she started crying, she knew she wouldn't be able to stop.

The room quietened as Deb took her place and looked out at them with her large dark eyes. "Welcome, everyone. Before we begin I'd just like to remind everyone that today is the anniversary of when we lost Barry." She cleared her throat, then looked up with an apologetic smile. "Hardly seems like a year, does it?" she asked, and several of the members gave murmurs of agreement. "I thought it only fitting that we light a candle in Barry's honor and have a moment of silence." She fumbled with a lighter until she set the candle aglow on the small table beside the podium, then looked toward the ceiling. "Barry, I hope you've found the peace you were never able to achieve here in this world." She stepped back and bowed her head.

In the heavy silence, Dana thought back to that horrible summer two years ago when that early morning telephone call Barry made to Joel was what probably saved her life. And poor Barry, so tormented by visions and dreams, tortured by losses in his own life he could foresee but not prevent, had rejoiced with them when he knew his gift had somehow finally made a difference to someone. But that was short-lived. In the months that followed, he had grown more and more depressed and stopped communicating with people from the group. Isolated himself from his few friends and remaining family. Until that night last year when he climbed to the roof of the eight-story First State Bank downtown and flung himself to the sidewalk below and finally managed to accomplish what decades of half-hearted attempts with pills and razors to the wrists had not. He had left a note in his apartment, but Dana had never learned its contents. And for the most part, she didn't want to know. Barry's death wasn't the first in the group, but it was the first suicide among them, and it hit many of them hard. Even now, a year later, as the candle sputtered in the front of the room she could hear the muffled sniffling of several people in the circle.

Finally, after what seemed an eternity, Deb resumed her position at the podium, dabbing at her watery eyes with a tissue. "All right. Let's begin. Mary Beth, can you give us the treasurer's report, please?"

* * *

When the business part was over and everyone had taken their turn at what her dad jokingly referred to as "psychic group therapy," and the crowd made its way toward the tables laden with food and drink, Dana remained in her chair. She felt numb. She hadn't spoken today in the group session, which wasn't unusual for her because she didn't normally have a lot to contribute at these meetings, but apparently her discomfort was enough for all to see.

"You okay?" Joel asked.

Everyone stop asking me that! "I'm fine," she said, knowing he didn't buy it for a minute, and knowing he would ask again on the drive home.

"I'm going to get some pie and coffee. You want anything?"

She shook her head. "I'm fine," she said again.

She watched him lumber toward the dessert and felt a pang of love in her chest that threatened another weeping spell.

"How are you doing, Dana?" said Deb, sliding into Joel's vacant seat. "You ready to have this baby?"

Dana laughed humorlessly and hid her teary eyes. "Absolutely."

"Tell me the truth," Deb said. Dana met her gaze and saw the seriousness in the other woman's eyes. "Something's wrong. I saw it the second you walked through the door."

Dana blew out a breath. There was no hiding from Deb. "I'm just scared," she said.

"Of what?"

Dana snorted. "I don't know, to be honest. I just

have this feeling of. . . "

Deb's gaze softened. "Dread?"

Dana nodded. "Yes. Dread. Like something is, I don't know, going to jump out at me at any minute."

Deb placed a hand atop Dana's. "Is everything all right with you and Joel?"

"Yes!" Dana blurted. "Oh, yes, we're okay."

"Have you told Joel how you're feeling?"

Dana sighed and looked at the floor, at the scuff marks across the beige tiles. "Not really. I don't want to worry him."

"But he knows something's wrong." It wasn't a question. It was a statement, and Dana knew Deb was speaking the truth. "If I saw it, if *Father Michael* could see it for goodness' sake, you know your own husband senses it. Even if he wasn't sensitive, it's written all over your face. You need to talk to Joel, and you need to be honest and open with him."

"I know that."

"Have you thought that if he knows something's wrong and you're not telling him about it that you're actually making things worse? That maybe all kinds of things are going through his head that are ten times more terrible than the truth?"

Dana shook her head. "No. I hadn't thought of that." She squeezed Deb's hand. "You're right. That's been so stupid of me. He has so much on him, I just didn't want to worry him with this."

Deb smoothed the dress across her thighs. "Look,

I've never had kids, so I don't know firsthand, but pregnancy can really mess with your hormones. Maybe what you're feeling isn't clairvoyant at all. Maybe it's physical. Have you told your doctor how you're feeling?"

"No," she admitted, somewhat ashamed. "I just assumed the feeling was coming from the outside."

"But you're psychoscopic, right?"

"Huh?"

"You read objects. You don't have the gift of precognition. Like Barry did. Or Joseph does."

"True."

"So why do you think you'd suddenly develop that ability?"

Dana shrugged. "I don't know. You're probably right. I'm sure it's just hormones."

Deb looked away, focusing on the far wall.   "Unless. . . "

Dana leaned forward. "Unless what?"

"Unless it's coming from the baby."

Dana squeezed Deb's arm. "Is that possible?"

Deb laughed. "Honey, anything's possible when you're dealing with this stuff. But to be on the safe side, you should talk to your doc."

"I will. Thank you."

Deb stood. "I'm famished. I want to get some of that apple pie you brought before it's all gone." She started toward the food, then turned back. "Everything's going to be all right, Dana," she said. "Don't worry."

Dana gave her a faint smile and watched her clack away in her black pumps. Deb was right of course. But why did the fear still weigh on her like a lead blanket?

* * *

3:35 PM

By the time the meeting concluded and he and Dana had said their goodbyes, the rain had returned. In the parking lot, Bonnie held her jacket over her head in the downpour and gave each of them a quick peck on the cheek. "You two be careful," she said. She glanced up at the sky. "I don't like the looks of those clouds."

Frank shook his head. "Come on, old worry wart, they'll be fine." He gave Joel a wink and opened the van door for Bonnie. "See ya, Papa."

Joel nodded, cringing as he helped Dana into the car. Frank had started calling him "Papa" right after they learned Dana was pregnant. Joel knew Frank meant it in an affectionate way, but it grated on him. The same way as when his mother had started calling him "Little Man" right after she got together with that bastard who would eventually marry her, break her, and ultimately kill her. What was wrong with just calling him by his name?

He slid into the Corolla's driver seat and started the engine, turning the defroster on full blast to clear the fog on the windshield. Dana was shivering in the seat next to him. "It'll warm up here in a sec."

"I just got chilled in the rain," she said.

They sat in silence for a bit and watched Frank and Bonnie drive off toward the street. "Sad day today, talking about Barry and all," he said.

She nodded. "Yeah. I can't believe it's been a year already."

"Poor guy. He just wanted to stop seeing things, I guess."

"Yeah."

He drummed his fingers on the steering wheel. The beat of some boy band song on the radio was barely audible. "I can't imagine what a burden it must be to. . . to *know* things and not be able to shut it off. Not like us being able to just avoid touching people or things. But to just have things invade your head like that with no control over it. To just constantly walk around with your mind be like a TV you can't turn off. Or a radio picking up random signals. And to see stuff that's going to happen and not be able to – "

"Shut *up*!" Dana suddenly screamed.

He looked at her, his mouth agape. "Wha –"

"Just shut up about it! I don't want to hear about it anymore." She reached down and snapped off the radio.

His stomach burned with confusion, then anger. "What's the matter with you? What did I say?"

She shook her head and stared out the passenger window. Tears glinted on her cheeks. "I'm sorry," she whispered. "I didn't mean to. . . " Joel reached over and took her hand, half-afraid she would jerk it away. But she didn't. Instead she squeezed his and looked back at him. "You were right," she said. "I've still been holding back from you. It's nothing bad. I just didn't want to worry you."

"What?"

She swallowed and looked at the rain washing across the front glass. "When I said I was scared, it's not just about being a parent. It's not just about childbirth."

"What is it then?"

She turned back to him. "For the past few weeks I've just had this. . . *feeling*. A feeling that something's going to happen. Something bad."

Ordinarily he would have smiled. Would have laughed at her being silly and worried about nothing. Would have blamed it on the pregnancy and hormones run amuck. But not today. Not after talking with Joseph. "Look, babe. There's something I need to tell you, too. I hope it's nothing, but. . . "

Her eyes widened, and he knew he'd frightened her. "What?"

"Well, you saw me talking to Joseph. I didn't exactly tell you the truth in there."

She nodded and stared at her belly, absently rubbing the bulge with her fingertips. "I know." She looked at him and tears were spilling down her cheeks. "It's bad, isn't it? We're going to lose Sofia, aren't we?"

He took her hands in his and kissed them. "No, it's nothing like that. Sofia's going to be fine. It's. . . "

"What?" Her eyes blared. "*What?*"

He squeezed her hands, unsure of how to proceed. "Joseph said he senses danger around you. Something vague. He's not sure. Something about the bedroom."

"The bedroom? What exactly did he say? Should I start sleeping somewhere else?"

"He said you should never be alone there. He said we need to get an alarm system. He said I need to reinforce the locks. He even. . . " Here Joel almost chuckled. "He even said I need to nail all the windows shut."

Dana looked at him, shaking her head. "Dear God. What – *who* – does he think is going to try to get in?"

"He doesn't know."

Dana blew out a breath, staring straight ahead at the fog that was beginning to dissipate off the front glass. "You know I wasn't exactly truthful with you either," she said. "I've had this sense of dread for the past few weeks. Something more than the pregnancy. Something bigger." She caressed her belly again. "Something that affects all three of us. What you said about Joseph kind of confirms it. I even talked to Deb about it today." She looked at him. "Joel, she thinks it's possible I'm picking up premonitions from Sofia."

Joel fought the urge to laugh. "From *Sofia*? How is that even possible?"

"I don't know. But it makes sense. I've never had the kind of gift Joseph has, but here I am sensing something – a threat, a *warning*. And if Sofia is sensitive. . .

"

Joel nodded. He'd seen crazier things since becoming acquainted with the group. "Well, one thing I want you to promise me."

"What's that?"

"No more secrets."

She smiled. "No more secrets."

* * *

The rain struck again about five miles from the Cedar Hill exit. As before, the pounding storm washed over the windshield until Joel could barely see the white stripe along the edge of the pavement. He switched the wipers to full-blast, then slowed down to fifty, then forty.

"Maybe you should pull over again," Dana said. He glanced at her and saw she was gripping the edge of her seat with one hand and the door pull with the other.

"We'll be all right," he said. "Besides, we're almost home. Just a couple more miles to the exit."

"I don't know how you can see the road."

"I don't think it's quite as bad as before," he said. He gave her a quick glance. "You know, I think – "

The tail lights of the semi suddenly appeared through the veil of rain. Joel had just enough time to stomp on the brake pedal and feel the vibration of the anti-lock brakes kick in, just enough time to feel the tires slip helplessly across the wet pavement –

. . . those damned bald tires I should have bought new ones months ago . . .

– just enough time to catch sight of the terror in Dana's eyes and hear her utter a short, sharp scream.

Then there was the bone-jarring impact as the Corolla slammed into the back of the trailer. The crash of breaking glass. The sudden numbness of his face as it smacked the airbag.

Then the awful, abrupt quiet.

* * *

5:05 PM

Earlier there had been a discordant wail of sirens in the distance, and vaguely she wondered what was going on and where, but the important thing was that the baby wasn't disturbed, and soon she forgot about it all and settled in to watch *The Great Ziegfeld* on the TV in the front room.

Over the past few days Kris had begun thinking of the baby as Eric. It was hard simply thinking of him as a nameless infant. It seemed too cold and clinical. He needed something that made him more human. She thought back to sixth grade, to her first crush. Eric Brown. Tall and gangly, with a comma of dark hair that lay over his forehead, and sleepy brown eyes that feigned indifference but always seemed to belie the deep thinker within. She would sit at her desk throughout Mrs. Lovingood's English class, gazing at the back of his head, at the small freckle on his right ear. She

longed to kiss the freckle and to feel the tiny downy
hairs of his ear against her lips. One day on the playground he and two of his friends cornered her in a
deserted section at the far end, away from where the
teachers could see, and glowered at her. "Why you always staring at me?" he spat. She opened her mouth to
tell him how much she liked him, how she loved looking at him and dreaming about holding his hand and
kissing his ear, but before she could get the words out
his fist shot out and the side of her face exploded in
pain. She fell in a heap onto the grassless dry dirt of the
playground, and she remembered how a plume of
brown dust burst into the air before it dissipated in the
breeze. "Freak!" he screamed at her, and then he ran
back toward the swings, cackling with the two other
boys. She waited for them to get out of earshot, then
climbed to her feet and dusted off her clothes. She
wasn't surprised to find blood trickling from her nose.
The next day a large purple bruise appeared across her
cheek, though her mother never noticed it. When
Grandma Hettie asked about it, she said she'd fallen at
recess. She never told anyone that Eric had hit her. And
she continued to watch him from afar, continued to
nurse the pang of want in her chest. But after that year,
he moved away to Indianapolis and she never saw him
again. She continued to think about him over the years,
though, even as she grew older and began to experiment
with boys (and sometimes girls), none could ever compare with the feelings that Eric Brown still stirred

within her.

Her thoughts were interrupted by a light tapping at the front door. She froze, her heart thumping in her chest. Had she imagined it? She muted the television. She could hear the hum of the machinery in the nursery and the beeps of the monitor. The tapping came again and she made her way to the door. The fanlight window was too high for her to see who was on the front stoop, and she pressed her cheek against the door, as if she could sense who was behind it. "Who's there?" she called.

"It's Maria," the muffled voice on the other side said.

She exhaled in relief and eased the door open. Maria stood there in a red suit and black blouse, her ebony hair perfectly coiffed and her olive skin flawless. "May I come in?"

"Oh, yes." Kris stepped aside and Maria stepped into the room, bringing with her the soft scent of mimosa.

"I'm sorry to drop by unannounced," Maria said. "I was on my way to mass. I thought I would stop to see what you need by way of supplies."

"I've made a list. It's in the kitchen." Kris headed toward the back of the house, and Maria followed, her heels tapping on the hardwood floors. "Would you like something to drink? I can make some coffee. Or would you prefer tea?"

"Nothing, thank you," Maria said. "As I said, I'm on my way to mass."

"Oh," she said, beginning to feel flustered. "That's right." She ripped the top sheet from the memo pad where she'd written down what she needed and handed it to the other woman.

Maria glanced over it, then smiled at her. "Do you need anything for yourself? Anything personal you'd like me to pick up?"

"No, I'm good."

"I'd like to see him," Maria said.

"Certainly." She led Maria to the nursery and silently swung open the door. "He's asleep at the moment."

Maria watched him for a moment, then looked back at her. "You've done well. He looks healthy."

"Yes, thank you."

"The monsignor will be pleased." Maria turned and headed for the front door.

"Will he?" she asked, following and admiring Maria's red suit.

"He's coming for the child tomorrow."

Kris's chest tightened. "Tomorrow?" So soon. She would have to give him up so soon. "Already?"

Maria paused at the door and studied her for a moment, the faintest trace of a smile on her lips. "His family is waiting."

"Yes, yes of course." What must Maria think of her? "A good family?"

Maria smiled in earnest now. "The best. Lovely Catholic parents. Very worthy."

She nodded. "That's wonderful."

"The monsignor is eager to meet you."

"Oh really?"

"He will have a new assignment for you."

"All right."

Maria stepped outside, then turned back to her. "You're not having second thoughts about our work are you?"

"No, of course not."

Maria looked at her, and her dark eyes were suddenly cold. "Good." She made her way down the sidewalk in the golden late afternoon light toward the black Jaguar in the narrow drive, her red heels clopping on the concrete.

Once Kris was alone again, she returned to the sofa and sank into the cushions. On the television, an elaborate Busby Berkley dance routine paraded silently across the screen. She leaned back and watched it for a moment. A new assignment. She took a deep breath. She hoped it would go as smoothly as the last.

MONDAY, OCTOBER 6

3:15 AM

THERE WAS A STEADY, rhythmic beeping. It was coming from somewhere on her left. It echoed inside her brain, relentless and piercing.

Her eyelids were so heavy. She couldn't open them. In fact, her whole body was heavy. And uncomfortably numb, as if she were encased in rubber.

The crash.

With every ounce of her strength she forced her eyelids open. Everything was gray and unfocused. She was in a hospital bed, that much she could tell.

Sofia.

Her belly was round and full under the white blanket. She moved her fingers toward the mound. Her arm weighed a thousand pounds. As her vision cleared a bit, she could see an IV tube snaking off from the back of her hand. At last her fingertips rested atop her stomach, and a surge of fear and adrenaline seemed to wash away the dullness in her head.

In the faint light she could see Joel sprawled in a chair next to the bed, his head lolling on his chest. Could hear him snoring above the incessant beep of whatever machine was next to her ear. He was here. He was all right. Tears brimmed in her eyes. "Joel," she croaked, surprised at the weakness of her voice. "Joel?"

His eyelids fluttered open, and he stared at her a moment as if trying to get his bearings. And then he was upon her. "Dana! Oh, my god!" He kissed her cheek and ran a thumb along her chin. "How you feeling, baby?"

A thousand questions flooded her brain at once. "The wreck. . . Sofia. . . "

"She's fine, baby," Joel said, and tears glinted in his eyes. "Sofia's fine."

Dana let out a breath she wasn't aware she had been holding. "Oh thank God, thank God." She relaxed against the pillow. "What happened? I don't remember. . . "

"We rear-ended a semi," Joel said. "Fucking idiot was stopped in the middle of the interstate."

She was suddenly aware of the cuts across his forehead, the bandage across his left ear. "Your face. . . "

"I'm okay," he said. "Just a little banged up. Not much you can do to make me any uglier."

She felt a relieved smile play on her lips. He was

okay. Sofia was okay.

"You're all right," he told her. "They just wanted to keep you overnight as a precaution."

She tried to swallow, and her throat was like petrified wood. "Thirsty. . ."

Joel poured some water from a hospital-pink plastic pitcher into a foam cup, then held it to her lips. The water was painfully cold but thankfully wet. "Not too much," he told her. "Don't want you to get sick to your stomach."

She closed her eyes. "I feel so weak."

"Probably the tranquilizers," Joel told her. "They had to sedate you."

"What? Why?"

"You kept fighting the nurses," he said. "You were screaming about Sofia. They barely got your IV in." He grinned crookedly. "You don't remember any of that?"

She shook her head. "No."

He gave a small snort. "It was pretty funny," he said. "Little pregnant Dana fighting off three good-sized women."

She blew out a breath. "Embarrassing."

His fingers traced up and down her arm. "Don't be embarrassed. You were just worried about Sofia."

"Mom and Dad. . ."

"They were here after you were asleep. I sent them home around ten."

"What time is it now?"

"A little after three. Go on back to sleep. You need

to rest."

"Are you sure we're all okay? You're not just saying that are you?"

His fingers tightened on her arm. "We're all fine. No secrets, remember? The Toyota's probably totaled, though."

She smiled. "I don't care about that."

"And we'll both probably be pretty sore for a while."

"As long as we're alive. And Sofia's okay."

He smiled down at her and stroked her cheek with his fingers. "Go to sleep, babe. Everything is fine. At least we know what Joseph's warning meant."

She nuzzled against his hand, and in a moment she was drifting away.

* * *

8:45 AM

Bob Richardson was furious. Halloran could see it in his furrowed brow and the flushed red of his face, which seemed to be getting darker by the minute. Even the whites of his eyes had turned a bright shade of pissed-off pink. "I want to know what you morons are doing down here," he said, his teeth clenched. "It's been almost a week since my little girl's murder. We bury her tomorrow and we haven't heard a word from anybody."

Beside him, his wife sniveled into a tissue, her green

eyes fixed on the edge of the desk. "We just want to know what's going on," she said, her voice cracking. Sue Richardson was a handsome woman, just beginning to show her age – early fifties if Halloran had to guess – with a shock of gray in the center of her otherwise naturally dark hair. "Everyone was so helpful when. . . when all this happened." She dabbed at her eyes. "And now –"

"Now nobody's returning our calls," Mr. Richardson spat.

Halloran had seen this before when an investigation stalled. And he felt for them. Their grief and anger was thick and heavy in the closed office. They just wanted answers. They wanted justice. Someone to blame. Someone to pay for what had happened. "I apologize that we haven't kept you informed," Halloran told them. "The truth is, there hasn't been much to report."

Mr. Richardson leaned forward, so close that Halloran could see small white hairs sprouting from the tip of his nose. "Then what are you doing? Why aren't you people out there combing the streets? Why aren't you going door to door looking for our grandson? You and I both know he's out there. Along with that sick bastard that killed our little girl."

"Mr. Richardson, calm down."

"I guess you idiots are too busy out there writing parking tickets and hanging out at the coffee shop."

His wife elbowed him in the ribs. "Bob! Stop it. You're not helping." She gave a sideways glance at him. "What would poor Addie think about how you're acting?" She broke into fresh sobs, then blew her nose. "She was such a sweet girl," she said to Halloran. "Always wanting to help people. She had such a bright future. At one time she wanted to be a teacher. If she'd only gone on to college."

"If she hadn't got mixed up with that white trash meth-head," Mr. Richardson muttered.

Mrs. Richardson shook her head and buried her face in a fresh tissue. "Bob. . . "

"We knew he was trouble as soon as we met him. We tried to talk to her. Reason with her." His voice broke and he looked away. "You have any kids, Lieutenant?"

"No, sir."

Mr. Richardson stared at a poster on the office wall. A smiling dad with a small boy sitting astride his shoulders. The boy was laughing. The copy read, "Talk to your kids about drugs. . . before someone else does." A single tear slid down Bob Richardson's ruddy face. "She was our only child," he said, his voice barely above a whisper. "Neither of us liked Billy Ray from the moment she brought him home. He was rough."

"She'd always dated nice boys before," Mrs. Richardson said.

"He was rude," Bob said. "Wouldn't shake my hand, wouldn't look me in the eye." He looked at Halloran. "I don't trust anyone who won't look me in the eye." He held Halloran's gaze for several seconds, testing him.

"Anyway, we weren't surprised when he lost his job at the toy factory. I couldn't believe they'd hired him in the first place."

"Addie tried to hide it from us, but we knew he was dealing drugs," Mrs. Richardson said. "Making it, or whatever they do."

"We could smell it on her," Mr. Richardson said. "You can't hide that smell. It seeps into your clothes. We worried about what being around it was doing to her. To the baby."

"If it helps," Halloran says, "the coroner didn't find any traces of drugs in Addie's system."

Both of them nodded and were silent for a moment.

"Her real name was Adele," Sue Richardson said suddenly. "Like the singer."

Halloran nodded. He'd seen the name on the coroner's report. "I promise you we're doing everything we can. Believe me. And we're doing everything possible to find your grandson."

Mr. Richardson looked at him. "Do you still think he's. . . " He swallowed hard. "You still think he's alive?"

"We have no reason to believe otherwise," Halloran said.

Mrs. Richardson dabbed at her eyes, keeping her gaze on the floor. "I was reading about missing persons," she said. "They say after forty-eight hours the chances of finding someone decreases by half. Is that true?"

"I will be honest with you. It's been five days and we have no solid leads. Yes, it becomes more difficult to find someone the longer they've been missing." He looked at them. "But I don't want you to give up. We've contacted the FBI and the state police, and we've notified all the hospitals in the area. Someone knows where he is. Sooner or later he will need medical care and he will be seen by a doctor or a clinic." He paused. "Had Addie decided on a name?"

Mrs. Richardson shook her head. "She said her and Billy Ray were arguing over it. She wanted to call him Robert Matthew, after her daddy and my daddy. Billy Ray wanted to name him Billy Ray Junior." She wrinkled her nose. "I never did like a boy being a junior. It's like the poor child can't have his own name." She shot him a glance. "Oh, I'm sorry. You're not a junior are you?"

He gave her a smile. "No, ma'am."

* * *

When the Richardsons had gone, Halloran made his way to the breakroom and poured a cup of black coffee. It had been sitting a while, and now it was scorched and thick. He considered starting a new pot, but fuck it. The visit with Addie Richardson's parents had drained him. He'd talked with grieving parents many times over the years, but the Richardsons were different. It was the loss of their daughter combined with the faint hope of finding their grandson alive. The roller coaster of emotions emanated off of them like waves of heat.

Brooks was buried in paperwork when Halloran peeked in, an intense look of determination across his face. Halloran knocked lightly, and Brooks looked up, his features softening. "Hey, what's up?"

Halloran sank into a chair and set his coffee on the edge of Brooks' desk. "Just had a visit from the Richardsons."

"How'd that go?"

Halloran shrugged. "'Bout like you'd expect." He took a sip of the coffee and winced as it seared his tongue. "I know this is a pointless question, but have we heard anything from any of the hospitals or clinics?"

"Not a damn thing," Brooks said, his face grim. "And nothing new from the Feds or state boys, to answer your next question."

Halloran stared at the steam rising from his foam cup. The coffee smelled like burned cereal. "I told the Richardsons I'd be at the funeral tomorrow. You want to go with me?"

"Of course."

"You don't have to."

"I want to. It'll be a good time to see if there's anyone there that seems out of place."

"Exactly." He lifted the cup to his lips, then set it back down. "I wonder though. . . "

"What?"

"There's the very real possibility that the perp left

here the same day Addie Richardson was killed. We know the person or persons had medical training. Most likely neonatal skills. Could be keeping that child alive somewhere. Depending on their level of skill, they could be nearby or. . . or anywhere."

Brooks chewed his pen. "How difficult would it be to travel with a newborn? I mean, one fresh out of the womb?"

"You're the dad," Halloran said. "You tell me."

Brooks continued to gnaw on the ballpoint. "Carly was healthy," he said. "Still, they wanted to monitor her for twenty-four hours. Something about some medication the doctor had given Diane while she was pregnant. Seemed like there were nurses constantly in and out, checking Carly's vitals, adjusting her IVs, something."

"So you don't think Addie's baby could be too far away?"

Brooks tossed the pen to the desk with a clatter. "I'm not saying it's impossible, I just think it would be damn difficult to go much of a distance with a baby a day or so old. And that's a healthy baby. You'd think Addie's baby might have suffered some trauma from being ripped out of his mother's womb in a parking lot. Trust me, that child is getting medical attention somewhere. I'd be willing to bet he's pretty close."

"If he's still alive," Halloran said.

"Yeah. If." Brooks leaned back in his chair, clasping his hands behind his head. "So. . . you still coming over tonight to meet one-legged Kelly?"

"I am," Halloran said. "Thought I might bring along some wood stain. That wooden leg of hers probably needs a touchup."

Brooks laughed. "I think you'll like her."

"I stalked her Facebook page," Halloran said, feeling his face flush.

Brooks' eyes widened. "You did? You dog, you!"

Halloran grinned. "She really is an attractive woman."

"Told you."

"What happened to her husband?"

"Not sure," Brooks said. "Accident maybe?"

Halloran rubbed his chin. "Is that how her son got the scar on his neck?"

"Hmmm. I don't know. I don't guess I knew he had one."

"I noticed it in her pictures. Some of the younger pictures of him he doesn't have it."

Brooks smiled broadly. "You really did stalk her Facebook, didn't you?"

"Hey," Halloran told him, "I had to see what you were getting me into."

"That's only fair, I suppose." He leaned forward. "Diane's looking forward to it. She thinks a lot of Kelly, and of course she loooooooves you."

"Well, of course," Halloran said. He waved his hands up and down his body. "Who wouldn't love all this?"

* * *

12:20 PM

"Easy does it," Joel said, lifting Dana up the front steps of the house.

"Let me get the door," Frank said, brushing past them. He fumbled with the keys, then dropped them on the metal threshold with a clatter. "Dammit."

"Calm down, Frank," Bonnie said from the yard. "No need to rush. Joel doesn't look like he's having any trouble carrying his load." She winked at Joel.

"We're good," Joel said. "For a pregnant woman she doesn't weigh a lot." He grinned at Dana, then kissed her on the nose. "Little mama."

She laughed. "Big daddy."

"All right, that's enough of that," Frank said, swinging open the front door. He stood aside as Joel carried Dana into the living room.

"I can walk, Joel," Dana said. "I'm on bed rest. I'm not a paraplegic."

"Hush," he told her, heading down the hall. He set her carefully onto the bed and fluffed the pillows behind her back. "How's that?"

"Thank you." She carefully stretched out her legs, wincing as she did so.

The OB/GYN had ordered Dana to stay in bed through the remaining weeks of her pregnancy. Although there was no indication that Sofia had been injured in the accident, Dana was to take no unnecessary chances. A bump, a fall, or – God forbid – another accident could send her into early labor, and that could be dangerous for both Sofia and Dana. Mandatory bed rest for three weeks, if Dana went until her due date. But that was really up to Sofia.

Bonnie appeared in the bedroom door, her chubby face flushed beneath her short blond hair. "Can I get you something? You want a drink?"

"No, I'm good."

Joel fished through the clutter on the bedside table and presented her with the TV remote.

She smiled up at him. "Joel always knows what I need."

He glanced at Bonnie, saw her grin at Dana's comment, and his face grew hot. He reached out and stroked Dana's hair. "You rest now." He followed Bonnie out to the kitchen. "I'm going to make some coffee. Would you guys like some? Or a Coke?"

Frank sat at the dining table, his readers perched on the tip of his nose and his pudgy face pinched in concentration as he stared at his phone. "Sure," he said, not looking up. "Coffee would be great."

Bonnie shrugged. "If you guys are having some, I guess I wouldn't mind a cup." She pulled out a chair and collapsed into it, blowing out a breath. "I feel like I can finally breathe easy, now that Dana's home and resting."

Joel glanced at her as he pulled the coffee from the cabinet. He wondered, not for the first time, about Frank and Bonnie's gifts. They'd never shared anything specific in the group meetings, only vagaries about feelings and hunches. Their intuitions were obviously not on the same par with their daughter's, or even his own. Maybe that was for the best. All this was hard enough without the two of them hovering over Dana like hummingbirds. And if Joseph had spoken his warning to them as he had to Joel, there would have been no getting rid of them. At least that was behind them now, and they could get through the rest of the pregnancy without a dire prediction hanging over their heads.

As the coffee maker gurgled to life, Joel sat down with Frank and Bonnie and gave a long, loud yawn before he could stop himself. Something hitched in his shoulder and he cried out, making Bonnie jump. "Sorry."

"I guess you'll be sore for a few days," Frank told him, eyeing him over the top of his readers. "You should probably take it easy yourself."

"I intend on it," Joel said, "but I've got to go back to work tomorrow."

"Well, don't you worry about Dana," Bonnie said. "I can stay here through the day while you're at work."

Joel looked at her. "You'd do that?"

"Of course I'll do that!" she snapped, then chuckled. "Honestly! She's my daughter. It's not like I have anything else to do."

"Except nag me," Frank muttered, still staring at his phone.

Bonnie shot him a glance. "I have my volunteering

at the nursing home on Tuesdays and Thursdays, but they'll just have to do without me for a while."

"Lucky them," Frank said.

"What are you doing, anyway?" Bonnie said. "You've been looking at that phone for three days." She looked at Joel. "Frank got that new phone Saturday, and I swear he hasn't said two words to me since. He's had his face glued to that thing the whole time."

"You should be thanking me," Frank said. He punched the screen with a stubby forefinger. "I took a picture of Dana this morning, and I'm trying to figure out how to put it up on Facebook."

Bonnie spun toward him in her chair. "Facebook! You took a picture of Dana in the hospital and you want to put it on *Facebook?*"

"Relax," he told her. "I just wanted to say she came home and everyone was all right."

"She'll *kill* you if she sees that!"

Joel watched them banter back and forth for a moment, unsure of whether to be more surprised by their good-natured ribbing or the fact that his father-in-law had a Facebook account. One thing was sure: Frank and Bonnie were still in love with each other, even after all this time. He looked forward to the day he would be sitting at Sofia's dining table shooting good-natured insults with Dana while his son-in-law looked on in envy. It was a thought that filled him with hope. And after the last two days, hope was a valuable commodity.

* * *

5:40 PM

The sound of car doors brought her instantly to her feet. She had known they were coming, of course, but there had been no set time. She'd been waiting for hours, tense and anxious. She turned down the volume on the television and smoothed out her scrubs, then checked her appearance in the hall mirror before stepping over to the front window and peering through the crack in the drapes at the black Jaguar in the driveway.

The monsignor was much shorter than she had imagined. Portly. A ring of dark hair encircled his head, leaving the top naked and shiny. Black eyes stared intently beneath thick eyebrows, and his face had that ashy look common to men with dark hair and heavy beards that no amount of shaving could lessen. Gray slacks. A tweed jacket over his black shirt with its white priest's collar. Maria was dressed smartly in a plaid wool suit and holding an infant carrier, a small tote bag dangling from one thin wrist.

She was instantly afraid, though she didn't know why. There was a light rap on the door, and her blood was suddenly cold. She took one last look at herself in the mirror, noticing the fright in her expression, and swung the door open wide.

The monsignor stood patiently on the stoop, staring

up at her. God, his eyes were dark. Darker than any she had ever seen. Black. An uncontrollable shiver rippled through her. She nodded at him. "Monsignor."

"It is good to meet you," he said, his accent thick. She struggled to place it. Spanish? Portuguese like Maria's? It was like nothing she'd ever heard before. He held out his hand, palm downward, and she stared at it a moment, at the large gold ring on the third finger, before she realized she was expected to kiss it. She took the hand in her own, surprised to find it warm and dry, and brought it to her lips. "I trust we have kept you comfortable," he said.

"Yes," she said, "very much." She moved aside as the monsignor and Maria stepped into the entryway. "How was your trip?"

"Uneventful," he said. His gaze flitted about the house, taking in the bare walls and secondhand furniture. The place wasn't well-furnished, but it was clean. He would see that, she thought with satisfaction. And he would know she wasn't lazy.

She smiled at Maria, standing behind the monsignor, but Maria's expression remained neutral and mannequin-like.

The monsignor's eyes met hers and her pulse quickened. "Where is the child?" he asked.

"Oh," she said, suddenly feeling foolish. "In here."

She led them into the front bedroom where the baby lay in the bassinet. He was awake and silent, his limbs jerking involuntarily as he watched the mobile spin above him. She lifted him up and placed him in the monsignor's waiting arms.

"Ah," the monsignor said, a smile playing on his lips as he gazed into the face of the infant. "What a beautiful baby boy."

Before she could stop herself, she blurted, "I've been calling him Eric." A look of disapproval passed quickly across Maria's features, and she knew she'd made a mistake.

The monsignor looked at her. "It is not up to us to name the children, Krystine."

Her face grew hot. "Yes, yes of course. I understand. I only call him that because. . . well, I felt I needed to call him *something*."

"I see." He gazed back into the face of the baby. "We must leave the naming of the children up to the new parents, Krystine."

"Yes. I'm. . . sorry."

"Kris has done an excellent job of caring for him," Maria said, locking glances with her. Again, her expression did not soften, even as Kris gave her another smile of gratitude.

"I can see that she has," the monsignor said. "Your choice to hire her was wise."

Maria nodded. "Thank you, Monsignor." She took the infant from his arms and placed him into the carrier.

The monsignor turned back to Kris. "Maria tells me you are ready for another assignment."

"Yes. Yes, of course."

He pulled a manila envelope from Maria's tote bag and presented it. "Samantha Jarvis."

A sting of panic stabbed her. "Jarvis?"

"You know her of course."

"Yes," she said, hoping she was wrong. "She's Daniel Jarvis's daughter. The senator. Right?"

"Correct."

She stared at the sealed envelope in her hands. A senator's daughter. This felt bigger than what she'd anticipated.

The monsignor was studying her. "You seem. . . reluctant."

She looked at him. "No. I'm fine. Just a bit surprised is all."

The monsignor's hand rested on her arm, and his touch was hot. He leaned closer, so close she caught the faint scent of peppermint on his warm breath. His eyes seemed to pierce her to her soul. "We must know that you are with us. There can be no question about your loyalty."

"No," she whispered. "Of course not."

He drew back, and she realized how his closeness had overpowered her. As if she had momentarily forgotten how to breathe. "There is no room for unreliability in this work, Krystine."

"Yes, Monsignor."

Maria opened the door and glanced back at her. "I'll be expecting to hear from you," she said.

The monsignor followed Maria out onto the front

stoop in the purple twilight. "Goodbye, Krystine."

"Goodbye, Monsignor," she said, but he had already closed the door.

She sank onto the sofa, watching the silent images on the television and listening as the Jaguar's doors thudded closed again. Once. Twice. Three times. Then the purr of the motor as it backed out of the drive and faded out down the street.

She looked at the plain manila envelope in her hands, feeling the bulky contents of folded papers inside. She took a breath and ripped it open.

* * *

7:05 PM

Halloran glanced at the clock on the dashboard. He was late. He knew he would be.

He had hurried home and jumped into the shower, and the nervousness and rushing had left him flushed and hot and sweaty. He had stretched out in his underwear on the bed to catch a quick smoke and cool off and had fallen asleep, only to awaken at 6:45 PM in a groggy panic. He pulled on his best khakis and a blue Oxford, then donned a light sweater to conceal the fact he hadn't ironed the shirt, and by the time he left the house, he was again coated in a film of sweat. He hoped the sweater wasn't a mistake.

He wheeled his Trailblazer into the drive and parked

behind a dark Toyota bearing a yellow "Lake County Junior High School Mom" bumper sticker. He turned off the engine and sat in the darkness for a moment. His heart was thudding in his chest and there was a knot in his stomach. His hands were slick and sweaty on the leather of the steering wheel, and he wiped them on his khakis. Sweaty palms would not make a good first impression.

He looked at with himself in the rear-view mirror. "Calm down," he said out loud. "It's not a date. It's just dinner." He took a deep breath. "Let's do it."

Brooks' house was a white two-story Cape Cod in one of the older subdivisions on the edge of town. The yard was small and neatly trimmed, and a row of box-woods ran the length of the front walk up to a small porch. Through the front window he could see into the living room. Brooks sat in a recliner, a bottle of beer in his hand and wearing a Packers sweatshirt. Diane was perched on one end of the couch, speaking rapidly and gesticulating with both hands. On the opposite end was Kelly, wearing a light-colored sweater and jeans; he watched her as she nodded and smiled at whatever Diane was saying while one hand idly played with a gold locket that hung in the center of her chest. She really was quite attractive.

Suddenly he felt panicked. He could, of course, turn around and head back home. Call Brooks and offer an apology. A stomach thing. Didn't want to take a chance of giving everyone some kind of bug.

No.

Because he knew if he did that, he would regret it. And not only because he would take a lot of ribbing from Brooks. He would regret it later tonight when he tossed in his sexless bed. He would beat himself up over the fact he had a chance to meet an attractive woman and he had shrugged it off. He would regret it next weekend when his Saturday night was spent alone and lonely.

He took a deep breath and climbed out of the Trailblazer. The early evening air was surprisingly chilly after the warm day, and it was hard to believe he and Brooks had been shirtless on the lake just two days before. The smell of burning leaves wafted along the slight breeze, and the thought flitted through his mind that Sunday's rain should have made everything too damp to burn. He stepped up onto the porch, gave one last glance at Kelly through the window and knocked.

Diane swung the door open wide, spilling light and warmth onto the porch. "Hey! We were starting to wonder about you."

"Sorry," he said, stepping into the room and suddenly remembering that he had planned on stopping to pick up a bottle of wine on his way over. The living room was close and stuffy, and the scent of dinner floated through from the kitchen. Somewhere Nirvana's "Smells Like Teen Spirit" was playing, echoing through the halls

Kelly had already locked glances with him, and she

was on her feet and extending her hand. "Hi, I'm Kelly."

He took her hand, marveling at how smooth and warm it was. "Mike." Her eyes were green, and there was a touch of mischief that made them spark. "Glad to meet you."

Brooks was up and across the room at once, shaking his hand. "Glad you made it." He lofted his bottle. "You want a beer?"

"Sure."

"I'll get it," Diane said. "You guys sit. I need to check on dinner anyway." She patted him on the shoulder as she passed by. "Hope you're hungry."

"Always," he said. He sank down onto the sofa, intensely aware of Kelly as she sat beside him. "So," he said, giving her a furtive glance, "Greg tells me you work at the credit union."

"Yeah. Only been there about three months. My son and I just moved back from Springfield."

"Oh really?"

"Yeah." Her fingers went back to her locket. It was oval and looked both old and expensive. "We moved there last year. Trying to get a fresh start, you know? After. . . "

"Greg told me your husband passed away."

She glanced at him and gave him a quick smile. Obviously it was still a sensitive topic. "I thought it would be good for Trevor – my son – to get away from here. Too many memories, you know?"

Halloran nodded. "You didn't like Springfield?"

She chuckled and shook her head. "Too big. I missed Cedar Hill. I thought we'd enjoy a bigger city. More stuff to do, more opportunities. But I wasn't happy there. And Trevor wasn't happy there. So we moved back here just before school started."

Diane returned with a bottle of Michelob and handed it to Halloran. "Dinner's just about ready," she announced. She settled onto the couch on the other side of Kelly. "So," she said, slapping Kelly's thigh, "you want another glass of wine?"

Kelly shook her head. "No, I'm good." She looked at Halloran. "So, Mike, have you got any kids?" Diane and Brooks laughed, and Kelly glanced back and forth between them, her face flushing. "What? Did I say something wrong?"

"None that he knows about," Brooks said, a little too loudly.

Halloran shot him a look. "They think they're being funny," he told Kelly. "No," he said, turning back to her, "no kids. Never been married."

"He's married to his damn desk," Brooks said, and Halloran wondered how many beers he'd downed already.

"Greg and Diane said you've been with the department a long time."

"Seventeen years now, detective for fifteen." He considered telling her about his years on the force, but decided against it. He didn't want to be a bore. "So what do you do at the credit union?"

"I work in bookkeeping," she said.

"Kelly handles our correspondent bank accounts," Diane said.

"Oh," Halloran said. "That's cool."

"Not really," Kelly said, and they both laughed. "It's a job. It's not like I'm saving humanity or anything."

Halloran took a sip of his beer. "Who was it that said, 'There are no small jobs, just small people?' Was that Ben Franklin?"

"No!" Brooks said, leaning forward. "It was that hotel bitch from the 'eighties. The one that got in trouble for not paying taxes. What was her name? Leona something. They made a movie about her. Leona Helmsley!"

"You're both wrong," Kelly said. "That's from *Gulliver's Travels*."

Halloran looked at her. "Really? Could have sworn that was Ben Franklin."

Diane smirked. "You'll learn it's best not to argue with her, she's always right."

"English Lit major in college," Kelly said.

"Seriously?" Halloran said. "How'd you end up in a credit union? Shouldn't you be teaching or something?"

Kelly shook her head. "Long story," she said. "I'll bore you with it another time."

Brooks leaned back in his chair. "Mike's got plenty of boring stories, too, don'tcha Mike?"

Halloran glared at him, but grinned in spite of himself. "Yeah, I guess I do."

"I bet your job is exciting," Kelly said.

Halloran shrugged. "It can be. It can also be pretty nasty sometimes. And sometimes it's boring as hell."

"Can't be any more boring that looking at numbers all day," Kelly said, shaking her head. She gave Diane an apologetic glance. "Guess I shouldn't be saying that in front of my supervisor."

Diane laughed. "Oh, honey, believe me, I know. You think any of us are thrilled to be there? I mean, besides Todd in Accounts Payable."

"Oh, he's the worst," Kelly said. She stuck her tongue out.

"Wait," Halloran said, "who's Todd?"

"This creepy guy that works at the credit union," Diane said. "He has a thing for Kelly."

"Stop saying that!" Kelly cried. She looked at Halloran. "I kinda feel sorry for him though. I don't think he has any friends."

"Except his cats," Diane said.

"He has cats," Kelly said. "How many, Diane?"

"Ten at last count."

"Ten cats," Kelly said. "Ten."

"That's a lot of pussy!" Brooks said.

Diane gasped. "Greg!"

Brooks laughed. "Well, it is."

"He smells like cats," Kelly said. "And his clothes are always covered in cat hair." She shuddered. "He asked me out once. And I'm ashamed to say I told him I already had plans with Trevor that night. And then I took Trevor to see a movie so it wouldn't be a total lie."

Diane laughed. "Kelly, you're hilarious."

Halloran took another sip from his bottle and glanced at Kelly from the corner of his eye. Her face was flushed and happy. She caught him staring and smiled at him. He smiled back and looked away quickly, already glad he had come. "I have a cat," he said.

"You have *one* cat," Diane said. "Not ten."

"True," he said.

"And you don't smell like cat pee," Kelly said.

"Just cigarettes," Brooks said.

Kelly looked at Brooks, then back at Halloran. "I don't smell cigarettes on you."

"I'm trying to quit," he said.

"He's been trying to quit since I've known him," Brooks said, laughing.

"It's hard," Kelly said. "My husband smoked. Tried to quit for years. Never could."

He looked at her and she held his gaze. "Well I have cut back," he said. "I'm down to half a pack a day."

"That's good," she told him. "Maybe you just need more motivation."

He smiled. "Could be."

* * *

The lasagna was excellent, and Carly made an appearance for dinner, happy to see her "Uncle Mike" and giving him a big hug. She was a pretty, petite ten-year-old, and Halloran knew Greg and Diane would have their hands full fighting off the boys in a couple of years. But she was busy with an art project on her computer, and she quickly scarfed down her dinner and returned to the sanctuary of her room.

The conversation flowed easily among the remaining four of them. Halloran was amazed at how comfortable he was with Kelly, almost as if they were old friends. He watched her with cautious glances as she took dainty bites of meat and noodles, once leaving a smear of tomato sauce on her upper lip that she dabbed with her napkin. Normally he would have felt like a clumsy oaf in the presence of someone as refined and mannerly, but there was nothing pretentious about her at all. Nothing forced or condescending. It was almost too easy to imagine how they would fit as a couple. Familiar roles that he had so often seen in others and had never really experienced himself. He had to remind himself that this was only their first date. And not even a date. Just dinner. Dinner with friends. And he was getting way ahead of himself. If he thought too much about it, he would panic. And if he panicked, he would run. And if he ran he would never know what might happen with her.

After dinner, Diane refused any help cleaning up, and they all made their way back to the living room with their drinks. Halloran took a spot in the corner of the sofa, and he was pleased when Kelly took a seat next to him. As relaxed as he was with her, she seemed more so with him. She spoke easily and freely, never failing to meet his eyes, and once touching him lightly on his forearm to make a point about something. He didn't know what. He wasn't paying any attention to what she was saying. All he knew was that he could spend the whole night listening to her talk. The rise and fall of her voice, the timbre of her inflections. It was like music.

"I know you can't talk about it probably," she said, "but are you guys working on that murder of the pregnant girl?"

Halloran jolted to reality at once. "Yeah," he said. "We are." He clucked his tongue. "Bad business." He thought again of the Richardsons in his office, desperate and demanding answers.

"Doesn't make me feel too wise in my decision to move back here," she said. But she gave him a crooked smile.

"Mike will protect you," Brooks said, and winked.

Halloran glared at him.

"What do you think happened to the girl's baby?" Kelly asked. "Do you think it's still alive?" But when she saw the emotionless expression on his face, she said quickly, "Oh, I'm sorry. I shouldn't ask about stuff like that. It's just like people asking me about credit union business."

"It's okay," he said. "We don't know," he answered her, giving her the same comment he'd given the press. "We hope so."

"I just can't imagine," she said, and shuddered. "You

know, when I was younger I used to enjoy horror and slasher movies. But when I got older I started seeing more and more real horrible things on the news and. . . I don't know. I just didn't want to fill my head with imagined horrors when there were so many real-life terrible things going on as well." She looked at him. "Does that make sense?"

"It makes perfect sense," he said. "The last thing I want to do is leave work and see more of the same. Give me a good comedy or some sci-fi anytime over that horror shit." He caught himself. "I mean, crap."

Kelly laughed and reached for her tea.

"You'll have to excuse him," Brooks said. "He's not used to being around a classy woman."

Halloran raised a hand to point at him, to tell him to hush, but his fingers collided with Kelly's glass of tea, upending it all over her and the couch. "Oh, my God, I'm so sorry!"

"It's all right," she said, standing and swiping at her tea-soaked sweater.

"Diane, we need a towel!" Brooks called.

Diane stepped into the room with a dishtowel. "What happened?" She hurriedly blotted the tea off Kelly's sweater.

"Mike decided to douse our guest," Brooks said, laughing.

"I'm so sorry," Halloran said again. He could feel his face burning all the way up to his ears.

"It's really okay," Kelly said. "No harm done."

"I'll pay to get it cleaned," he said.

"I'll just throw it in the washer," she said. "It's not a big deal."

Diane stooped to blot the tea on the carpet. Halloran bent down. "Here, let me do that."

"You want one of my tops to put on?" Diane asked Kelly.

"No, that's all right." She glanced at her watch. "It's almost nine and I probably should be going anyway."

"Oh, don't go yet," Diane said.

"Yeah," Brooks chimed in. "We'll make Mike leave and then we'll spend the rest of the night laughing at him."

Kelly smiled and Halloran felt his face get hotter. "Well, Trevor's home alone, and I should really get back. I mean, I trust him and all, but, you know… He's thirteen."

"I think I've got you blocked in," Halloran said, handing the tea-soaked towel to Diane.

"I'll just get my jacket," Kelly said, heading toward the hallway.

Diane followed. "Here, let me try to dry you off a little more with a bath towel."

Brooks stood looking at Halloran. "Well, you sure fucked that up."

Halloran glared at him. "Shut up." He glanced back to make sure the women were still preoccupied elsewhere. "I like her," he said.

Brooks nodded. "Yeah, too bad you're never going

to see her again."

Halloran shook his head.

Diane and Kelly returned, with Kelly now wearing a light windbreaker. "Thanks, guys, for dinner," she said, digging her keys out of her purse.

"Yes, thanks," Halloran said.

"You going, too?" Diane said, and her disappointment seemed genuine.

"Yeah. I think I've messed up enough things for one evening."

"Well, we'll have to do this again," Diane said. "I've had fun."

"Me, too," Kelly said.

"Me, three," Halloran said, then immediately felt idiotic.

They said their goodnights, and Halloran followed Kelly outside, standing by as she unlocked her car. "I really did enjoy the evening," he said.

She turned and gave him a grin. "Yeah, me, too. In spite of getting drenched."

"I am so sorry."

She touched him on the arm. "Stop apologizing. It really isn't that big of a deal."

"I would. . . um. . . "

"Yes?"

He chuckled at his awkwardness. "I'd like to see you again."

"Yeah," she said. "I'd like that, too."

"You would?"

"Sure." She pulled out her phone. "What's your number?" And as he told her, she keyed it in and his phone dinged in his pocket with a text. "Now you've got mine, too."

"You have plans for this coming weekend?"

"I don't think so, but I'll have to check my busy social calendar."

"I'll give you a call."

"Yes. Do that." She gave him a final smile as she climbed into the Toyota and started the engine.

Reluctantly, he made his way to the Trailblazer and climbed in. Yes, he thought. Coming tonight had been a good decision.

* * *

11:40 PM

Joel awoke with a start, and for a moment he had no idea where he was. He had been running from something, something with blades for fingers, like Freddy Krueger or Edward Scissorhands. Something that was slashing at him and wanted him dead. His face and chest were coated in a light cold sweat.

He was in Sofia's room, sitting in the rocker. The nightlight threw a revolving cavalcade of soft stars across the ceiling and walls. He sat for a moment, letting his pounding heart subside to its normal rhythm, listening to the nighttime sounds of the house – the tick-tocking of the clock in the bathroom, the thrum of the furnace, the clicks and pops of the walls settling.

He eased out of the rocker, its wooden frame groaning with the strain, and turned out the nightlight, then padded barefoot down the hall to the kitchen. He pulled out the milk and drank from the jug, then wiped his mouth on the back of his hand and headed back toward the bedroom, maneuvering his large frame carefully to avoid the creaking floorboards.

Dana was resting on her side with a pillow between her knees, snoring lightly. On the TV screen Loretta Young glided about an impeccable sitting room, a chiffon gown billowing out behind her.

He eased onto the bed and lay beside Dana. The flickering light from the television played across her features, giving the illusion of a fluid bevy of emotions crossing her sleeping face. He resisted the urge to touch her and peer into her, even though he knew touching a sleeping person never gave him anything but a jumble of random images and thoughts, none of which meant anything, and none of which made sense. And it was still an invasion of privacy – seeing into her at her most vulnerable, almost as if looking at her naked and exposed – and the idea of it filled him with shame. So he lay facing her, content to watch her eyes flutter beneath her lids, to listen to the steady breathing of her deep sleep, to feel the warmth emanating from her body beside his. It was a moment he wanted to never end. He could lie like this forever, could die right here, right now, and know he would never feel more content.

He closed his eyes, feeling the tension of the past few hours ease out of his throbbing shoulders and back. He would probably feel worse tomorrow, if past injuries were any indication. He would dope himself up on Motrin and try to push through the workday. It was all he could do. But for now, he just wanted to lie here and drift off to the drone of the television and the breathing of the woman beside him. Fragments of the day flashed before his eyes, and he knew he was falling over the edge into sleep. And just when he was almost gone, something jolted him awake.

He opened his eyes, and Dana was staring at him, her eyes wide and panicked. She was gasping for breath.

He sat up. "Dana! What's wrong?"

She looked at him, her hands clenched to her chest. She rocked back and forth frantically, and Joel suddenly understood she was trying to sit up. He eased her upright, clasping her hands in his. "Jo. . . Jo – " she stammered, staring straight ahead at the television, but he knew she wasn't seeing it.

"I'm here, babe," he said.

She shook her head, still trying to catch her breath. "Jo. . . Joseph."

"What about him?"

"We were wrong." She looked at him. Her eyes were glassy, and tears brimmed over the lids. "It's still here. I feel it."

He was halfway between fright and exasperation. "What's still here? What are you talking about?"

Her hands squeezed his tighter. "He wasn't trying to warn us about the accident, Joel. What exactly did he tell you?"

He took a deep breath. His heart was hammering in his chest. "That there was some kind of danger associated with the bedroom. That – "

"The *bedroom*," she said. "It wasn't about the *car*. It wasn't about *driving*. It was the *bedroom*. That's why I still feel it."

"I don't understand what you're saying. You're not making any sense."

"Don't you see?" she said, clearly frustrated. "He didn't warn us about the accident because that's not the danger he saw. He saw something else. Something here in this house. In this room. That's why I still feel something looming over us. Whatever it is hasn't happened yet." She looked at him and placed her trembling hands on either side of his face. "I – we. . . we're still in danger." She swallowed, and the brimming tears finally spilled down her cheeks. "Sofia's still in danger."

TUESDAY, OCTOBER 7

7:50 AM

AFTER ALL THE EVENTS of the past few days, Joel was almost relieved to head back to work. Bonnie arrived a little after 7:30, and immediately began buzzing about the house like a worker bee, fussing over Dana and tidying up. He was glad it was Dana who would be dealing with her and her incessant energy rather than him. And despite the damp chill in the early fall air, he enjoyed the drive across town to the office through the morning traffic. The sun was deceptively bright, and the heat from the travel mug of coffee he'd brought with him warmed him up considerably by the time he reached the parking lot of Cable-Com.

He pulled in beside Wade's truck, where his brother stood leaning against the back fender taking in one last cigarette before heading inside. He nodded in greeting as Joel put the truck in park and climbed out with his coffee. "Mornin', sunshine."

Wade grunted and took a draw off his cigarette. "Mornin'. Welcome back."

"Thanks." Joel leaned back against his own truck and took a sip of coffee.

"How's Dana?"

"Still sore, but she's doing all right. Bonnie's there."

"Yeah, you told me her mom was gonna stay with her."

"Insurance adjuster is supposed to go by the body shop today and look at the car. I think it's probably totaled."

Wade whistled softly. "You two are lucky you didn't get killed."

"Tell me about it." Joel ran a thumb along the rim of the travel mug. "How was yesterday? Were you busy?"

"Nah." He took a drag off his cigarette and blew a plume of smoke into the air. "Got that new modulator in and hooked up. I think we had three escalated service calls. Everything else we just put off 'til you got back."

"Well, thanks for covering for me."

"No sweat. I'm just glad you guys are okay." He looked off into the distance, at the diner across the street and its lot full of cars and pickup trucks. "Sorry I didn't make it to the hospital."

"No problem. I know it was late by the time you got back from the lake. Besides, there wasn't anything you could do, and they only kept her overnight." He took a sip of his coffee. He wasn't even sure he would have wanted Wade hanging around anyway. He probably would have just been on his phone sexting with women and only communicating with everyone else by way of grunts and profanity. "So – and I almost hate to ask this – but how was *your* weekend?"

A grin crept across Wade's face and he shot Joel a look. "Pretty wild."

"Oh yeah?"

"Man. . . Parker. . . " He gave a guttural moan. "It was hot. *She* is hot. We stayed naked just about the whole two days. And Sunday it rained like a mother-fucker, so there was nothing else to do but stay inside and screw."

Joel felt his face burn. "Sounds awesome," he said, turning away. He downed the rest of his coffee and headed toward the side door of the building. "We better get inside before Betsy gets on the warpath."

Wade flicked away his cigarette butt. "Yeah," he said, following him. He clapped Joel on the shoulder – enough to sting but so quickly that Joel couldn't read him. Still, Joel knew it was meant as a friendly gesture, and as much as he sometimes detested Wade, it felt good that his brother was showing him some semblance of affection.

Just inside the door they clocked in, and as they headed up the hall to the front desk, Wade popped into the men's room. "Be there in sec. I gotta take a whiz."

Joel made his way past the darkened doorways of

several now-empty offices, wondering how long it would be before Cable-Com moved them to a smaller building or closed up shop in Cedar Hill completely and ran everything here remotely. Up front, Rhonda was signing into her computer, a fresh cup of steaming coffee and a half-eaten glazed donut on a paper towel beside her. She glanced up at him and broke into a wide smile. "There you are! Are you okay? How's Dana?"

"We're both okay," he said, already weary at the anticipation of going over every detail of the accident and its aftermath.

Rhonda brushed a strand of dark hair behind her ear. "When Wade told us about your wreck yesterday – "

"Joel?" Behind them, Betsy stood in the doorway to her office, looking austere in a navy suit and with her blonde hair pinned back. "Glad to have you back."

"Thanks."

"Can I see you for a moment?"

"Of course." He gave Rhonda a glance. She raised an eyebrow and turned back to her computer. He followed Betsy into her office.

"Shut the door and have a seat," she commanded, slipping behind her desk.

Joel did as he was told. He hated these one-on-one conversations with Betsy. He knew he'd done nothing that would deserve a reprimand, but being called into the boss's office was still a nerve-wracking event.

Betsy leaned forward and folded her hands on her desk. "First, I want to tell you I'm so glad the two of you are all right. Is Dana's mom staying with her while you're at work?"

He nodded. "Yeah, she's going to stay every day through the week until the baby comes. We're lucky she can do that."

"Absolutely," Betsy said. She leaned back. "Look, I've been thinking about when the baby comes. How long do you plan to be out?"

"Just a couple of days. I won't miss too much work."

She gave him a crooked smile. "A couple of days? Joel. . . This is your first child. You need to take longer than that. At least a week. Take two if you want to."

He shifted uncomfortably in the tight chair. "Well. . . "

"Under the Family Medical Leave Act you know you can have up to twelve weeks of leave."

"I don't need twelve weeks," he said. "Besides, Dana couldn't stand me being home that long." He chuckled and Betsy smiled. "But two weeks sounds pretty good."

"Then plan on it," Betsy said. "Your job will be here waiting for you when you get back."

"Thanks."

"And this won't count against your vacation time."

He gaped at her. "Seriously?"

"Corporate may squawk about it, but I'll find a way to work it out for you." She leaned forward again. "You're a good employee, Joel. Probably the best one I've got. And honestly, the only reason I put up with your brother is because of you. I want you to know I've got your back, and I want to make sure you're treated well."

"Well, thank you," he said, feeling overwhelmingly grateful.

"Do you need to take some time off right now?" Betsy asked. "To be with Dana and deal with all this?"

"Oh, no," he said. "We've got everything worked out. And it's just a couple of weeks until the baby comes. We'll be fine."

"Okay, Joel," Betsy said. She rose from her chair, indicating the meeting was over. "But if you need anything, you let me know. You know can confide in me."

He nodded. "I appreciate that."

He turned to leave and saw Rhonda and Wade watching him through the glass window of Betsy's office. They both looked away quickly and Joel felt a chuckle escape him. He emerged into the lobby and headed toward the kitchenette to refill his coffee mug, aware that Wade was trailing after him.

"What the fuck was that all about?" Wade said in a half-whisper. "Everything okay, buddy?"

"Relax," Joel told him, grabbing the coffee pot and pouring his travel mug full. "She was actually being nice. We were talking about me taking some time off when Sofia gets here."

"Oh yeah?"

Joel ripped open two sugar packets and sifted the contents into the mug. "Yeah." He glanced up at Wade. "She's not always a bitch, you know."

"If you say so, bud."

* * *

10:35 AM

Worthington's Funeral Chapel was located on the southern edge of town, just barely in the city limits. And while, according to the Richardsons, Addie had all but withdrawn from most of her family and friends, it was easy to see they had not forgotten about her. Every space on the paved lot was full, and Halloran was forced to park in a mowed grassy field next to a few other latecomers. He and Brooks climbed out of the sedan and made their way across the mushy ground to the pavement. His shoes would need a good shining tonight when he got home.

"Hey, hold up," Brooks said behind him. "Hold still."

Halloran felt Brooks arrange the collar of his suit jacket before giving him a pat on the shoulder. "Thanks."

"You really need a woman," Brooks said, catching up to him.

"Yes, I know. And you keep trying everything to make sure I don't forget it."

"Just trying to help."

The line of mourners stretched out the front door of the chapel. Halloran and Brooks took their place in line and shuffled along into the airless funeral home with its suffocating stench of flowers. Halloran was reminded of an old silent movie he'd seen once, *Metropolis*, where the city workers lumbered into work each day as a cohesive unit, not talking, not looking up, just moving toward the task at hand. Likely as not, most everyone here was still in a state of shock. He noticed many young people, probably in their early twenties and experiencing the loss of one of their peers for the first time. As the group wound through the funeral chapel and toward the pearl-colored casket, many of them broke down in tears. Some were trembling. One or two left the line and made their way to the chairs set up in the chapel.

Both of the Richardsons looked pale, drawn and exhausted. Halloran took Sue's hand in both of his and found it cool and dry. "I'm so sorry," he said, knowing his words were woefully inadequate. She nodded and dabbed at her eyes with a wadded tissue. Bob Richardson nodded at him and shook his hand but could not meet his gaze.

Addie looked peaceful. She wore a pink linen dress, and her honey-colored hair flowed about her face and shoulders. She had really been a lovely young woman, and Halloran felt a pang of sadness as he thought of Sue Richardson saying she'd wanted to be a teacher, and how her son would never know his mother. If he was still alive. But they would find him, Halloran told himself. If the baby was out there, they would track him down and bring him home to the Richardsons.

Halloran and Brooks took seats at the back of the chapel to observe the crowd. Compared to the funerals he'd attended of older folks, this bunch was subdued. Many elderly people he'd encountered at funerals had treated the event as a social occasion, sometimes being boisterous and jovial. But those times were different; the deceased had usually lived a long and fruitful life, was remembered for his or her contributions to the community, and was discussed fondly. Addie Richardson had been cut down in her youth, her infant ripped from her body. Her potential had been erased like a stray pencil mark. There was no joviality here. No wistful smiles. Nothing but grief. Somewhere an organ began to play, dragging and despairing, punctuated by swells that intensified the air of gloom in the chapel. The Richardsons gave one final hug to the last mourner at the casket, then took their seats in the front row for the service.

When the funeral ended, Halloran and Brooks followed the motorcade to Oak Grove Baptist Church, where Addie would be laid to rest. In the clammy October air, they watched from two rows over as the mourners gathered beneath the large green tent covering the gravesite. The Richardsons emerged from the funeral chapel's black limo and were escorted to their spot in the front row of the green felt-covered folding chairs. Sue Richardson looked as if she had aged five years in the past hour.

"Don't look now," Brooks muttered, "but we're being scoped out." He jerked his head to his right.

About two hundred yards away a slim older man in faded jeans and a grubby white T-shirt leaned against the boom of a backhoe, drinking a Coke and watching them behind sunglasses. The gravedigger. Halloran nodded at him, then was dismayed to watch him shuffle toward him. "'Mornin'," he said. "You guys cops?" He stood before them, effectively blocking any view they'd had of the crowd at the graveside.

"That's right," Halloran said. "Detectives."

"Thought so." The gravedigger grinned, showing impossibly white perfect teeth. "This is that girl what was murdered, ain't it? The one whose baby got took."

"Yes, sir," Halloran said, trying to hide his growing irritation.

"Dewey," the gravedigger said, sticking out his hand. "Dewey Cavanaugh."

Halloran shook the man's dusty hand and fought the urge to wipe his palm on his slacks. "Lieutenant Mike Halloran. This is my partner, Greg Brooks."

Halloran could see the man's eyes widen, even behind the dark glasses. "Halloran. I seen you on TV before."

"Probably."

"Yeah, yeah, I remember now. Back when those other girls got killed."

"Yes."

Dewey sipped his Coke. "This ain't part of that

again, is it?"

Halloran blew out a breath. "No, sir."

"'Cause you all caught that guy, didn't you?"

"Yes, sir."

Brooks stepped toward Dewey. "If you don't mind, sir, we're here on official duty."

Dewey smacked his forehead so hard that his mousy brown hair fluttered. "Oh, of course. I'm sorry, officers. I'll let you get back to your investigatin'." He started toward the backhoe, but then turned abruptly. "Say, you know, I been hearing for years now there was a cult in Cedar Hill. Heard they worshipped the devil and sacrificed babies and stuff. Is that true? You think they might have done this?"

Halloran held up a hand. "I assure you, sir, we're following up on every lead."

Dewey nodded and marched back toward his perch against the backhoe's boom, taking a swig from the Coke can.

Brooks shook his head and chuckled. "Good Lord."

Halloran jerked a thumb behind them at the sedan. "Let's get out of here. I'm not seeing anything interesting."

Twenty minutes later, sitting in their usual spot at Grace's and waiting for their food, Brooks stirred his Diet Coke with his straw. "You know, that weird little guy at the cemetery is the second person to bring up a Satanic cult."

Halloran rubbed his temples. A dull throb was growing behind his eyes. "Who was the other one?"

"That O'Dowd lady at the baby shop where Addie was killed."

"Oh yeah."

"You think there's anything to it?"

Halloran looked at him. "Greg, I'd be willing to bet dollars to donuts there is no cult in Cedar Hill. A bunch of superstitious nuts, but no cult. I looked into the O'Dowd woman's suspicions, but I couldn't find anything. You know that."

"Still. . ."

"Look, if it makes you feel any better, make some calls to the boys over in Springfield. See if they know anything about a cult operating in this area. Or any other fringe religious sect that might have recently set up shop."

Brooks nodded. "I might do that, if you don't mind."

"Sure, go ahead." Halloran picked up his glass of water and took a sip.

"Watch out," Brooks said. "Don't drench me like you did poor Kelly last night." He laughed.

Halloran grinned in spite of himself. "Wow. That was brutal." He chuckled. "I was so embarrassed."

"She seemed like a good sport about it." He leaned back in his chair. "So we haven't had much of a chance to talk about it. What did you think of her? You given any thought to going out on a real date? Provided she wants to see you again, of course."

Halloran nodded. In truth he had barely thought of

anything else. And if Addie Richardson's murder wasn't looming before him right now he most likely could have been consumed by the idea of dating again. "I liked her," he said. "Wonder what she thought of me?"

"You mean besides the fact that you're clumsy as hell?"

"Come on."

"Well, you two seemed like you were getting along pretty well. Diane and I talked about it the rest of the night."

"Oh yeah?"

"I'm sure Diane will get the scoop today at work."

"You let me know what she says."

"I will." Brooks looked at him squarely. "So. . . you gonna call her?"

Halloran felt a grin creep across his lips. "Thinking about it."

"You think too much, bud," Brooks told him. "She's gonna be gone, and you're gonna be left holding the bag. All alone. You don't want to be alone the rest of your life, do you?"

"I'm not alone," Halloran said. "I've got Mel."

"Mel's a cat," Brooks said. "Don't end up like that poor schmuck Diane and Kelly work with."

"Todd."

"Yeah, Todd. Don't be a Todd."

Halloran glared at him. "I'm not going to be a Todd."

* * *

3:20 PM

Sam Jarvis emerged from the elevator into the airless vestibule of The Fourth Street Building, her arms loaded with a stack of mortgages to be filed at the county clerk's office across the street and her purse slung over her shoulder. She stood for a moment, barely noticing the whisper of the elevator door closing behind her, watching through the glass panels as the girls behind the teller line in the first-floor bank gossiped and joked. She envied them in some ways. Going home to their families, having their nightly rituals of cooking dinner and helping with homework and maybe later an early bedtime with their husbands to make love and get up to do it all again the next day. There was something comforting in that. Routine. Safe. Numbing.

The teller on the end, Beth, caught sight of Sam and waved. Sam smiled and nodded at her. Beth usually waited on her. Beth was thirty and blonde and petite, the mother of twin boys and the wife of Jeffrey, who owned a construction firm in town. Beth was always smiling and happy. Always quick to talk about the latest adventures of her "men." And always immaculately dressed and coiffed.

Sam hated her. There was such a thing as being too perfect, and Beth was it. Beth had probably never had a bad day her whole life. Had probably wanted for nothing since she had been born. And would probably live to be a hundred and her skin would still be flawless and her hair the same shade of blonde.

Ugh.

Sam let out a deep sigh. The vestibule smelled of stale cigarettes and urine. All she wanted to do was drop off the mortgages for recording and then head home early, prop up her swollen feet, and relax with a cup of hot tea and that James Patterson novel she'd started last night.

Outside the air was brisk and heavy with the scent of autumn. She stepped quickly across Fourth Street, though there was no need to rush. Traffic was always light in Cedar Hill, despite being the seat of Lake County, and no one here got in a hurry. It had been the perfect place to disappear after law school. The perfect place to get away from the society hubbub in Washington. The perfect place to hide from her father's shadow.

J. Daniel Jarvis, Republican. Republican with a capital "R." Always eager to cozy up to any crony who would scratch his back for a good cause. Especially when "good cause" meant any kind of special interest that would result in more money in the Jarvis coffers. It made her sick, all the political cock sucking (both figurative and literal) that went on in D.C. When her mother died while Sam was still an undergrad, good old J. Daniel had wanted – no, *expected* – Sam to step in and take her place. To be the ever-dutiful daughter and to accompany the senator to his state dinners and political soirees. No, thank you.

She'd attended one black-tie affair with J. Daniel at the Virginia estate of some well-to-do medical executive, and that had been enough for her. She'd taken a wrong turn on her way back from the restroom and found herself in a remote parlor where a chubby, hairy shirtless freshman senator from Mississippi was snorting cocaine with one of the female servers. He'd invited her to join them, suggesting that after another line they could all three sneak off to one of the upstairs bedrooms. She'd stumbled out of the parlor and wandered around the house for half an hour before finding her way back to the party. By that time she was nearly hysterical, and she had refused to ever attend any event like that again.

After law school, she remembered Cedar Hill, where she'd once spent a summer with a college roomie. She remembered its small-town charm and laid-back pace, its proximity to Harper's Lake and all its outdoor activities. But mostly she remembered how far removed it was from her father's world, and how peaceful she had felt while she was there. She quietly made some inquiries to several law firms, never disclosing who her father was, and found a position as a staff attorney at Carlton and Bartholomew, "Lake County's Real Estate Legal Experts!" She practically saw the trademark symbol flash before her eyes every time she heard the phrase.

There wasn't much to the job, really. Title searches and preparing mortgages and deeds. Walking across the street daily to the courthouse to file paperwork with the county clerk's office. Occasionally closing a mortgage loan for one of the larger banks. It didn't pay much – staff attorneys around here averaged around sixty thousand a year – but since she had no debt, it was enough to keep her in groceries and a spacious leased townhome in one of Cedar Hill's nicer riverfront areas. And pay for her black Mustang convertible. And most importantly, it kept her away from her father and out of his liability.

The old man had remarried last summer. Evelyn Winifred Smythe from Darien, Connecticut. ("It's pronounced '*Dairy-Ann*,' my dear.") Old money. Widowed for twenty years. Had never worked a day in her life. And, Sam thought, probably never had an orgasm either. She had no children of her own, and when she married J. Daniel she remarked about how now she would finally have a daughter. Um, no. Sam had no desire to be part of that snobbish set or have anything to do with that woman. Especially when she found out Evelyn had made J. Daniel sign a pre-nup. And while she could understand the legal reasons, it was insulting. For all his shortcomings, her father had his own money and his own investments. And if she thought she was protecting her money from Sam, she was not only a bitch but a stupid one at that. The world of the rich was not one Sam cared to be part of. Not in the least.

Besides, now she had more important things to think about. She touched her swollen belly and couldn't help but smile. When little Berkley got here everything would be different. She would try her best to keep J. Daniel and Evelyn's influence out of her daughter's life, but she knew it would be difficult. J. Daniel was excited about his first grandchild. He'd talked about moving Sam up to Connecticut to stay at Evelyn's house for a few weeks after Berkley was born so Sam could have some help with the baby, and while the offer had been tempting, Sam was determined to do this on her own. She had friends here in Cedar Hill, friends who had volunteered to help her out. And she already had a nanny lined up. She could do this. She didn't need J. Daniel's help. And she certainly didn't need or want Evelyn's. Not that Evelyn would have given any. J. Daniel let it slip that he'd asked Evelyn to plan a baby shower in Darien, but Evelyn had refused. "My dear, she's not *married*. That just isn't done here." What a bitch.

She also knew she wouldn't ask for anything from Bryce. He had his own issues dealing with the disintegration of his ten-year marriage, and he couldn't be bothered with the pregnancy of the fellow attorney he'd knocked up during a three-day fling while his wife had been out of town. Goddamn Bryce Nelson. He was one of the best defense attorneys in the county, but God he was stupid and selfish. That Friday night in February at the party celebrating Judge Adams' retirement they'd seen each other across the Judge's great room, and owing to the wine, their mutual loneliness, and her own horniness, they'd slipped out and made their way across town to her place. She'd seen him around, of course. Knew he was married and had two little kids. But that night she didn't care. She needed someone to hold and make love to, and it had been three years since she'd been with anyone. And, as she had practically regrown her virginity, she wasn't on the pill and had no need to keep condoms on hand. They'd stayed in bed all day Saturday, going out only to drive over to Harper's Lake to grab dinner. "Somewhere nobody will know us," he'd said. And Sunday had been the same. They'd fucked one last time early Monday morning. And yes, she thought of it as fucking because there was nothing to it but unadulterated lust. Then he'd left, she got ready and went to work, and they never talked again. When she found out she was pregnant, she came close to calling him, but she didn't. She didn't really want him in her life. Wasn't sure she really wanted a baby either. She'd explored her options with her doctor and discovered the only place she could get an abortion was halfway across the state. And after thinking about it, she decided she would keep the baby after all. But she wouldn't tell Bryce the baby was his. In fact, she hadn't told anyone. Even her closest friends. She'd only said the father was an "old friend from back home" and left it at that. No one had pried. No one had asked any more questions because no one here gave a damn. It was another reason she loved Cedar Hill.

Inside the courthouse, she made her way downstairs

to the lower level toward the clerk's office. The smell down here was overpowering – stale disinfectant from the restrooms and numerous air fresheners the workers down here used to try to cover it – and she wondered how the girls who spent day after day here stood it. Or maybe it was just because she was pregnant. Either way, she stifled a gag and stepped into the office and held up the bundle of papers. "Who wants me?"

Annie Childers, the Lake County Court Clerk, rose from her desk and maneuvered her considerable bulk toward the counter with a smirk. "I'll do it, you little pregnant bitch."

Sam laughed. "No need for name calling, you old whore."

Annie guffawed and slapped the counter. "God, I haven't been called a whore in twenty years."

"More like fifty," Carla Tipton muttered next to her in stage whisper, then gave Sam a wink.

Annie clucked her tongue. "Oh, shut up."

Carla was the deputy clerk. The three of them had become well-acquainted over the past couple of years and had formed a bond of sorts. All three were single, and occasionally they met up for drinks or dinner, always ready to commiserate about their jobs, their lives, and their lack of men. Annie was close to retirement age, and she'd held this office for close to thirty years. Carla had been here for ten, ever since graduating high school.

Annie took the mortgages from Sam. "You want to

pick these up tomorrow?"

"Yeah. I don't want to wait," Sam said. "I need to get home and put my feet up." She reached down and massaged her throbbing ankle, noticing it had swollen significantly since the morning.

"Bless your heart," Carla said. "When I was pregnant with Timothy I could barely stand up by the end. And then I had those horrible hemorrhoids."

"Dear God," Annie said. "Not this again."

"Well so far I haven't had those," Sam said.

"You're lucky," Carla said. "I think I spent the last two weeks of my pregnancy in a sitz bath."

Annie blew out a breath. "Carla, as much as we'd love to hear about your ass, I'm sure Sam has better things to do."

Sam laughed. "We still on for Friday night? Don't know what I would do without my weekly glass of Chardonnay."

"Absolutely," Carla said. "Thinking about that is all that's keeping me going today."

"I'll have to check," Annie said. "I may actually have a date."

Sam gaped at her. "What?"

"Annie has a new man," Carla said with a grin.

Annie blushed and gave a self-conscious smile. "His name's Bobby."

Sam clapped her hands. "Annie, you slut! Where'd you meet him?"

"I took my car in for an oil change and he was working the service counter. He just moved here. He retired from Purina and he's working at the Ford dealership part-time. Said he couldn't take sitting at home every day with nothing to do."

"Well, look at you," Sam said. "You be careful, you'll end up in my condition."

Carla snorted. "I told her she'd better pack some rubbers."

"So is this your first date?" Sam asked.

"Actually, we had lunch yesterday," Annie said with a slightly embarrassed grin.

"She was twenty minutes late getting back," Carla said.

"Oh, Annie!" Sam said. "I'm so excited for you."

"Well, thanks," Annie said, blushing again. "We'll see how it goes."

Sam shifted uncomfortably on her feet. "Well, I've got to get home before my ankles give out."

"You take care, now," Annie said.

Sam climbed back up the steps to street level and emerged from the courthouse into the early afternoon sun. Despite the brightness, the breeze was chilly, and Sam hurried back across the street toward the parking structure, giving a wave to Mr. Jessup in the booth at the entrance. He nodded at her and gave her wide smile, his perfect teeth stark white against his ebony skin. How he could sit alone in that tiny space day in and day out she could never understand.

She passed into the shadow of the garage, and the

wind rushing through became colder. Here, even during the baking humid heat of Lake County summers, the air was always chilly and dry, and the breeze funneling through the structure whistled and moaned like something from an old horror movie. She gathered the collar of her blouse around her throat and trudged toward her car. Even though her spot was on the first level, it was still all the way at the back of the garage facing Fifth Street and the block of buildings across the way. Why they couldn't cut out a simple entrance to the street for pedestrians she didn't know. She hated parking garages, not only because she feared getting flattened by an idiot careening around the levels, but the gloom and the silence creeped her out. Anything could be hiding in the darkness between all those parked cars. A murderer, a rapist. . . anything.

She spotted the Mustang and reached into her purse for her keys.

"Samantha."

She froze, then whirled around. There was no one there. The voice had seemed far away yet nearby at the same time. A kind of hoarse whisper. She felt a sudden tingle at the base of her spine. Her eyes darted to the dark spaces between the vehicles, but she could see nothing. Maybe she had imagined it. She had, after all, just been thinking about someone hiding there. And after what had happened to that girl last week –

"Samantha."

No. She hadn't imagined that. She straightened up

and walked briskly toward her car, hitting the unlock button on the fob and feeling a slight sense of relief as the Mustang's taillights flashed. "I don't know who you are," she said forcefully, "but I've got a gun with me." She didn't, of course, although she knew a couple of women in the office had their concealed carry permits and kept handguns in their purses at all times. She'd never felt the need for such a thing before, especially here in Cedar Hill. But whoever was whispering her name didn't know that. She hoped. She did, however, have a can of pepper spray. Blindly, she fumbled for it in the clutter of her purse with her free hand.

She was twenty feet from the Mustang now. God, her feet and ankles were killing her with every step. She thought of running, but she knew her swollen joints and the heels she was wearing wouldn't allow it. A burst of anger hit her for panicking. She should have asked Mr. Jessup to walk her to the car. He would have done it. *Where the fuck was the pepper spray?*

"Samantha!"

This time the voice came from directly behind her. She didn't dare turn around. In desperation, she hit the panic button on the key fob, and the Mustang's horn blared a deafening tattoo throughout the garage, its lights flashing like a strobe. She was ten feet from the car now. Almost within grabbing distance.

Her fingers closed around the small canister of pepper spray in the bottom of her bag. She pulled it out just as something caught about her throat. The pepper spray and her keys flew from her hands and clattered to the concrete. She grasped at her neck. A cord of some kind. Her mind raced through all the self-defense training she'd half-dozed through over the years. She kicked behind her, hoping to connect with the attacker's shin, but her aim was off, and the swollen ankle on her other leg gave way. She slumped toward the concrete, the sharp pain of her impossibly-bent ankle nearly unnoticed as she struggled to get her breath.

* * *

3:45 PM

Ray Jessup cocked his head when he heard the car alarm go off. Damn idiots were always setting them off accidentally. He didn't even bother checking them out anymore. There was never anyone around, and most of the time the sound stopped before he could find the vehicle. And if someone did break into a car, that wasn't his problem. Fools needed insurance. That's why the signs were up all over the garage: NOT RESPONSIBLE FOR UNATTENDED VEHICLES. People knew what the risks were parking in public, but most of them were just idiots.

After what seemed an interminable time, the blaring alarm was silenced, and Jessup decided either the car shut it off automatically or the moron finally figured out how to stop it. In any event, it stopped.

Later he would comment to the police, "I sure wish I'd gone and checked. I sure do. I might coulda saved her."

* * *

4:05 PM

Bonnie was snoring.

Dana lay on the bed, staring at Dr. Phil on the television but not really watching. Some punk teenage girl was refusing to obey her mom, and the audience had let out a collective groan when they saw pictures of the girl's trashed bedroom. Dr. Phil was saying something to her, but Dana couldn't hear him over Bonnie's snoring from the chair in the corner. She looked about for the remote, but she'd apparently lost it over the edge of the bed while she'd been napping herself. It didn't matter. Nothing Dr. Phil or anyone on this show said was that important.

She rolled onto her back and stared at the ceiling. Popcorn. A popcorn ceiling. Yuck. They'd meant to redo the ceilings in this house at some point, but it was a project that had been put on the backburner when she got pregnant. Instead, they'd poured their money and effort into turning the spare bedroom into Sofia's nursery. And now it looked like the ceilings would wait a while longer. It didn't really matter anyway. She could live with it, no matter how ugly it was.

Earlier, Amy Jo Carter had dropped off a fat manila envelope for her. Dana had lain on the bed, listening to Amy Jo as she talked to Bonnie at the front door, that sing-song voice that Amy Jo's second-grade students loved, but that Dana and the other elementary teachers secretly imitated in the teachers' lounge when Amy Jo wasn't there. Bonnie told her that Dana was asleep, for which Dana was grateful. As much as she despised lying here bored out of her wits, she just wasn't sure she could take Amy Jo's bouncy demeanor right now. Amy Jo was a good friend and confidant, and when she and Dana started teaching at Cedar Hill Elementary last year they formed a close bond. Rookie teachers and all that. Dana still loved Amy Jo, but she could only take her in small doses.

Now she reached for the unopened envelope on the bedside table where Bonnie had laid it. Her name was written across the front in Amy Jo's loopy script and adorned with a hastily-drawn daisy. God. She tore open the flap and a stack of folded papers spilled out onto the bed. Notes and letters from her students, most written on lined notebook paper, some on thick creamy stock from the art room. She picked up the first one.

Dear Mrs. Roberts, Sorre about your acident. Hop you fil better soon. Love, Ryan

The next one was written in tiny, precise script:

dear mrs. roberts, please get better soon. we miss you.
love, eileen margaret simpson

She thumbed through the rest, enchanted by the drawings, the words of encouragement, and the innocence and caring she sensed through her touch of the bundle. The penciled messages began to blur, and she realized her eyes were tearing up. Lying here isolated from the world was one thing, but being away from the kids was even worse.

She leafed back through until she found Eileen's note and ran her fingertips over the words, feeling where Eileen's number two pencil had pressed hard on the paper in machine-like fashion. He wasn't doing it anymore, her stepfather. Dana had scared him. Good.

She'd first noticed the change in Eileen about a month ago. Her hair, dark, long and naturally curly was no longer neat and clean, and sometimes it looked as though she'd been sent to school in clothing dragged out of the dirty laundry. She questioned Eileen about her home life, and discovered that Eileen's mother had recently remarried. Eileen was terrified of her stepfather. She hadn't told Dana this, but Dana had sensed it through the impressions she picked up from Eileen's schoolwork – bits and pieces of conversations, yelling, slamming doors, that kind of thing. But one day when Dana was grading math tests, she picked up Eileen's paper and was hit with a visual flash. Eileen in the tub, a hulking shape in the bathroom door. Eileen struggling to cover her nakedness with her washcloth and the Mr. Bubble suds. The shape, half-hidden in the shadows, watching her. He hadn't done anything yet, but the way he watched Eileen, Dana was sure he was contemplating it, because she knew with certainty this wasn't the first time he had watched his stepdaughter in the bath. Dana feared for Eileen's well-being, but she was helpless to do anything. After all, she couldn't very well go to the police with nothing but what they would consider a hunch, no matter how strongly she knew it was more than that.

But the next week was parent-teacher conferences, and to her amazement, Eileen's mother and stepfather both attended. Eileen's mother was tiny and birdlike, much like Eileen herself, and wore rimless glasses. One of the lenses, Dana noticed, was chipped on the corner. The stepfather was large and bear-like with an unkempt tuft of blondish-red beard sprouting from his chin. He sat uncomfortably and defiantly in the hard plastic student chair at Dana's desk, his arms crossed and his eyes cold as two stones. Dana could barely look at him through the conference. She could feel the danger – the *evil* – radiating from him like heat, and it frightened her.

But when the conference was over they stood to leave, Dana surprised herself. She grabbed his shoulder. It was like plunging her hand into a ball of twisted, intertwined snakes. "Hey."

He turned and regarded her, his eyes dark with malice. "Yeah?"

Feeling a surge of courage, she stepped closer to him, her heart thudding in her chest. "I know what you're doing to her."

His eyes narrowed. "Who?"

"Eileen."

He looked at her for a moment, long enough for a flush spread across his cheeks. "I ain't doin' *nothin'* to Eileen." He pointed a finger at her, and she could sense how badly he wanted to jab her with it. "You best be careful, makin' accusations against people." He followed his wife out the door. "Stupid bitch."

But Dana knew she had touched a nerve, which proved she was right. He hadn't said much else because it was true. She had seen a glimmer of fear in his eyes. And it pleased her immensely. And now, judging by what she was picking up from Eileen's note, the bastard was leaving her alone.

Good.

She set the stack of letters aside and looked back toward the television. It was a commercial for some kind of cleaning product. An impossibly slim and happy mom was dancing through her sun-lit kitchen with a mop. Lord.

She flopped on her back and stared again at the popcorn ceiling. Two weeks. Two more weeks. If she had to lie in this bed for that long she would go insane. And now she felt pressure in her bladder. Great.

She placed her hands on her belly. "Come on, little

girl. Your mom can't take much more of this."

She glanced at Bonnie, still snoring in the chair, her head drooping onto her chest. A thin string of drool hung from her lips and pooled on her blouse. Dana fought an urge to giggle. She hated to wake Bonnie to help her to the bathroom. Maybe, if she was careful, she could do it on her own.

She rolled onto her side and eased her legs off the bed, then pushed herself up to a sitting position, keeping her gaze on her mother. Bonnie wasn't moving. Good. Dana could get to the bathroom, pee, and get back to the bed without Bonnie ever even knowing.

She braced a hand against the bedside table and pushed herself to her feet. The pain in her legs and back was nearly blinding. Some of it had to be from lying on the bed so long. She shuffled out the door into the hallway, then into the dark bathroom. She barely got her sweats and panties lowered before she sank to the toilet and the urine gushed out of her. The sense of relief was overwhelming. She hadn't realized she'd needed to go so badly.

Back in the hallway, she realized her mouth was dry and papery. A drink would be good. A Sprite or even water. Steadying herself against the wall, she made her way toward the kitchen. Every step was excruciating, and the pain she'd first mistaken for stiffness from lying on the bed she now realized was from the wreck. And it was getting stronger with every footfall.

She just made it into the kitchen before she lunged

toward the dining table and collapsed into a chair. This had been a mistake. She shouldn't have tried to do this on her own. Not this soon. Now she knew why she'd been put on bedrest. "Mom!" She listened. Bonnie was no longer snoring. "Mom!"

"Dana, where are you?"

"In here. In the kitchen."

Bonnie appeared in the doorway, looking a bit disoriented from her nap. "What are you doing up?"

Dana felt a rush of guilt. "I had to pee."

"Well why didn't you wake me?" She rushed to Dana's side. "Are you okay?"

"I'm all right. My legs just nearly gave out. I'm really hurting."

Bonnie gave her a quick hug. "Can you make it back to the bed?"

"I think so."

"Here, let me help." She managed to get Dana to her feet and held her up as they eased back down the hallway to the bedroom. "We'll get you back on the bed and I'll get you one of those pain pills."

"They don't do much good."

"Well, maybe it will help you sleep."

There was a sinking in Dana's chest. "I don't want to sleep. I'm so tired of being in that damn bed."

Bonnie clucked her tongue. "I know, baby, I know."

They reached the bedroom, and Bonnie eased her back onto the mattress. "I can't do this for two more weeks," Dana said, angry that she felt close to tears. "I can't."

Bonnie patted her shoulder. "Let me go get your pill. You want anything else?"

"No," Dana said, then caught Bonnie's arm. "Yes. Sprite. Bring me a Sprite."

Her mother nodded and shuffled back down the hallway. In a moment Dana could hear her rattling around in the kitchen and heard ice cubes falling into a glass.

She lay back with her eyes closed so she wouldn't have to look at that damned popcorn ceiling. Everything within her wanted to cry, to just let loose and allow the tears to flow. But it was almost half past four, and Joel would be home in a little while.

She had to put on a brave face.

* * *

4:40 PM

Halloran stood inside the Fourth Street parking garage and surveyed the scene – the covered body in a pool of blood next to the black Mustang, the spilled contents of Samantha Jarvis's purse, the yellow tape that had been strung up around the crime scene. The sun was now behind the downtown buildings, and the dim fluorescents in the garage did little to illuminate the area. "And nobody saw anything?"

He'd said it more to himself than anyone, but Aldridge, a fresh-faced rookie who'd been first on the scene and now stood beside him, answered. "No, sir. Garage was empty at the time."

Halloran blew out an exasperated breath. "Jesus."

A hundred yards away, Brooks was talking to Ray Jessup who had been manning the entry booth. He shook the man's hand and headed back toward Halloran. "He didn't see anything," Brooks said, looking over his notes. "He's pretty shook up."

"I bet."

"Said he heard a car alarm, and that it went on for a while. He didn't know anything was wrong until the Wentworth lady came up screaming at him."

Halloran glanced over at Kathy Wentworth, a heavyset woman who had happened upon the scene as she was headed to her car after work. She was now seated in the open doorway of an ambulance holding a bottle of water with a gray blanket draped about her shoulders. Her face was drained of color and reflected back the flashing lights almost like a movie screen. It would take her some time to get over this shock.

"Another pregnant one," Halloran said. "Jesus Christ." He glanced about the structure. "Any security cameras?"

"No," Brooks said, almost apologetically. "First thing I asked Mr. Jessup."

Halloran shook his head. "Well, you can bet your ass there'll be some now."

"We'll get a subpoena for the credit card records

from the entrance booth," Brooks said, "although I'm not sure what that will tell us. Mr. Jessup says nobody left the garage after he saw Miss Jarvis enter."

"I don't imagine he was even in a car," Halloran said, nodding toward the short concrete wall around the first level. Outside on the street a perimeter had been set up to cordon off the sidewalk from onlookers. "He probably just climbed in and waited for her."

"Lieutenant!" Halloran turned to see one of the officers – Tate, he believed – headed toward them from the entrance. "People want to know how much longer. They want to get in here and get their vehicles so they can go home."

Halloran blew out a breath. "Tell them we'll be done when we're done, and they can hold onto their goddamn horses."

Tate's eyes widened. He threw his hands up and turned back toward the front of the garage. "Yes, sir."

* * *

10:05 PM

Krystine sat rocking in the stillness of the darkened house, the sleeping baby nestled against her breast. She had barely made a sound since Kris had brought her home, but she had taken a small bottle and already had her first bowel movement. This little girl would be a survivor. She was pink and healthy, and during the short time she'd been awake earlier, she had gazed wonderingly about the room without so much as a whimper. Such a good baby.

"I think I'll call you Sarah," Kris whispered to her. She bent down and kissed her gently on the forehead. "Little Sarah."

Like "Eric," the name "Sarah" had come to her from the past, this time from tenth grade, when Sarah Collins had befriended her and brought about her awakening. Kris had been experimenting with makeup and clothes, and in her awkwardness had drawn the unwanted ridicule of girls and boys alike. Sarah came to her one day at lunch, like something from a dream, and offered to help her with fashion, to teach her how to properly apply makeup and fix her hair – something Grandma Hettie was too ill to help with by this time. She remembered the thrill of sitting at Sarah's vanity while Sarah used her skills to transform Kris into a beautiful young woman with thick lashes, luscious lips, and perfect hair. She remembered the shock of seeing herself wrapped in one of Sarah's beautiful dresses, how the deep blue of the material brought out the color in her eyes. And she remembered the surprise and pleasure when Sarah had kissed her, the shivering pleasure when Sarah peeled the dress down Kris's body and made love to her with her mouth. After that first time, Kris and Sarah were together nearly every day, and when they had the chance, they would lock themselves in Sarah's room. Sarah would work with Kris like an oversized doll, then they would undress and slip naked between the sheets of Sarah's bed.

Kris had never experienced anything like that before. Had never experienced anything like that since. Gradually, she and Sarah saw less and less of each other, and Sarah began dating Jeremy Utley, whom Kris found out later she'd married right after high school. And by that time, Grandma Hettie had died and Kris was moving on.

She thought of Sarah from time to time, and she wondered if Sarah's husband knew what she and Kris had done in the privacy of Sarah's bedroom. She also found herself wondering how differently things might have turned out had she and Sarah kept seeing each other. Whether they would have remained lovers. She also wondered if Sarah saw her as nothing more than a living sex toy, something to feed her fantasies to help her get off.

But it was pointless to wonder about such things.

Right now, Kris had more important things to do than think about sex – whether it was with men or women. She had a mission to carry out. A purpose.

Work for God.

WEDNESDAY, OCTOBER 8

9:20 AM

DANA LAY ON THE BED, her feet stretched out in front of her, and her back supported by pillows. She was on her third cup of coffee, even though she knew she would pay for it later, both in terms of Sofia being restless and repeated trips to the bathroom. Bonnie had come early today and fixed breakfast before Joel left for work, and it made her happy (as well as a bit guilty) to see him head out the door with a full belly. Most days he got by with a Pop Tart, and he was lucky to get that.

Bonnie came into the room holding her own steaming mug of coffee and eased into the chair next to the bed. "Okay, got the dishes all washed. Thought I might work on your laundry here in a bit."

"Mom, you don't have to do that," Dana told her,

though she knew it was futile. "Joel can do that when he gets home."

Bonnie gave her a dismissive wave. "Nonsense. What else am I going to do? Watch you sleep? Look at these stupid talk shows and game shows on the TV all day? No, thanks."

Dana smiled and sipped her coffee. "All right, you win. But don't dry Joel's work shirts. I'm afraid they'll shrink. And God knows he's about to bust out of them as it is."

Bonnie giggled and lowered her voice to just above a whisper, as if Joel might hear her across town. "I swear I think he's gained a few pounds since you got pregnant."

Dana blew on her steaming coffee. "He has. About fifteen to be exact." She took a small sip. "We're hoping once Sofia gets here we can both start being active again. And maybe next summer we can start going out to the park and stuff." She looked at Bonnie. "You know what I miss? Picnics."

"Really?"

"Yeah. Sitting out on the grass in the fresh air and sunshine. Having a sandwich and a cold drink. Watching the kids play. Hearing the birds. I don't think Joel and I have done that since before we got married."

Bonnie chuckled. "Well, that's how it is when you get old."

On the television, the *Today* show faded out for a local news cutaway. Dana pointed at the screen. "Turn that up. I want to see the weather. I hear it's supposed to get colder by the weekend."

Bonnie reached for the remote and inched up the volume. But instead of weather, the female anchor was leading off with a story from Cedar Hill. Another murder. Another woman. Another *pregnant* woman. An attorney. And a senator's daughter.

"Police are not confirming whether there is a link to the murder of Addie Richardson last week," the anchor said, "but if the two are connected, it would be the second time in two years the sleepy college town has been the scene of serial killings."

"Turn it off," Dana said, her mouth suddenly dry.

"But don't you want to – "

"Turn it off!"

Bonnie sighed and switched off the television. She looked at Dana. "Are you all right?"

"I'm okay," Dana said, though truthfully she didn't know *how* she felt. A knot was in her stomach, burning and nauseating.

"I don't understand it," Bonnie said. "This really scares me. The whole world has just gone crazy."

Dana held out her coffee to her mother. The smell of it suddenly repulsed her. "Can you take this? I think it's making me sick."

"Sure."

"Take it to the kitchen."

Bonnie took the mug and headed toward the bedroom door. "You want something else?"

Dana shook her head.

Bonnie looked at her closely. "You sure?"

"Yes. I'm fine."

Bonnie shuffled on down the hall toward the kitchen. "I'm going to get started on the laundry then."

Dana sighed and lay back against the pillows.

She was not "fine." She didn't know exactly what was wrong, but she knew she was definitely not fine.

* * *

12:35 PM

Halloran sat looking at the club sandwich nestled on a plate with soggy fries and a limp pickle. He'd taken one bite of it, and it felt lodged just above his stomach. He sipped at his Diet Coke, but it did little to loosen the lump he felt in his throat.

Earlier he and Brooks had met with J. Daniel Jarvis. The senator had caught a flight from D.C. last night and made it to Cedar Hill about two this morning. When he met with them, he was bleary-eyed and disheveled and damned angry and smelling faintly of whiskey, demanding answers, threatening lawsuits, questioning the department's investigative skills. Even going so far as contacting the FBI, who told him in no uncertain terms that as of now, his daughter's murder was still a local police matter. Jarvis was furious. "You will find this bastard," he told Halloran, "or I will see you and every member of this monkey outfit strung up by your balls."

Halloran got the impression that Jarvis wasn't joking. And with the senator's connections, he had no doubts such an act could be accomplished.

At 3:00 Halloran and Brooks were scheduled to meet with Gerry Friday, the security officer at the First State Bank across the street from the parking garage. Halloran wanted to get a look at the footage from the bank's security cameras in the hopes one of them had picked up the attack. It was a long shot that any of them had something useful; after all, those cameras were notoriously bad at long distance clarity. They simply weren't designed for that.

Brooks shoveled a forkful of mashed potatoes into his mouth. "You think Jarvis is serious about bringing in investigators from the outside?"

"I do," Halloran said. "God knows he's got the clout. And I guess you can't blame him, wanting his daughter's killer caught as soon as possible."

"True."

"Not hungry today?" Grace said behind Halloran, resting a hand on his shoulder. "You want me to box that sandwich up for you for later?"

Halloran slid his plate over to her. "Would you care? Not the fries though."

Grace nodded. "My pleasure." She grabbed the plate and started toward the kitchen, then turned abruptly, looking slightly sheepish. "Look, I know you can't tell me anything, but everyone in town is saying these two murders are connected."

"Well, that's what we aim to find out," Halloran told her.

"Folks are scared."

"I know."

She looked from him to Brooks, then headed toward the kitchen.

Brooks shook his head. "I don't like this, Mike. There's too much talk in town. It makes us look inept."

"Well, it *is* a small town, Greg. That's just how things are."

Yet, he and Brooks both knew the murders were connected. The same M.O. The same type of victim. The same kind of weapon – a cord of some kind used to strangle both women. But why? And *who*? Once Scotty finished the autopsy, they would make an official announcement that Samantha Jarvis was most likely killed by the same perpetrator that murdered Addie Richardson. But it was too early now. Halloran wanted all the information he could get before that kind of statement.

* * *

2:20 PM

Wade took a drag off his cigarette and blew a plume of smoke into the air. "So Parker has a new scheme going."

Joel took a sip of his Mountain Dew. "Oh yeah?"

"Uh huh."

They were parked in the side lot of the Gas-N-Pack, Joel sitting sideways on the driver's side of the work truck, the door propped open, and Wade leaning against the side panel, his feet crossed. Their scheduled work for the day was done, and now they were just killing time until five o'clock. They seemed to be doing this a lot lately. Not enough to keep them busy for a whole eight hours. Joel wondered again whether this time next year he and Wade would even have jobs. It was a sobering thought, especially with Sofia on the way. But he remembered his conversation with Betsy and her reassurance that she had his back. As long as Betsy was with the company, he knew he would stay employed. But what would happen if the whole operation shut down? Where would he go? What would happen if Dana couldn't go back to work? If he allowed himself to dwell on the possibilities, he would find himself spiraling into a panic. And there was no reason to do that just yet. Still, he wondered if he should be scouting around for other employment opportunities if the need arose. He also wondered whether he should voice his concerns to Wade. But he felt sure Wade would have no trouble finding other work; if nothing else, he could bullshit his way into just about any job he wanted.

Wade adjusted his cap. "She's rented a cabin somewhere in the woods up in Indiana."

Joel looked at him. "Oh really?"

Wade nodded. "Says there's no TV, no cell service. . .

nothing but trees and some trails."

Joel chuckled. "Well, you don't need any of that anyway, do you?"

Wade grinned. "Probably not."

"It does have plumbing, right?"

Wade snorted. "God, I hope so. If not, I guess I'll be taking a shit in the woods with the bears."

"Better pack your toilet paper," Joel told him.

Wade thumped the ashes off his cigarette. "You know, I think she may be getting too serious. I think. . . " He looked at Joel. "I think she wants more than I do."

"How long you two been dating now?"

Wade rubbed a thumb over his stubbled chin. "Let's see. . . we went to that Fourth of July thing at her friend's house. We'd been on a couple of dates before that." He grunted. "Christ. Longer than I thought."

"It's still just a few months," Joel said. "But if you think she wants something serious and you don't, you need to tell her, man."

"Yeah, I know," Wade said, "and I will eventually. But not before this weekend." He took a drag off the cigarette and winked at Joel. "Honestly, the sex is just too goddamned good."

* * *

3:05 PM

Gerry Friday was a slim African American who barely stood five-and-a-half feet tall, and his age could have been anywhere between thirty and sixty. He showed not one gray hair, not even in his wispy mustache, but his demeanor was straight-forward and mature. And if Halloran had been a gambling man, he would have bet Friday had had some martial arts training. There didn't appear to be one ounce of fat on the man's body; his forearms were hard and sinewy with muscle, and no doubt he probably sported a six-pack that would put a Calvin Klein underwear model to shame.

Friday met them in the busy bank lobby and led them down a shadowy hall to an unmarked door. "When I saw the news I started wondering if our ATM camera might have picked anything up, so I wasn't really surprised to get a call from you."

Behind the door, Friday ushered them behind a desk where half a dozen computer monitors blazed with security camera feeds. He nodded to two empty desk chairs. "Have a seat."

"Quite a setup you have here," Brooks said.

"State of the art," Friday said, obviously proud. "We don't spare any expenses here when it comes to security."

He took a seat at the desk and with a few keystrokes brought up a full-screen color image on the largest monitor. "As soon as I got here this morning I started going through the footage. I think you'll like what I found." The scene was the bank parking lot in the foreground and Fifth Street and the rear of the parking garage beyond. The parked cars in the structure were in shadow, but the quality of the image ensured a passable level of detail. The video was paused, according to the time stamp in the lower right corner, at 3:42 PM.

"Now," Friday said, glancing up at them. "You're going to see a customer drive up to the ATM. As soon as she pulls away, focus your attention on the row of cars just inside the garage." With a click of the mouse, he started the video.

An older woman wearing sunglasses pulled up to the ATM, and they were treated to an unflattering view of her nostrils as she inserted her card and stared at the screen to complete her transaction. She pushed buttons. She stared at the monitor. She pushed more buttons. Finally, her business complete, she settled back into her seat, rolled up her window, and glided out of frame.

Friday placed his finger on the screen. "Now watch."

The dark blue fender of the customer's car pulled out of frame, and the camera adjusted its focus. Right where Friday's finger pointed, Halloran saw a figure walking briskly toward a dark Mustang. Although the image was grainy, Halloran knew instantly it was Samantha Jarvis. The Mustang's lights were flashing, meaning Samantha had already triggered the car's alarm. Suddenly from behind, a second figure appeared and looped something around Samantha's neck.

"Is that another woman?" Brooks said.

Halloran and Brooks watched as Samantha Jarvis struggled with her assailant, which appeared to be another woman with light blonde hair, though the facial features were unclear. She fought hard, grabbing at whatever was around her throat. With the distance from the camera it was impossible to see, but Halloran knew that like Addie Richardson, Samantha Jarvis had been strangled with a nylon cord. Samantha Jarvis slumped out of view behind the low wall of the parking structure, and the attacker hovered over her and also disappeared from view. They watched the screen in silence for a full two minutes. The Mustang's lights stopped flashing. In a moment, the blonde woman reappeared, standing upright and holding a small bundle. She looked about her, then disappeared back into the shadows of the parking structure.

"There's more," Friday said.

Nothing happened on the screen for over three minutes. Then they watched as a heavyset woman neared the scene. It was Kathy Wentworth. Her hands flew up to her face in horror. She staggered backwards, fell to the ground, then scrambled to her feet and took off running toward the entrance of the structure, out of sight. There was no sound on the video, but Halloran knew she was screaming. At that point, a Ford pickup pulled up the ATM, blocking the camera's view of the garage.

Friday paused the video. "Unfortunately, the customer at the ATM heard the commotion across the street and left his vehicle to see what was happening. He didn't come back to move his truck until after you guys were already on the scene."

Halloran took a deep breath. He had certainly seen more horrible video of killings – suicides and full on execution-style murders – but this one was chilling. The assailant's face, though blurred from the distance, never changed expression. Never seemed to convey that the attack was taking any effort at all. Halloran leaned forward. "Can you run it back for us?"

"Certainly," Friday said.

"Start it just where the woman at the ATM drives away."

Friday clicked a few buttons, and the screen blazed up with the footage.

Just as the car pulled out of frame, Halloran laid a hand on Friday's shoulder. "Stop it right there. Can you zoom in any?"

"I can," Friday said, "but the resolution will be shit."

"That's okay," Halloran said. "Do it anyway."

Friday clicked some buttons on the keyboard and the figure of Samantha Jarvis grew larger. And blurrier.

"Okay, play it," Halloran said.

They watched the video a second time, and just as the second woman grabbed Samantha, Halloran had Friday pause the playback again. "How tall was Samantha Jarvis?" he asked Brooks.

Brooks scratched his head just above the temple. "Trying to remember. Five-eight, five-nine maybe. Little on the taller side for a woman."

Halloran pointed at the screen. "This second woman

towers over her. She's a good eight inches taller than Samantha."

Brooks squinted at the screen. "Looks like it. But could that be because Samantha is bent backwards?"

Halloran shook his head, keeping his gaze locked on the smeary image of the struggling women. "I have no idea. Even so, this second woman is damned tall." He nudged Friday. "Okay, play it."

The murder played out again on the monitor, and this time when the perpetrator stood upright with the bundle which could only be Samantha Jarvis' baby, Halloran could see a splash of blood on her face. She looked furtively about her, then took off.

But not before Halloran noticed something else.

"Run it back," he told Friday. "Just to where she stands back up." Friday did as he was told, and just as the woman reappeared, Halloran had him pause it again. "Can you zoom in just a little more?"

"I can," Friday said, "but like I told you, you won't be able to see any more detail. This isn't like *CSI*."

"Humor me," Halloran said.

Friday gave an almost inaudible sigh and clicked a button on his keyboard. The blond woman's face, now just a jumble of pixels, grew larger.

"Can you play this in slow motion?" Halloran asked.

"Whatever you want," Friday told him.

Halloran pointed to woman's head, to her hairline. "Keep your eye right here," he said to Brooks. "Watch her hair when she looks back and forth."

The woman's head moved side to side. Her hair shifted slightly. Unnaturally.

An expression of understanding crossed Brooks' face. "That looks like – "

"It's a wig," Halloran finished for him. "She's wearing a wig."

* * *

7:30 PM

She was beginning to love this time of the evening. Even though in the beginning the dark unnerved her, the house was quiet and there was no noise from the street. Here in the nursery the only sound was the steady beep from the baby's heart monitor. The room was dark except for the warm yellow light that filtered in from the living room across the hall. Little Sarah, having had her bottle, slept deeply on Krystine's bosom. Kris pressed her cheek against the baby's head, then kissed her tiny forehead.

She'd always thought she would have made a wonderful mother, had she been able to bear children. And if she'd had babies, how different things might have been. Right now she might be helping her kids with their homework. Cooking dinner for them. For her husband. What would it be like to set a meal on a kitchen table for your family? To listen to them talk about their day, to make plans for the weekend? Or to lie in bed at night next to your spouse and discuss having a couple's getaway? Or a family vacation next summer? It was all too wonderful to imagine. She envied those mothers she saw in the grocery pushing their children in the cart, talking to them about what they were buying, what they were going to have for dinner, what they were going to tell Daddy when he came home from work. She would smile at them, and sometimes they would catch her eye and smile back, and they would share a look, as if they were both women connecting with the bond of mother-hood. Those were moments that never failed to give her a thrill.

Little Sarah gave a small whimper, and Kris moved slowly to lay her down in the bassinet. She watched her for a moment, and when she was sure the baby was still sound asleep, she let out a breath and tip-toed out to the hall. It was time for her evening tea.

It wasn't until after the kettle screeched and she was pouring the steaming water over the tea bag in the cup that the thought hit her. An idea. A plan. She sat down at the table and dunked the bag in the cup, watched the water darken with the color of the tea.

She could leave. It was simple. She could pack up the baby and all the necessary medical supplies and start driving. Head for the west coast. For California. Maybe she could make it to Hollywood after all. She could find a job as a nurse. Tell everyone she had taken some time off to have the baby and now she was ready to get back to work. Start a new life as a single mother.

Sarah's father had been killed in an accident. No. . . A divorce. Sarah's father had divorced her. Or better yet, they'd never been married. He took off when he found out Kris was pregnant, and now she had no idea where he was or how to get in touch with him. That could fly. They'd believe that. After all, that kind of thing happened all the time. No one would know. In L.A. there'd be no one to draw a connection between Kris and Sarah and the daughter of a senator no one but those inside his district had ever heard of.

But *they* would find out. *They* would track her. Find her in California and take the baby. She couldn't even imagine what they might be capable of. Maria had told her about the Network. Dozens of women across the country just like Kris. All working for the same cause. All doing God's work. All saving the children and finding them loving, good, *decent* homes. And if the Network was as large as Maria intimated, there was no limit to their power. They might even be able to find her before she reached California. And then what?

She shuddered.

And then what?

* * *

9:05 PM

Halloran lay stretched out on the sofa, the box from Grace's open on his chest and a beer on the coffee table next to him. Mel was perched on the back of the couch, his gaze fixed on the remains of the club sandwich. Halloran picked up a small crumble of bacon and brought it to his lips while Mel's eyes remained locked on it. Halloran chuckled. "You crazy cat." He offered the bacon to Mel, who sniffed it as if deciding whether it was worth his time, then flicked his tail and jumped down to the floor. In a moment Halloran could hear him crunching on his cat food in the kitchen.

"All right," Halloran called to him. "But I'm going to tell Charlie you turned up your nose at his cooking."

He took a bite of the sandwich. It was cold, but he figured heating it in the microwave would only make the toasted bread soggy. Well, soggier than it already was after sitting on top of the sliced tomato all day. But he was starving, and he figured no matter how bad the sandwich was, it was nothing the beer couldn't wash down.

Earlier, Scotty had called him about the Jarvis girl's autopsy. He was officially ruling it a homicide (no surprise there), and from what he observed in the bruising on the neck, she had been strangled with the exact same kind of cord that had killed Addie Richardson. The cuts on Samantha Jarvis's abdomen had been made with the same medical precision, and most likely with a surgical-grade scalpel. Halloran called Brooks to give him the update, and there was no doubt in their minds that whoever killed Addie Richardson had also murdered Samantha Jarvis. Tomorrow morning they would issue an official statement to the public. It was a thought that filled him with dread. Not only would the department have to deal with investigating serial murders, they would also be under the scrutiny of an unforgiving and panicked public. Even the horror of two years ago couldn't compare to this. Because now the residents of Cedar Hill would demand to know how it could happen again.

He took one last bite of the sandwich and closed it up, dusted the crumbs off his hands and grabbed up his beer. Too much thinking on this. It was making him crazy. But the surveillance video had opened up new possibilities. And a new angle on the investigation. The fuzzy frame grab with the perpetrator's face, as indistinct as it was, had been released to the media earlier this evening in time for the nightly news, and he hoped it would spark some new leads. They could always hope.

He lay back and pressed the cold bottle against his forehead. He needed something to get his mind off this for a while. He picked up the remote and clicked on the television. An old rerun of *The Big Bang Theory*. He could deal with that. Something mindless and silly.

His phone dinged and he groaned inwardly. But when he looked at the screen he was pleasantly surprised to see a text from Kelly. *Hey, what's up?*

Not much, he responded, and he couldn't help but smile at the slight thrill that shivered through him.

Gotta a few minutes to chat? she wrote.

He started to type out a response, then stopped. Screw it. He hit the call button.

"Hey!" she said, and he could hear the smile in her voice.

"Hey there. Thought I'd just call instead of texting if that's all right."

"Sure. What's going on tonight?"

"Nothing," he said. "On the couch. Got the TV on. Just vegging."

"Me, too. Had a horrible day."

He sat up and turned down the TV volume. "Oh yeah? What happened?

"Oh nothing that you'd understand," she said. "I just couldn't get one of the accounts to balance. Worked on it all day long. Had to call the correspondent bank. Talked to four different people trying to find out what happened. It was just frustrating." She chuckled. "It sounds silly when I try to explain it."

"It doesn't sound silly at all," he said. "I know what it's like to get frustrated over something little."

"It's just that it took all day to get straightened out. Not to mention all the time spent on the phone, waiting for people to call me back, sitting on hold. I was exhausted by the time four o'clock came around."

"I can imagine."

"Anyway, I just got settled for the night so I thought I would text you. It wasn't too late was it?"

"Oh, no, not at all," he said.

"I didn't know what kind of schedule you keep."

"Nothing really set anymore, not with all that's going on."

"Oh, yeah," she said. "I saw the news. That's horrible what happened to that senator's daughter."

"Yeah. We've been pretty busy with all of it."

"Well," she said, "I know you can't talk about it, but I hope it's all over soon."

"So. . . " he said, wanting to change the subject, "I had a great time the other night. I really enjoyed meeting you."

"Same here," she said. "Greg is a hoot."

"He's something, all right."

"And I just love Diane. She's one of the best people I've ever worked for."

"Yeah," he said. "I've gotten pretty close to them since Greg and I became partners."

"I can see why. They seem like a lot of fun."

"Yeah."

He sat silent for a moment of palpable awkwardness. He could almost feel Kelly tensing up over the empty static on the phone. "So, yeah," he said, and his words seemed to trip over his tongue. "I was wondering if I could see you again. And this time without Greg and Diane. Maybe we could – "

"Yes," she said, interrupting. "I'd love to."

A laugh of delight escaped him before he could stop it. "Oh yeah?"

"Yeah," she said, and again he could hear the smile in her tone. "You're a nice guy, Mike. I just. . . I haven't met too many of those since Ronnie died. You know? You just seem like someone I'd like to get to know a little better. Just to do things with. Dinner and things. Maybe a movie occasionally. Just somebody to hang out with. More of a friendship. Not necessarily for *dating*, although I'm not ruling that out either, you know, if the chemistry is right and we click." She stopped abruptly, letting the last word hang in the air with all its implications and gave an anxious chuckle. "Sorry. I kinda rambled on there for a second."

"It's okay," he said, letting the grin play on his face.

"I'm just nervous I guess."

"Don't be nervous." He thought of the gold locket hanging around her neck and then with a cringe remembered soaking her with the tea. "I'm the one who should be nervous after giving you a tea bath the other night."

She laughed. "Don't worry about it."

"Did it stain your sweater?"

"It came out. No harm done."

"Good." The tense silence overtook them again, and before he could stop himself, he said, "So what about Friday?"

"Friday?"

"Yeah," he said. "You want to go out on Friday night?"

"Sure. I'm free all weekend. Trevor's spending Friday and Saturday night with a friend, so either night is fine with me. You're the one with the crazy schedule these days."

"Well let's plan on it then. Dinner, then maybe catch a movie afterward. Just typical date stuff. How does that sound?"

"Sounds wonderful. I like 'typical date stuff.' Seems like everybody wants to do something new and different these days. One guy wanted to take me to a rock climbing wall. No thanks. I'm an old-fashioned girl and I like old-fashioned dates." She laughed. "Does that make me old?"

"Not at all," he said. "I like it. I like old-fashioned." He took a sip of his beer. "I'll pick you up around seven. Will that work?"

"Perfect." She paused. "Aren't you forgetting something?"

"What?"

"You don't know where I live."

He laughed. "Oh yeah, I guess that would help." He grabbed a tablet and a pen and jotted down the address as she rattled it off to him. Waterwheel Way. He knew where that was, in one of the nicer neighborhoods on the west side of the city. "Okay," he said. "Guess I'll see you then. If something comes up I'll call you. You never know with an investigation when something might break."

"I understand. I know it's crazy for you right now."

"Good night, Kelly."

"G'night, Mike."

He disconnected the call and stared at his reflection

in the blank screen. He was still smiling. It felt good.

* * *

11:25 PM

She'd been lying awake for an hour watching the minutes tick by on the digital clock and listening to Joel snore beside her. They had started watching the news – more coverage about that awful murder of the senator's daughter. The senator's *pregnant* daughter. Thirty-seven weeks along, just like Dana. Just like the other girl last week. Joel switched off the television before the story was over, and though she knew it was to keep her from hearing more horrible details about the murder, it angered her nonetheless. He drifted off to sleep immediately as usual, but she couldn't shake the unease. And Joseph's warning still echoed in her ears.

She glanced at Joel. He lay on his side, his back to her. She could barely see the shape of his head in the darkness, squat and round, and his smallish ear sticking out like an almost perfect half-circle. She resisted the urge to reach out for him, even though she longed to touch him. If it weren't so uncomfortable and her back wasn't throbbing with pain she would roll onto her side and spoon up against him. But she'd practically been confined to this bed for three days, and everything – her arms, her legs, her back, her neck, her head – everything was hurting. And Sofia was dancing on her bladder. Maybe she would take one of those pain pills. But first she needed to pee.

She rolled up onto the edge of the bed, then managed to pull herself to her feet. She didn't feel the rush of dizziness the way she had yesterday morning, and she managed to maneuver around the bed in the darkness without any light-headedness and, more importantly, without barking her shin on anything or tripping over Joel's clothes in the floor by his nightstand.

In the bathroom, she switched on the light and blinked in the sudden brightness. She sat on the toilet, her panties twisted around her swollen ankles and looked at the large bruise on her right thigh. It was still purple, but now it was tinged with green. And still tender to the touch. She pulled up her underwear and rinsed off her hands, then lifted up her gown to gaze at the shocking blotch of dark reds and violets that stretched from just under her right arm down to her hip. The doctor had told her she was very lucky, and that she had been smart in making sure her seatbelt was around her hips and not her belly, because that would have been, in his words, "disastrous." She didn't need to think very hard to understand what he meant.

She shuffled into the kitchen, pulled a glass from the cabinet, and filled it with tap water. The bottle of pills was on the ledge by the sink, although she wondered why she was even bothering to take one. They were only glorified Tylenol, and in such a low dosage that they barely knocked any of the pain. Still, she fingered one from the bottle and washed it down with a swallow of tepid water, then gripped the edge of the counter until the nausea and the urge to vomit passed. The pills made her a little sick to her stomach at first, but it always passed quickly. She leaned back against the counter and took another sip of water, staring out the window at the dark, quiet neighborhood.

Apparently old Mr. Benson next door was also having a sleepless night. The kitchen light blazed on, and Dana could see him through window, futzing around in his bright yellow kitchen, wearing baggy boxer shorts and a tank-style T-shirt, his white hair splayed over the top of his head. She watched him for a moment, feeling a pang of guilt for being a peeping tom. He pulled a cup from the cabinet and filled it with water, then stuck it in the microwave while he dug around for something in a drawer. He produced a teabag and waited for his water to finish heating, staring at the microwave with an expression of defeat. Or exhaustion. He glanced out the window, toward her house, and though she knew he couldn't see her in the darkness, she quickly turned away.

Back down the hall, she felt her way into Sofia's room and found the rocker in the darkness. She was glad when she realized she'd felt none of the weakness she'd experienced yesterday when she needed her mother to help her back to the bed. She sank into the seat and rested her hands on her belly. Sofia had settled down and seemed to have gone back to sleep.

Dana closed her eyes and rocked gently, wondering for the millionth time how different it would be to sit here cradling Sofia in her arms and not in her belly. And she found herself thinking again about Joel's words: *Joseph senses danger around you. . . He even said I need to nail all the windows shut.*

She shuddered. Something was out there. Some kind of evil. It was a faceless, nameless, shapeless mass lurking in the dark, scratching at the windows like a wolf. Begging for her to let it inside. And what if she didn't recognize it when it came? What if instead of keeping it locked out she unintentionally invited it in? What if the cause of the danger Joseph sensed wasn't something outside, but something *inside*? What if it was Joel? What if it was herself?

Something splashed onto her arm, and she realized she was crying. She hadn't even been aware of it. She dabbed at her eyes with the sleeve of her gown, surprised at just how damp the material was when she felt it.

"Dana?"

Joel stood in the doorway, a hulking darker shape in the blackness of the room. She could barely descry his white briefs in the shadows. She swallowed a sob.

"Babe, what's wrong?" He moved closer to her and knelt beside the rocker.

"I can't do this," she said, her voice cracking just above a whisper. "I just can't. I thought I could but I can't."

His massive hand swallowed her tiny one. "It's going to be okay, baby."

"What was I thinking? What were *we* thinking?"

He leaned forward and rested his chin on the arm of the chair. "We're going to be fine," he said. "I'm scared, too. But we'll be okay." He placed his warm hand on her belly and caressed it with his thumb. "All of us."

She took his hand in hers and brought it to her lips and kissed it. "I'm terrified," she said. "It's not just being pregnant. These murders have got me all shook up, and I keep thinking about what Joseph said to you – "

Joel sighed and pulled his hand away. "Stop thinking about that," he said, his voice suddenly sharp. "I wish to God I'd never told you about it. It's all bullshit. You know he was talking about the accident."

"But what he said about the bedroom. And the windows – "

"Baby, the man's in his eighties. He probably got it confused with something else. A dream or something."

"But I feel it, too, Joel. Something bad. It's not over."

Joel stood, and from her spot in the rocker he seemed to tower over her like a giant. "You're getting yourself all worked up over nothing. Nothing is going to happen. Your hormones are working overtime. You're emotional. And I think you're still a little mixed up from the wreck."

Rage suddenly filled her. "I am *not* mixed up. I

know what I'm feeling, and I tell you, *something is wrong!*"

Joel took a deep breath. "Okay," he said, taking her hand. "Let's get back to bed."

She jerked her hand away. "I don't want to get back to bed," she spat. The last thing she needed was him trying to coddle her and spying in at her thoughts.

Even in the darkness she saw him shaking his head. Angry, confused, hurt, or all three she wasn't sure. He turned his massive frame and headed for the hallway. "Fine," he said with a wave of his hand. "Stay in here all night."

She sat rigid as he lumbered back to the bedroom and fell onto the mattress with a complaining creak from the bedframe. In a few moments, much quicker than she would have thought possible, he was snoring again. Her eyes stung, but they seemed drained of tears, and her neck and back were still screaming in pain.

To hell with it; she was getting another pill.

THURSDAY, OCTOBER 9

9:10 AM

SAMANTHA JARVIS'S TOWNHOUSE was in Waverly Estates, right on the riverfront. Halloran hadn't had much need to be out here over the years as it was an exclusive gated community with little crime, plus no one he'd ever associated with personally could afford to live here. The quiet street wound through perfectly manicured lawns and shrubs, past the centralized clubhouse, tennis courts, and pool, then circled around down by the river.

Beside him, Brooks was ogling the neighborhood like a young woman picking out an engagement ring at Tiffany's. "I've never been inside here before," he said. "These homes are gorgeous."

"Pricey, too," Halloran grunted. "Most sell in the low three-hundreds."

Brooks gaped at him. "For a *townhouse*?"

"Yep. Even higher as you get closer to the water."

Brooks clucked his tongue. "Guess that's why Samantha Jarvis was only leasing."

"Hell, I couldn't even afford *that*, probably," Halloran said. He pulled the sedan into a parking space between a blindingly polished silver Mercedes and a black Chevrolet Tahoe. The architecture of the homes was a mixture of styles – Georgian, Colonial, traditional – meant to give the impression the neighborhood had been here forever, and though they were all joined together, each townhouse had its own distinct look. Samantha's modest red-brick affair was offset with a copper-roof capped bay window. Beyond the row of houses, the Red River crawled sluggishly along on its course toward the Mississippi, its waters dull and dark.

Halloran rang the bell and was greeted by the senator wearing jeans and a bright yellow polo. The jeans were creased, as if they'd been ironed. "Come on in," he said, his voice strained and thin. "My wife is in Sam's bedroom looking through her clothes." He led them toward the staircase, then stopped and regarded them. "You have some news?"

"Of a sort," Halloran said.

Senator Jarvis gave them a grim emotionless smile and nodded, then headed up toward the bedroom. "Evelyn, they're here."

Evelyn Jarvis stood in the center of the bedroom, one hand on her hip. She was thin and tanned, and her shoulder-length blondish hair looked as if it would withstand hurricane-force winds. She stared at three dresses laid out on the unmade bed before her – one black, two navy blue – not acknowledging that anyone had come into the room. "What do you think, Daniel dear?" she said finally. "Black or blue? Samantha always looked nice in blue."

The senator raised his hands. "Whatever you think." He looked at Halloran and Brooks. "It's a surreal feeling, trying to figure out what to bury your daughter in."

"I think we'll go with this one," Evelyn said, sweeping one of the blue dresses off the bed. It had a white lace collar, and Halloran thought it looked like something a twelve-year old would wear to a tea party. "She wore this one to our wedding, remember?"

Jarvis sank into an overstuffed chair in the corner. "No," he said. Halloran thought the man looked considerably smaller than he had the day before, as if all his bravado and anger had spewed out of him and left him wilted.

"'No' you don't remember, or 'no' to the dress?" Evelyn said.

"I don't remember," he said.

Evelyn floated toward them. "My apologies, detectives," she said, extending her hand. "Evelyn Smythe-Jarvis."

Halloran took her hand. It was cold and bony like touching a corpse. "I'm Lieutenant Mike Halloran and this is Detective Greg Brooks."

"They said they had some news," Jarvis said from the corner.

"Nothing big," Halloran said quickly when Evelyn raised an eyebrow. "We're issuing a statement to the press this morning and wanted to tell you first."

Evelyn leaned back against the bed. "Good news, I hope," she said.

"After seeing the coroner's report, we're fairly certain your daughter was attacked by the same individual that killed Addie Richardson last week."

Daniel Jarvis's face went rigid. "'Fairly certain?' What the hell does that even mean? Either he did it or he didn't."

"Well," Halloran said, "without saying too much, we know the methods used were the same. And at this point, after watching the surveillance video we still don't know whether we're looking for a male or a female. I'm sure you saw the frame grab on the news."

Jarvis shook his head and looked away. "Sick bastard either way."

"Have you received any calls about the picture you released?" Evelyn said.

"No, ma'am," Halloran told her. "But it's only been twelve hours." He looked at them. "I do have a question for you though. Who is the father of Samantha's baby?"

The Jarvises exchanged a glance, and J. Daniel let out a deep sigh. "We don't know," he said.

"She would never tell us," Evelyn said.

"Her co-workers seem to think the father was from

D.C.," Brooks said. "At least, that was the impression she gave them."

"Sam never dated anyone in D.C.," the senator told them. "And she was never there long enough in the past few months to. . . "

"I understand," Halloran said. "So you don't know if she was still in communication with the father."

"No," Evelyn said. "She told us very little about her pregnancy." She cut her eyes at the senator, who nodded. "Except that at first she was considering. . . termination."

"An abortion," Brooks said.

The woman winced. "Yes."

"What changed her mind?" Halloran asked.

"We're not sure," Jarvis said. "But the last few weeks she seemed excited about the baby. A girl. She was going to name her Berkley." Jarvis's eyes brimmed with tears. He had completely changed from the blustering heavyweight that had vowed to have the whole Cedar Hill police department declared incompetent. He hung his head.

Evelyn Smythe-Jarvis clucked her tongue and moved to her husband's side. "Oh, Daniel dear," she cooed, smoothing his hair.

Beyond the uncurtained bedroom windows, a coal barge was making its way upriver. Halloran watched it for a moment, thinking. "Do either of you know who Samantha's OB/GYN was? Was it someone here in Cedar Hill?"

Evelyn smiled coldly. "As we've told you, Lieutenant, Sam told us very little about her pregnancy. She and I weren't very close, and visits to the gynecologist aren't something a girl tends to confide to her father about."

Halloran prickled. "I only asked because I thought her doctor might have information on the baby's father. A name at least. And we'd like to talk to him."

"Well," Evelyn began, "as I said – "

"Majmadar," J. Daniel blurted. "Dr. Majmadar."

Evelyn gave him a shocked glance. "Daniel, how did you – "

"She's an OB/GYN here in Cedar Hill," he went on, ignoring his wife. "Sam loved her."

Halloran worked to keep the smile off his lips. "Would you happen to know her number? Have an appointment card or anything?"

"She shouldn't be too hard to find," the senator said.

Halloran thanked them, promising to call if there was more news, and he and Brooks made their way downstairs and out to the unmarked sedan. "No love lost between those two," he said, unlocking the car and sliding into the driver's seat.

Brooks climbed in and fastened his seatbelt. "Wow," he said. "What a cold bitch. Wonder what else he hasn't filled her in on?"

Halloran started the car and began the circle back to the main road. "I want you to locate this Dr. Majmadar, then file for an emergency warrant for her records. I'd like to get in there today if possible. We need to find the father of this child."

"Will do," Brooks said.

Halloran pulled up to the gate at the end of the drive and waited for it to open. "In the meantime, I've got another angle I want to pursue."

* * *

Back in his office, Halloran punched a number into his desk phone and listened to the ringing on the other end. Finally, the phone picked up and Bob Richardson's voice answered. "Hello?"

"Mr. Richardson, this is Lieutenant Mike Halloran at the Cedar Hill Police Department. How are you doing, sir?"

"Ah, Lieutenant. We're. . . we're muddling through. It's been pretty rough."

"I can only imagine," Halloran said.

"Pray you never have to bury your child," Bob Richardson said. "You don't know what heartache is."

"Yes, sir," Halloran said. "I'm. . . terribly sorry."

"Do you have any news?"

Halloran told him about the statement to be issued to the press and promised to call if the photograph from the security video prompted any new information. "And. . . one more thing," he said. "Would you or your wife happen to know what doctor Addie was seeing? I mean, her OB/GYN?"

"I don't," Bob said, "but Sue might. Let me get her to the phone." Halloran heard him shuffling through the house, calling for his wife, and then heard him whisper something unintelligible followed by, "No, nothing new."

And then Sue Richardson said, "Good morning, Mr. Halloran."

"Good morning, Mrs. Richardson. How are you doing?"

"Oh. . . I don't know. Still kind of numb. Bob said you had a question."

"Yes ma'am. Addie's OB/GYN. Do you know who she was seeing?"

"Yes, sir, I do. Dr. Majmadar at the women's clinic on the east side."

Halloran felt a thrill shoot through him. "Dr. Majmadar. You're sure?"

"Oh, yes. Addie thought the world of Dr. Majmadar. She's Indian, you know."

"I gathered."

"I went with Addie to her first few visits. She's a lovely woman, Dr. Majmadar. And I don't think she has any children of her own. Do you know," Sue went on, "she actually came by the funeral home?"

"Did she now?"

"Yes. Wasn't that sweet?"

Halloran made a note of it on his scratch pad. "Indeed," he said.

* * *

11:40 AM

Little Sarah had just drifted off to sleep after her bottle, lulled by a full belly, a warm onesie, and the steady rhythmic beeping of the monitor. Kris placed her carefully into the bassinet, then moved to the windows and pulled down the shades, leaving the room in semi-darkness. She tip-toed out, leaving the door open just a crack behind her, and stepped lightly down the hall toward the kitchen, wincing with every creaking step on the hardwood.

It was almost time for lunch. There was some deli ham in the refrigerator along with some leftover salad from last night; a good sandwich and a glass of tea would go well with watching the noon newscast to see whether the police had come up with any new leads.

Last night the top stories on all the local stations had been the fuzzy shot of her in the downtown parking structure, along with the supposition that she was wearing a wig. A mixture of excitement, terror, and anger had roared through her. Why had she not taken into consideration the ATM across the street? She knew bank ATMs concealed security cameras inside. That the picture of her had been as clear as it was (which was not very) had itself been an unfortunate miracle. But the fact that some sharp-eyed detective could tell she was wearing a wig was downright unbelievable. Unless, of course, it was all speculation. A guess. A theory thrown out to the wind to see if it would lead to any information. She didn't know. But she had lots of wigs, and changing her appearance was something she had mastered. Wigs and makeup could mask many things, but the one thing she couldn't hide was her height. Hadn't the police noted that in their statement, surmising by the height of the wall of the parking structure that she must be at least six-foot-five? They weren't far off; in her stocking feet she actually towered above most other women at six-feet-three. But now she would have to be careful. It would be even more important to keep to herself and go out of the house only when necessary, at least until the mission was complete.

Her cellphone vibrated in her pocket with an incoming call. She pulled it out and her heart jolted when she saw it was Maria. She accepted the call and slowly brought the phone up to her ear. "Yes?"

"I'll be arriving at five today for the infant," Maria said, her voice distant and clinical.

Kris felt a pang shoot through her stomach. "Already? But I just got her."

"You were careless, Krystine," Maria said. "Have you seen the news?"

"Yes, I saw the picture," she said, trying to keep the rising panic out of her voice. Maria had never sounded so cold to her before. "But my face isn't clearly visible. I don't think anyone can tell that it's me."

"I meant the other news that came out this morning."

Kris's breath caught in her throat. "What news?"

"They've linked the Richardson girl's death last week with the Jarvis girl's."

"Well we knew that would happen eventually," Kris said. Her mouth was suddenly dry. "You said so yourself."

"Yes," Maria said, "but now they have your picture. The stakes have changed, Krystine. We have to do everything possible to protect the infant. That's why I'm coming today. We have an eager family, one that is most worthy. And we can't risk waiting and having anything happen to that baby."

Kris's eyes welled with tears. "I understand."

"The job here is over."

"But there was one more assignment. If I can complete it this weekend – "

"It's over, Krystine," Maria said, and her voice was firm. "I'll see you at five. You should start making plans to vacate the premises." With that she disconnected the call, and Kris was left listening to dead air.

She sank into a chair at the kitchen table. Tears were spilling down her cheeks now. One splatted on the yellow vinyl placemat. Over and done. And now what would she do? Maybe Maria would still give her the full payout they had agreed on. It would be enough for a new start in a different city, maybe even enough to get her to California. But what if Maria said she didn't earn the entire sum? Or what if she refused to pay anything?

But Kris had completed two of the three anticipated assignments. Surely that was worth two-thirds of the promised sum. Or at least half. Even half of the money she had anticipated would be enough for what all beginning a new life would require – new identification documents, transportation, moving costs.

If they gave her anything at all. She had complicated things. Had put the entire operation in jeopardy. What if they wanted to tie up all loose ends? What if they wanted to be sure she would never make any further mistakes? That she would never reveal anything about what had transpired? The idea sent chills through her.

She thought of little Sarah, sleeping away in the nursery. Kris had toyed with the idea of running away with Eric, but dismissed it eventually as an impossible folly. Again, she considered the same with Sarah. Bundling up the infant along with the necessary supplies and heading out of town. But there was no time to prepare. Maria would be here in a little over five hours. And even if she left she knew the odds were high they would catch up to her. They wanted the baby. They wanted Sarah. And Kris knew they would not deem her honorable of adopting the infant. Not a single mother. Not someone who had killed – even in the name of God – to protect the innocent. They would do whatever it took to place Sarah with a decent, respectable family. They would never let anyone like Kris keep her.

She held her face in her hands and wept.

* * *

2:30 PM

The sun was warm and comforting against Dana's skin, but the breeze blowing in from the west had a slight bite. Summer was officially over, even if most of the trees had yet to turn. It had been a dry summer; the weatherman said there would be no vivid colors this autumn, that everything would just fade to brown and die. Somehow that seemed fitting, considering all that had happened in the past week.

Dana and Bonnie sat outside on the patio behind the house. The previous owners had assembled the patio themselves from brick leftover from the construction of the house. It was rustic and moss-covered and uneven, and Dana loved it. She had purchased some inexpensive patio furniture – two rockers and a cocktail table – and had planted a border of knockout roses around it, and although the summer had proven too hot to sit out and enjoy it much, today seemed perfect. Along with the slight chill, the breeze brought with it the unmistakable scent of fall – the faint whiff of wood smoke and the earthy smell of natural decay. She closed her eyes and breathed it deeply, then brought the cup of coffee to her lips and sipped it. It had cooled somewhat but was still too hot without blowing on it.

"What's on your mind?" Bonnie said.

Dana opened her eyes. Her mother was staring at

her with an amused grin. "Nothing," she answered. "Just enjoying being outside."

"It really is nice out here."

"Joel and I haven't been able to be out here much. This side of the house faces the southwest, so it always gets the afternoon sun. And I just couldn't take the heat this summer, not with being pregnant and all."

Bonnie nodded and set her empty coffee cup down on the glass-topped cocktail table. "Yeah, I didn't have that trouble since I was pregnant with you through the winter. I loved being pregnant."

"I hate it," Dana said, and realized at once how bitter she sounded. "I mean, I can't wait for Sofia to be born, but I'm just tired. Tired of being pregnant and not able to do things."

"I know."

"I mean, I'm tired of sitting in the house," Dana said, ignoring her mother's attempt at empathy. "I want to go out to dinner. Go the park again. Go the movies. Just get out of this place and even just go to the damn grocery."

Bonnie chuckled. "You'll get to do those things again. You and Joel will get to do all that and more."

"Yes, but it will be different," Dana said. "We'll have Sofia with us."

"Ever hear of babysitters?" Bonnie said. "I promise as soon as you're able, I'll stay here with the baby and you and Joel can go out on a date."

Dana set her cup down. "I feel really bad about how

I treated Joel last night. I was a real bitch."

"Now, honey you know I don't like that word."

"Sorry, Mom, but it's the only way to describe how I acted. I know he was just checking on me. I know he was concerned." She traced her finger around the pattern of the pebbled glass of the table. "I really need to apologize to him."

Bonnie nodded. "Yes, you do."

Dana stared at the rose bushes. They needed trimming. "I just hope he understands. He hardly said two words to me before he left for work."

"He'll be fine," Bonnie said. "Joel loves you more than anything. Anyone with half a brain can see that."

"Sometimes I don't know what I did to deserve to him," Dana said.

* * *

3:15 PM

The Center for Women's Health was located two blocks from the hospital in what had once been an abandoned strip mall. Halloran remembered the area being rundown and littered with graffiti and drug activity in the past, but the construction of the new hospital in the late 'nineties had given the east side of the city a new vibrancy. Coffee shops, small diners, and a couple of boutiques lent a young hipster feel to the streets, and a developer had just announced plans to turn a deserted

warehouse into loft apartments. Cedar Hill was growing, and though that was good for the city's economy, it
also meant increasing crime and an increased workload
for the department. Today was no exception.

Halloran and Brooks announced their arrival to the
receptionist, and they had just taken seats in the waiting
room when a nurse appeared at the doorway to the ex-
amination rooms and called them back. She led them to
a small meeting room equipped with a long oak board
table and upholstered chairs and no windows. The walls
were decorated with reproductions of paintings depicting medical procedures – gruesome and disturbing, and
Halloran wondered why anyone would choose them as
a design choice.

The board table held legal tablets and pens with the
center's logo and a cluster of chilled bottles of water on
a glass tray. Brooks took one of the waters and drank
half of it in one gulp.

"Thirsty?" Halloran said.

"Dry." He screwed the cap back onto the bottle and
set it on the table next to the folded warrant he had
pulled from his interior jacket pocket.

The door to the room opened and a squat gentleman
with a gray goatee and a dark blue suit entered. "Gentlemen," he greeted, extending his hand. "I'm John
Trent, the center's attorney."

Halloran shook his hand. "Lieutenant Mike Halloran, and this is my partner, Detective Greg Brooks."

Trent shook Brooks's hand. "It's a pleasure." He

took a seat at the table opposite them. "Dr. Majmadar will be joining us shortly. I trust everything is in order with the warrant?"

"Yes, sir," Brooks said, sliding the papers toward him.

Trent donned a pair of reading glasses, opened the folded warrant and read through it. He set it on the table and nodded. "Seems satisfactory."

The door whisked open and a young Indian woman stepped in. She was small and petite, and her long dark hair was pulled back into a pony tail. Her white lab coat was nearly blinding against her brown skin.

All three men stood, and Trent said, "Dr. Majmadar this is Lieutenant Halloran and Detective Brooks."

Dr. Majmadar nodded. "Very nice to meet you," she said and took a seat next to Trent.

"I assume this won't take long," Trent said. "I know Dr. Majmadar has patients waiting."

"Not long at all," Halloran told him, pulling out his notepad. "First off, I appreciate your meeting with us on such short notice. Any information you can give us will be of help."

"It's my pleasure, Lieutenant," Dr. Majmadar said, her accent thick. "I am happy to be of any assistance. I was very saddened by what happened to Miss Richardson and Miss Jarvis."

"What do you know about them personally?" Halloran said.

Dr. Majmadar took one of the bottles of water and

uncapped it. "I know Miss Richardson was not in the best of circumstances. She talked to me several times about her boyfriend, but I did not realize what was really happening until it all came out in the news. If I had known she was around all those drugs, all those *chemicals*, I would have pushed her to leave that place."

Halloran nodded. "Was there anything unusual about her pregnancy?"

Dr. Majmadar took a sip of her water. "Nothing, although early on she asked me about termination."

Halloran looked up. "Abortion?"

"Yes," Dr. Majmadar said. "But only in general terms. At the time I wasn't sure why, and it concerned me greatly."

"How so?"

Dr. Majmadar studied one of the gruesome prints on the wall for a moment. "Because she seemed happy about her baby. But she seemed so unsure of what would become of them all after he was born. I think she was truly torn at first about what to do."

Halloran tapped his pen against his notepad. "Do you have any idea what might have changed her mind?"

"I think at first it was the cost," Dr. Majmadar said. "Miss Richardson was on Medicaid, and even if she had not been, insurance will not cover abortion. And for most people in similar financial conditions, the cost of terminating a pregnancy is prohibitive."

"I see." Halloran made a note of that.

"But at her last visit, she told me she was thinking

of leaving her boyfriend."

Halloran looked at her. "Oh really?"

"Yes," Dr. Majmadar said, nodding. "And she seemed very confident in that decision."

That was most interesting, Halloran thought. Billy Ray Fields had said nothing about either abortion or her decision to leave him when they questioned him. Either he was holding back that information or he wasn't aware of it. Even Addie's parents hadn't mentioned any of that. "What about Samantha Jarvis?" he asked Dr. Majmadar. "What do you know about her?"

"She was quite different from Miss Richardson," the doctor said. "Professional. Wealthy. And she was not happy at all about being pregnant."

"And she also discussed an abortion with you, correct?"

Dr. Majmadar took another sip of water. "Yes. And in the end she decided to take the pregnancy to term."

Halloran leaned back in his seat. "Did she ever discuss the baby's father with you?"

"Of course."

"Did she ever say who he was?"

Dr. Majmadar glanced at Trent, who gave an almost imperceptible nod. "No," she said. "Not specifically, other than to say he was in her same profession."

Halloran sat up. "Another attorney?"

"Yes."

"Here in Cedar Hill?"

"She didn't say."

"I see." Halloran scribbled *Atty CH?* on his notepad, then looked at Dr. Majmadar. "One more thing. Do you have any idea why Samantha Jarvis decided against terminating her pregnancy?"

Dr. Majmadar sat still for several moments, staring at her water bottle. She was motionless for so long Halloran began to believe she was not going to answer the question. Finally she looked at him, and her gaze was cold. "Honestly, Lieutenant, I think it was out of spite."

"Why do you say that?"

She took a deep breath. "Samantha Jarvis was not a very nice person. She seemed to hate everyone and everything. I do not remember her looking forward to the birth of her child, and I do not remember her having anything positive to say about her whole experience. I think she saw having a baby out of wedlock as a personal affront to her father and his wife. She absolutely despised his wife. She only ever referred to her as 'that woman.'"

Halloran tried to control the grin creeping across his lips. After meeting Evelyn Smythe-Jarvis, he could understand. "Anything else?"

"Yes," Dr. Majmadar went on, "I do not know this for a fact of course, but I almost got the impression. . . "

"Yes?"

"I almost got the impression she was going to use the baby against the father somehow."

"The baby's father or her own?"

Dr. Majmadar looked at him. "The baby's."

Halloran leaned forward. "You mean, *blackmail*?"

"That's enough," Trent said. "I think we're done for today."

Halloran nodded at him. "Of course," he said. "But one last thing." He pulled out the photograph from the bank security camera and slid it across the table. "Have you seen this woman before?"

Dr. Majmadar examined the picture and shook her head. "No. I saw this on the news, but I don't recognize her." She stood, and the men followed suit. "If you will excuse me, gentlemen, I must get back to my patients."

"Thank you very much, Doctor," Halloran said.

"You are most welcome. If you will see Julia at the front desk, she will get those records for you." She nodded at the three men and slipped out the door.

Halloran shook Trent's hand. "We'll be in touch."

* * *

4:50 PM

Kris sat with Baby Sarah in the rocker in the nursery. The baby slept peacefully in her arms as Kris rocked and wept silently. It wasn't fair. It just was *not fair*. She'd had so little time with her, and now they were going to take her away already. She bent down and placed a gentle kiss on Sarah's forehead.

The sound of a car door in the driveway outside filled her with panic. She glanced at the clock on the nursery wall. Ten minutes early! No. Definitely not fair! She stopped rocking and sat motionless, not daring to breathe.

A light tapping came at the front door.

Kris remained still. Maybe if she didn't go to the door, Maria would go away.

Knocking again. Louder this time.

This was silly. She couldn't sit here forever holding the baby. Maria had a key. She could just come in.

The knocking was more insistent now. "Krystine?" Maria's voice was muffled through the door.

She shrugged and wiped her eyes against the upper sleeve of her T-shirt and rose from the rocker. She would just have to do what was expected of her, whether she liked it or not. She made her way to the front door and eased it open. "Sorry," she said when she saw Maria's stone-like expression. "I just got her to sleep."

"Let me in, Krystine," Maria said coldly.

Kris stepped aside and Maria entered holding the baby carrier. "I didn't expect you yet," Kris said. "We were rocking. She enjoys it so, and I – "

"Is everything packed?"

Kris nodded toward the tote bag sitting by the front door. "It's all there."

Maria held out her arms for Sarah. Kris hesitated and reluctantly handed her over. Wordlessly, Maria strapped the infant into the carrier. Sarah never woke.

"You did say she's going to a good family, right?" Kris said.

Maria stood upright and looked at her. Even though Kris was at least a foot taller, Maria seemed gigantic. Threatening. "She's going to a most worthy family," Maria said.

Kris averted her eyes. "I could be worthy," she said, and was angry when her voice quivered.

Maria continued to stare at her. "You're not worthy, Krystine."

Kris felt something loosen in her chest. "I could," she said, and tears welled up in her eyes. "I *could* be worthy." A lone tear crawled down her cheek. "It's just that. . . I want a baby *so bad*, and I thought since I've helped with the mission you could – "

"You will *never* be worthy, Krystine," Maria repeated, her face beginning to flush. She took a step toward Kris, and Kris backed up instinctively. "You know," she said, "the monsignor expressed his doubts about you after he met you, but I was able to convince him you were the right one for this job." Her eyes darkened. "Don't make me regret defending you."

Kris had backed into the wall. She stared at Maria's shoes. They were black leather and unmarked, and Kris was certain they were expensive. "I'm. . . sorry," she stammered. "I just – "

"I told you before you couldn't get attached to the infants." Maria finally broke her gaze and reached for her purse – also black leather – where it sat next to the baby carrier. "In any event, this was your last assignment. This mission is over." She pulled a small white envelope from the handbag and offered it to Kris. "Here."

Kris took the envelope and opened it. There was cash inside. Crisp hundreds. She quickly thumbed through it. Her face burned hot. "What's this?"

"Your payout for the mission."

Kris trembled. "This isn't even a tenth of what was promised to me," she said. Her vision clouded with rage. "I did everything I was told. I completed two assignments. I – "

"You jeopardized the operation, Krystine," Maria spat. "You put countless people – *babies* – at risk. The entire nationwide Network is at risk because of you." She turned and picked up the carrier with the sleeping infant. "You're lucky to get anything at all."

Kris moved toward her. "But – "

Maria whirled to face her. "You have to be out of the house by Sunday morning. Leave nothing personal behind, nothing that can be traced to you or the Network."

Panic rose in Kris's chest. "But where am I supposed to go? This money won't even buy me a plane ticket."

"That is not our problem," Maria told her.

"But you promised you'd relocate me after the mission was completed. You said – "

"The mission was *not* completed," Maria said, opening the door. Outside the sounds of happy children playing on the next block drifted through the thickening twilight. "I'm sorry," Maria said, her voice softer, "but that's how it is. Goodbye, Krystine." She stepped into the gloom and headed toward the sedan parked in the drive.

Kris watched her until her vision completely blurred with tears. She shut the door and sank to the floor sobbing.

* * *

5:05 PM

Maria buckled the infant carrier into the back seat, pleased that the baby never woke through her conversation with Krystine. She shut the door and climbed into the driver's seat and glanced at the house, at the lit windows, and was surprised she didn't see Krystine watching her drive away. She started the car and backed carefully out into the street, then headed toward downtown, breathing a sigh of relief as the brick house and Krystine faded into the dark of the evening.

She turned left into the heavy traffic of Laurel Avenue, punched a button on her steering wheel, and waited for the ding. "Call the monsignor," she said, and listened as the voice activated control dialed the number and the phone rang on the other end.

"Yes?" the deep male voice answered.

"It's me."

"Yes? Do you have the infant?"

"Yes. I'm on my way now. Krystine was very upset with the payout."

The monsignor sighed. "As we knew she would be."

"Well, it will be recovered soon," Maria said, eyeing the traffic and signaling to change lanes. "Again, Monsignor, I apologize. My intuition failed me this time."

"You will have more chances to redeem yourself, Sister. Have you purchased your plane ticket yet?"

"I have. I fly out tomorrow morning at 11:30."

"Good. And Krystine?"

"I told her to vacate the house by Sunday."

The monsignor grunted. "Excellent. I will arrange the elimination."

Maria's hands were suddenly heavy on the steering wheel. "Monsignor. . . "

"Don't worry, Sister," the monsignor said, "she will not suffer."

* * *

5:45 PM

Dana glanced at the clock and worry gnawed at her. Joel was late. Either something last-minute had come up at work or he was still angry with her. And as much as she knew job issues irritated him, she hoped that's all it was. She couldn't take more of his silence.

Bonnie had left at five, anxious to get home and start Frank's supper. She was reluctant to leave Dana alone, but Dana had convinced her she would be fine, that Joel would be home in just a few minutes. And now, as she lay atop the rumpled bedspread and listened to the newscaster drone on about the Middle East and foreign policy, she realized how much she had come to depend on someone else being with her the past few days. It wasn't that she was afraid of being alone (Joseph's warning aside), it was just the lack of human interaction that left her to her own thoughts. And some-times that was a dangerous world to get lost in.

On Joel's nightstand was the book he'd been read-ing, some science fiction novel with a battered space ship on the cover. She rolled over onto her side and reached out for it, snagged it by one corner of the curled cover and dragged it across the bed to her. She was do-ing what they had sworn never to do – peek. Her heart pounded, as if she were going to do something lecher-ous or evil. But she had to see. She had to know.

She held the paperback against her chest with both hands, inhaling the dusty scent of the paper and feeling the emotions snaking out to her like tendrils of smoke. What she expected, she saw; what she feared, she did not. Joel's love for her radiated from the book like warm sunlight. No anger, no jealousy. No resentment. Only love. Strong. Pure. She laid the book down and the intensity of what she had felt lingered, as if she'd dipped her hands in a warm bath and still felt the heat in her fingers.

She settled back against the pillows, and the TV screen blurred as the tears welled up in her eyes. He loved her. And if her reading were to be believed, it was a love that transcended both the physical and the emotional to a plane she'd never known existed. A love so strong that she almost feared it. Because she wondered if her feelings for him could ever be that powerful.

The back door rattled open, and she hurriedly wiped her eyes with her fingertips. "Joel? That you?"

"Yep," he called, and she heard his heavy steps trudging down the hall. "Your mom already gone?"

"Yeah, she left a little after five. She said she – "

She broke off as Joel entered the bedroom. He was carrying several plastic grocery bags. He looked at her. "She said what?"

Dana stared at him. "You went shopping? I wondered where you were. I was afraid something had happened at work. And I knew you'd be in a bad mood when you got home – "

Joel leaned down and kissed her on the lips, then held up the bags. "I brought home dinner." He gave her an awkward smile and fished something out of one of the bags. It was a cheap plastic red-checkered tablecloth.

"What's all this?" Dana said.

Joel ripped open the package and spread the tablecloth across one side of the bed. "We're going to have a picnic."

She looked at him. "What? Here?"

"Yep." He pulled out two deli sandwiches and a large bag of potato chips, then produced a couple of bottled soft drinks. "I know how much you've been missing getting out and doing things. I know how much you hate being stuck here in the house."

She narrowed her eyes. "Have you been talking to Mom? Did she put you up to this?"

He gave her a look of confusion. "What? No." He unwrapped one of the sandwiches – ham and Swiss on a sub roll – and handed it over to her. "I know how restless you are." He offered one of the soft drinks, and she took it. It was ice cold and beaded with condensation. "I just thought we could do something fun."

She looked down at the plastic bottle in her hand and the tears she'd been holding back spilled down her cheeks. God, she loved this man. She didn't deserve him. And he didn't deserve someone as self-centered as her.

Joel saw the tears and placed a large, warm hand on her arm. "Hey. . . you okay?"

She nodded, letting the tears hang in droplets from her chin. "I'm so sorry I was nasty to you last night. I had no right to talk to you that way."

He traced a finger along her arm from her wrist to her elbow. "No, it was my fault really. I just kept on. Hounding you. I should have left you alone."

She looked at him, leaned forward, and he met her

with a kiss. "I love you," she said.

"I love you, too."

She looked at the spread of food on the bed. "And thank you for this. It really means a lot."

He shrugged. "It's nothing really."

Suddenly, she felt a sharp movement in her belly. "She's kicking!" she cried. She grabbed his hand and placed it on her mounded abdomen. "Feel it?"

Joel's face lit up with a wide grin. "Yeah. I do." His gaze met hers.

She leaned forward and kissed him again.

* * *

8:40 PM

Kris sat in the living room, staring at the television. It was tuned to the classic movie channel again, and this time it was a gritty noir movie from the early 'fifties. The sound was muted, and Kris stared at the flickering black-and-white images on the screen and listened to the stillness of the house. It was painfully quiet. Even the usual thrum of the HVAC unit was silent.

She looked about the room. Maria had told her to be gone by Sunday, and to be sure not to leave anything personal behind. She really didn't have that much. Her clothes, her wigs. A few keepsakes from Grandma Hettie that she'd lugged from place to place over the years. Nothing she couldn't box up in a couple of hours and fit into her car.

But now she was faced with the dilemma of where to go. She'd counted the money from the envelope again and again, each time hoping more bills would miraculously materialize. There was barely enough to drive cross-country with. And nowhere near enough to start a new life on.

Maria's words echoed in her head: *You'll* never *be worthy, Krystine.*

On the screen, a detective had grabbed a suspect by his lapels and shoved him against the wall of the interrogation room. She couldn't hear what was being said, and she couldn't read the actor's lips, but she could see the anger in the actor's eyes. She wondered how it would have been to grab Maria by the collar of her tailored suit and push her into the bare walls of the hallway. To hear the drywall crack beneath the older woman's back. To see the fear in Maria's eyes. To pull the length of nylon clothesline taut around her throat and feel the woman's powerless struggle to free herself. To watch her eyes bulge with panic and see her face bloom purple as she strained in vain to catch her breath. She had watched these things happen with the others, and she had taken no pleasure in it. But with Maria there would have been much pleasure in the woman's suffering. Great pleasure.

You'll never *be worthy, Krystine.*

Every time she thought of those words, anger seared through her, hot and cutting.

And then, as she sat watching the silent scuffle play out on the television, she happened to remember something. And the plan formed in her mind almost before she even had time to think about it.

She made her way to the kitchen and filled up the kettle with fresh water, then put it on the stove to boil. The laptop she had barely used while in this place sat silently on the dining table. She pushed the power button and it began its boot-up process. Her purse sat on the kitchen counter by the back door. She reached inside and fished around until her fingers found what they were searching for. A tiny thumb drive. She pulled it out and took a seat at the table in front of the laptop, then plugged the thumb drive in and waited for the laptop to finish booting. Maria didn't know about the thumb drive; Kris had wisely made a duplicate of the one she had passed along to the Network. Pages of information the organization had used to determine Kris's assignments.

She opened the folder and looked at the files it contained:

Richardson, Addie

Jarvis, Samantha

There were two more, and she hovered the cursor over the next on the list:

Roberts, Dana

She clicked.

On the stove behind her, the kettle began to scream.

* * *

11:10 PM

Halloran lay in the darkness under the sheets of the bed, smoking the last cigarette of the day. He took a drag and the tip grew bright and orange. At the foot of the bed he could barely make out the sleeping lump that was Mel, though he could hear the cat's soft purring. As was the case every night, Mel would start out at the foot of the bed, but by morning he would end up on Halloran's pillow, sometimes curled around his head. "Stupid cat," Halloran muttered, blowing his smoke into the dark.

Tomorrow night was his date with Kelly, and every time he thought about it a raw bolt of panic shot through his gut. He couldn't even remember the last time he'd been out with a woman. And sex? Not for at least a couple of years. And the idea of things leading to spending the night with Kelly tomorrow night (as slim as the odds were) practically terrified him. He knew his equipment still worked. At least it did when he was alone. But who knew what would happen once he was naked again beside a woman?

He took a deep breath. He was putting the cart way, way ahead of the horse. They hadn't even gone out yet and here he was, already putting himself in bed with her. But he supposed that's what guys did when they reached a certain point. A date at this stage in life wasn't just a date. It was validation, a sign that you still had. . . *something* that made you desirable. And once you felt that positive response from a woman you found attractive, you clamped down on it like a starving dog with a bone. It was the same flawed logic that led to a man becoming clingy and desperate, traits that inevitably pushed away any potential partner.

Still, he was forty-two years old, and the time to meet someone and start a family of his own was slipping quickly by. Kelly had Trevor. And though he hadn't met the kid, Trevor looked like a decent young man in Kelly's Facebook photos. Ending up with Kelly would give him a ready-made family. Not what he'd always envisioned for himself, but it was something. And there he was again, putting too much emphasis on a simple date for dinner and a movie. It was no wonder he didn't go out much. He was placing too much pressure on himself and too much importance on what should be a carefree evening. Women could smell that kind of desperation a mile away.

He took one last drag on the cigarette and stubbed it out in the ashtray on the nightstand, then double-checked to be sure his alarm was set. He settled back against the pillow and closed his eyes, waiting for sleep. But his mind was restless, and thoughts about the Addie Richardson and Samantha Jarvis case circled through his brain like a carousel.

Tomorrow he and Brooks would begin sifting through the records provided on a disc from Dr.

Majmadar's office. He had no idea how much information was there. The warrant had been for six months' worth of records, and he was sure there was a ton. How long would it take to sort through it all? A few hours? Days? And even then there was no guarantee a connection between the killings and Dr. Majmadar existed. It could simply be another dead end. But it was one that needed to be explored, even though the thought exhausted him. But if a connection *did* exist, what did that mean?

The light tread of Mel slinking up toward his pillow brought him back to full consciousness. "Hey, you stupid cat," he said. Mel curled up in the crook of Halloran's arm, licked his forepaw twice, and settled in, purring contentedly. Halloran gave him a scratch between the ears, closed his eyes again, and soon he was drifting off.

FRIDAY, OCTOBER 10

5:40 AM

THE SUN HAD NOT YET RISEN, but the sky to the east was just barely beginning to lighten. All along the block, the modest homes were still dark. Except for one. And it was that one Kris was most interested in.

After a busy and sleepless night, she had driven across town in the pre-dawn stillness, following the directions on Google Maps to the address that had been listed on the patient record of Dana Roberts. She had parked two houses down and sat in the chilly car, shivering and sipping the hot tea from her travel mug, watching the brick ranch for any signs of life. She did not have to wait long.

After a few minutes, a light winked on in the rear of the house and through the window she could make out the silhouette of a bearish man moving around a kitchen. From the notes she had jotted down while reading the patient records, Kris knew the man was Dana Roberts's husband and that his name was Joel. She also surmised from the work truck parked in the driveway that he was employed by Cable-Com and that he would be leaving for work soon. She didn't see any other vehicles in the drive, and she wondered if Dana would be home alone all day. If so, that would give her a perfect opportunity.

The plan was simple. Get into the house, find Dana, take the baby and head out of town. Everything was already packed in the car – all her personal effects, her clothes, supplies for the care of an infant. . . everything. And she had left a nest in the center of the back seat where an empty carrier awaited Dana Roberts's baby.

No, she thought with a sudden thrill. Not the Robertses' baby. *Her* baby.

She wondered if the infant was a boy or a girl. Dana Roberts had visited Dr. Majmadar so early in her pregnancy that the sex was unknown at the time. Kris hoped for a girl, but a boy would be wonderful, too. It didn't matter, really. It would be her baby. *Her baby*. The Network was finished with her now. They would have no reason to track her, no reason to know her whereabouts. And now she wouldn't have to kowtow to Maria or the monsignor in the hopes of someday being worthy, which Maria had assured her she would never be.

But now she didn't need Maria's approval. Or the

monsignor's. Or the Network's. She was on her own. She had no one to answer to but herself. And soon a baby.

She took a sip of the tea, which had now become tepid, and squinted at the lit kitchen window to get another glimpse of Dana Roberts's husband but he had moved out of view. She pictured him making coffee and breakfast, maybe taking it to Dana while they watched the morning news together. She wondered what Dana looked like, what the baby would look like. She had not been able to see any of the husband's features, but from his outline he looked large and intimidating. All she knew of Dana's physical features was that she had been five-foot-two and weighed a hundred and twenty pounds at her visit to the office in March. She would be easy to overpower, and being inside the house would give Kris ample time to work without fear of discovery. She could take her time and make sure her baby would emerge unscathed. Then she could clean the infant up, wrap him or her into a bundle, and be off.

A movement to her left caught her eye. An older gentleman in a light gray jacket was walking his small white terrier down the sidewalk, headed right in her direction. She froze. *Shit!* All she needed was for someone to notice an unfamiliar car and an unfamiliar face in the neighborhood. He hadn't really looked in her direction yet, focusing instead on his dog and pulling it out of a neighbor's yellow mums. She slouched in her seat, though she knew her height made it all but impossible for her to become invisible. Maybe if she remained still he would pass right by without paying her much attention, like she was part of the landscape.

But the dog didn't ignore her. When pulled from the flower bed it looked right at her and gave a sharp yap. The man's gaze followed, and Kris locked glances with him. His eyes widened in surprise, and he gave her a hesitant nod. *Damn it.* She nodded back.

Suddenly panicked, she started the car and pulled away. In the side mirror she saw the man watch her drive off. *Shit. Shit, shit, shit.* Why was she so stupid? Now she had all but implanted a crystal-clear vision of her car in his head.

A block away, she turned down a side street and slowed to a crawl, then put the car in park. She had no idea what to do now. Why had she become so flustered? Even if he had failed to remember an indistinct car parked along the street or the anonymous driver (she at least wasn't wearing a wig or makeup), he would definitely recall the car speeding off.

She took a deep breath and realized she was shaking, her heart hammering in her chest. She needed to calm down and drive out of here before someone else spotted her. The neighborhood was waking up now, and it would only be a matter of minutes before the streets would be active with people heading to work and school. She would have to come back later. When most people had left for the day and the neighborhood had quieted down again.

She put the car in drive and eased up the street, then stopped. There was an alley here that bisected the block the Roberts house sat on. On a hunch, she turned down it and rolled quietly past toy-strewn back yards, privacy fences, and garages until she spotted the back side of the brick ranch. The yard was edged with lanky shrubs, but she had a clear view of the house. A screened back door led out to a small patio, and next to that was a step-down entrance to a basement. That was intriguing. Because if she could park here in the alley and enter the house through the back, no one on the street would see her at all. And she could take Dana by surprise.

Joel appeared in a small double window above the patio, and Kris realized she was looking at the kitchen again, this time from a different angle. She could see his face clearly this time. Round and ringed with a dark beard. Not particularly attractive but not repugnant either. Again, she wondered what Dana looked like. But then, as she had seen in her years as a neo-natal nurse, sometimes even the ugliest people had the prettiest babies. Joel was doing something at the sink. She tensed, waiting for him to look in her direction and spot the car, but he paid her no attention. After a minute or two, he disappeared into the bowels of the house.

There were other windows back here, all of them curtained, and she wondered what rooms they were in. Bedrooms? A den? And would whoever was in there see her parked back here in the alley?

A knock on her driver's window startled her. It was the gentleman with the dog. Scowling at her with dark gray eyes. She'd been so engrossed in the Robertses' house she hadn't noticed him coming up behind the car. "Can I help you?" he said sternly, his voice muffled by the glass. "Are you lost?"

She shook her head and waved him away, then threw the car into drive and roared down the alley. She glanced in the rearview mirror and saw him jerk the dog close and throw her the bird.

Well, that cemented it, she knew. She would be lucky if he didn't alert the cops.

She pulled out of the alley and circled around the block, passing by the Roberts house again. But now along with the cable truck an older Dodge Caravan sat in the driveway.

Kris turned out of the subdivision and headed back across town. The plan would have to wait for another time. Maybe even another day.

* * *

10:30 AM

Halloran and Brooks had been poring over Dr. Majmadar's records all morning. The amount of information was overwhelming. So far they had found that both victims had been to the Women's Clinic in March – Addie Richardson on the fifth and Samantha Jarvis on the eighteenth. Both had discussed terminating their pregnancies. But what that meant, Halloran didn't have a clue. It could be crucial to the investigation or it could be nothing. But before they dug deeper, he had more questions for Dr. Majmadar. He had left a message for her to call him at her convenience, and by the time she returned his call, Brooks had another name, another pregnant woman who had discussed an abortion. Laura Kesterson.

"I remember Laura Kesterson very well," Dr. Majmadar told him. "I remember her because she died not long after her appointment."

Halloran sat upright. "Died?"

"Yes. Most unfortunate. A brain aneurism. Very sudden. Very unexpected."

"Do you know how long after her appointment with you that happened?"

Dr. Majmadar was silent for a moment. "No, I can't say that I do. But it wasn't long."

"Do you know if she was still pregnant when she died?"

"I don't know," Dr. Majmadar said. "But she had seemed most matter-of-fact about terminating the pregnancy. She and her husband had only been married a few months. She had great concerns about starting a family so soon."

"I see." Halloran scribbled the information down. "Let me ask you something. Do you have many women discuss terminating their pregnancies with you?"

"No," the doctor said, "not at all. And most of the time they are only seeking information and weighing options. But it seems there were several around that time last spring, and I remember thinking it was some kind of epidemic."

"Really? That's interesting. That may actually be helpful to us." He jotted down *Ck records spring*.

"And I'm actually glad you called, Lieutenant," Dr. Majmadar said. "After you left yesterday I happened to remember something. I was going to call you but I got busy and it slipped my mind."

"What is it?"

"It is probably nothing, but I wanted to pass it along. We had someone working for us about a month ago. Krystine Halpern. I hired her personally. She only worked for four days."

"What happened?"

"I fired her."

"For what?"

"She was looking at patient records," Dr. Majmadar said. "Records she had no business reading. I believe she was data mining."

A thrill shot through him. "Do you know why?"

"No. And when I confronted her, she denied it. Be that as it may, we could not risk a HIPAA violation. I let her go immediately. She started work on a Monday and she was fired that Thursday."

"Interesting. Krystine Halpern, did you say?"

"Yes. Spelled K-r-y-s-t-i-n-e. But she preferred to go

by Kris. She spelled it with a 'K.'"

Halloran wrote the information down and leaned back in his chair. "But you don't think she's the woman in the security camera footage?"

"I don't know," Dr. Majmadar said. "The photo was pretty blurry."

"How tall would you say Krystine Halpern was?"

"Oh, very tall," Dr. Majmadar said, sending a jolt through Halloran's gut. "I'm quite short, as you saw, so everyone seems tall to me. But Kris was almost a giant. Over six feet, I would say."

"I appreciate the information, Dr. Majmadar."

"Well, as I said, it may be nothing but I thought you should know."

"We will definitely check it out," he told her.

He hung up and stared at his notes. Krystine Halpern's height was a close match to the woman in the security footage. It had to be more than coincidence. He tore the sheet of notes from the pad and headed down the hallway to find Brooks.

* * *

1:15 PM

Lunch was done and the kitchen cleaned, and now Dana lay on the bed as some talk show played out on the television. Something about learning to love yourself through researching your past lives or some nonsense. She wasn't really paying attention. Bonnie was in the chair next to the bed, dozing, and Dana felt her eyelids getting heavier and heavier as she drifted toward sleep.

The phone trilled on the nightstand, and she was instantly awake. The landline. No one ever called them on it. She felt for it and pulled it up to her bleary eyes. The caller ID display read "Cedar Hill Police." Panic shot through her. "Hello?"

A male voice said, "Dana Roberts?"

"Yes?"

"Mrs. Roberts, this is Lieutenant Mike Halloran from the Cedar Hill Police Department. I'm not sure if you remember me or not. . . "

In a flash, she was standing back in the kitchen of Joel's old house with the gun to her head, locked in the grip of a madman, focused only on Joel's pleading gaze as he begged for her release. Her heart seemed to twist in her chest, and nausea instantly seized her. "Yes, Lieutenant," she said, her mouth suddenly dry, "I remember you."

"Are you going to be home this afternoon?"

Dana glanced at Bonnie, who was stirring in the chair as she recognized the anxious tone in Dana's voice. "Yes," Dana said, "I'll be here."

"My partner and I would like to swing by and talk with you and your husband."

"What about? Is it something to do with our accident?"

Halloran paused. "Accident?"

"Our car accident," she said. "Joel and I were in a wreck Sunday. Totaled our car."

"Oh," Halloran said. "No, it's nothing to do with that. But let me ask you something. . . Are you pregnant?"

The question startled her. "Yes. I am. In fact, I'm on bedrest for the rest of the pregnancy. Have been since the accident Sunday." She glanced again at Bonnie but ignored the look of confused concern in her eyes. "What's all this about?"

"Well," Halloran said, "I'd rather not talk about it over the phone. Is your husband home now?"

"He's at work right now," Dana said. "He'll be home a little after five. But my mom's here – "

"Would it be all right if we come by after your husband gets in?"

"Sure." She hesitated. "Is everything okay?"

"I think so."

"Can't you tell me what it's about?"

"I don't mean to be so mysterious, Mrs. Roberts," Halloran said. "It's just not something I feel comfortable discussing over the phone. Hopefully it's nothing to worry about."

She realized she was holding her belly protectively, as if shielding Sofia from whatever this was. "Is. . . is it about the murders?"

"Again," Halloran said, "we'll talk about it when we get there."

She disconnected the call and squeezed the phone in her hand. "That was the police," she told her bewildered mother. "They want to come talk to us about something."

Bonnie sat up straight. "The police? What do they want?"

Dana shook her head. "I don't know." She grabbed for her cellphone. "I'm calling Joel."

* * *

5:20 PM

When Dana called him, a hint of panic in her voice, Joel rushed home, telling Betsy he had an emergency at the house. After their talk on Tuesday he was sure she would have no qualms about him taking off early, and he was right. He apologized to Wade for leaving him alone the rest of the afternoon and told him to enjoy his Indiana weekend with his girlfriend (whatever her name was), and headed across town to the house.

He expected Dana to be hysterical, but she was surprisingly calm. Unnerving considering her frame of mind lately, and he longed to touch her to reveal her true emotion. They sent Bonnie home with the promise they would call her later and fill her in on the visit from the detectives, reassuring her it had to be nothing.

But now as he and Dana sat pressed together on the sofa and eyed Halloran and Brooks in the chairs opposite, he wasn't so certain. Halloran remembered Joel, and remembered that he never shook hands "because of germs," but Joel was convinced Halloran knew the real reason. Especially after the climax of events two years ago.

Halloran appeared younger than before, and Joel realized it was because he'd shaved off his mustache. He was a bit paunchier, though he still moved with the agility of someone who'd once been an athlete. A baseball player perhaps. Brooks was shorter and beefier, but he looked to be all muscle, and Joel had no doubt that Brooks could easily take a man of Joel's own size down.

Halloran pulled out a small notepad and leafed through it. "I didn't mean to alarm you, Mrs. Roberts. I just thought we should discuss this in person."

"Of course," Dana said, and Joel detected a slight quiver in her voice.

"Is your OB/GYN still Dr. Majmadar?"

"No," Dana told him. "I see Dr. Connolly. Elizabeth Connolly. She's over by – "

"But you did see Dr. Majmadar at one time, correct?"

Dana shot a glance at Joel. "Yes. I mean. . . I saw her just one time."

"Can you tell me the nature of your visit?"

Joel was suddenly filled with unease. "Does she have to?" Halloran and Brooks both looked at him. "I mean, this isn't anything we need an attorney for, is it?"

"No, sir," Halloran told him. "This isn't a formal questioning. We're just on a fact-finding mission." He turned his gaze to Dana. "We have the records from Dr. Majmadar's office, Mrs. Roberts. We know why you saw her."

Dana gave Joel a tight-lipped smile. "It's okay, Joel." She took a deep breath and turned back to the detectives. "Well then as you know I saw Dr. Majmadar because I was thinking of terminating my pregnancy. It just wasn't something I felt comfortable discussing with Dr. Connolly. She's been my OB/GYN since I was fourteen. I wanted. . . I wanted to talk about it with someone who didn't know me. And I wanted to weigh all my options before telling Joel I was pregnant." She gave Joel a fleeting look. "We've. . . already talked about it."

"I see," Halloran said, and wrote something on the notepad. "Well, we needed to speak to you because you saw Dr. Majmadar during the same time period as Addie Richardson and Samantha Jarvis."

Dana gave a slight gasp. "The women who were murdered?"

"Yes, ma'am."

Joel's dread ballooned to fear. "So what's going on? Is she in danger?"

"We don't know at this point," Halloran said. "We're just taking precautions."

Brooks produced a glossy photo and handed it to Dana. It was the grainy security camera photo of the woman from the parking garage. The one who had murdered Samantha Jarvis. "Have you seen this woman anywhere?"

Dana took the photo with trembling fingers and studied it. "This is the picture that was on the news, right?"

"Yes, ma'am."

Dana shook her head and handed the picture back. "No. I haven't seen her. But then I've been confined to the house for the past week."

"What about before that?" Halloran said.

"I don't know. I don't think so," Dana told him. "But then some things before the accident are a little fuzzy."

"Well, do us a favor, okay? If you see this person anywhere, you give us a call immediately." Halloran dug out a business card and handed it over to Dana. "My cell number is on there. Call day or night. In the meantime, I'll request some extra patrols for this area. Just to keep an eye on things."

Dana nodded, staring at the card, and Joel knew it was taking everything she had to not cry. He didn't need to read her to know that.

* * *

6:55 PM

The talk with the Roberts couple had gone well, Halloran thought, though he hoped he hadn't alarmed them unnecessarily. They had appeared concerned but grateful for the promise of extra patrols, but Halloran remembered from his previous encounters with Joel that the big man kept up a massive defense shield. It was impossible to know what Joel Roberts really thought. But one thing was certain: he was fiercely protective of his wife and unborn child, and after what Halloran had seen of him during the trouble of two years ago, he had no doubt Dana Roberts was in good hands.

A search of the state and national criminal databases had turned up no records for Krystine Halpern, and as much as he hated to think about it, there was the possibility that the lead from Dr. Majmadar was another dead end. Krystine Halpern's last known address was a loft apartment downtown, and the building's supervisor had neither a forwarding address nor any other information about her. "One day she was just gone," he said. But the possibility nagged. Even though Dr. Majmadar apparently did not recognize the woman in the security photo, the heights matched up. It was simply too great a coincidence to ignore.

He rushed back to the apartment for a quick shower, hastily pulled on some jeans and a button-down shirt he hoped looked casual but dressy, and now he cruised through the upper-scale Calumet Acres subdivision in the fading sunlight, looking for 722 Waterwheel Way. He found it at the end of a cul-de-sac, a small brick-and-vinyl cottage with a friendly cut-out ghost decorating the red front door and potted yellow mums on the front stoop. A blue bike – presumably Trevor's – stood at the edge of the curving sidewalk.

He gave his hair a once-over in the rearview mirror and stepped out into the early twilight. Wood smoke drifted on a crisp breeze, and he was glad he'd brought along a light jacket. It might be chilly when they came out of the movie.

He tapped on the door and an athletic-looking young man with tousled brown hair answered. Halloran recognized the facial scar from Kelly's Facebook photos. "Trevor?"

"Hi," Trevor said with an affable grin. He stepped back. "Come on in."

"I'm Mike," Halloran said, extending his hand. Trevor shook it, and Halloran was surprised at the kid's grip.

Trevor motioned toward the living room just off the entryway. It was spacious and homey with a large comfortable-looking sectional and a brick fireplace. Above the mantle a TV blazed with a cartoon. *The Simpsons*, Halloran noted with amusement. "Mom's almost ready," Trevor said. "Have a seat."

Halloran sank onto the sofa, which was much softer than it looked, and Trevor sat on a corner opposite. "So Kelly tells me you're spending the weekend with a friend," Halloran said.

"Yeah," Trevor said. "My friend Mark."

"Doing anything exciting?"

Trevor shrugged. "Probably movies or video games tonight," he said. "Then tomorrow Mark's dad is taking us on a hike over at Harper's Lake."

"Well that sounds fun," Halloran said. "I love Harper's Lake."

"Yeah. When Dad was alive we went a lot. Now, not so much." Trevor absentmindedly ran a thumb down the pink scar along his jaw.

"Well, I'm sure you'll have a good time."

Kelly appeared looking flushed and excited, wearing a simple blouse and dark slacks. "Hey."

Halloran stood awkwardly. "Hey. You look nice."

She smiled. "Thank you." She glanced from him to Trevor and back. "You two getting to know each other?"

"He was telling me about his big day tomorrow."

"Oh, good." She reached out and smoothed Trevor's hair. "You got everything packed?"

"Yep."

"You sure? I don't want to have to make a midnight run to Mark's house because you forgot your toothbrush."

He blew out a breath. "I've got it," he said.

From the street came a muffled car horn. "There they are," Kelly said.

Trevor shot from his seat and grabbed a black duffle by the front door. "'Bye, Mom."

"Be good!"

"Nice to meet you, Mike," Trevor called, and he was

gone out the door before Halloran could respond.

Kelly stood at the front windows, watching until the sound of the vehicle outside faded away. She turned and gave Halloran a quick smile. "You ready?"

* * *

He'd chosen Whiskey Fish, a catfish and steakhouse overlooking the river, and though it was dark by the time they were seated at their table by the window, the lights from the passing barges gave a romantic feel to the atmosphere. Halloran chose a moderately priced bottle of red wine upon recommendation of the young blue-eyed waiter and had to admit it was better than the cheap stuff he usually ordered.

"Promise me you won't try to drown me again tonight," Kelly said with a smirk.

He gave a snort. "I'm not promising anything," he said. "I'm too clumsy."

"Fair enough," Kelly said. She looked out at the riverwalk lights reflecting on the water and sighed contentedly. "This is nice," she said. "I've never been here before." She looked at him coyly. "Is this where you bring all your dates?"

"Oh, yes," he told her. "Sometimes I'm here two or three times a week."

"Oh yeah?"

"Mm-hm. A different woman each night of course."

"Of course."

They both chuckled, and Halloran said, "I haven't been here in a couple of years. In fact, I think the last time I was here I was with Greg and Diane."

Kelly sipped her wine and looked at him directly. "So. . . I get the impression you don't go on a lot of dates."

"Why?" he said, feeling his face flush. "What did I do?"

"Oh, nothing," she said. "I just meant with your schedule and all, you probably don't go out a lot."

"That's true," he said, running a fingertip around the edge of his wineglass. "Most of the time I'm way too tired. And I really don't get many opportunities to meet people. I mean, let's face it. Most of the time I'm talking with a single woman it's because she's either in trouble or someone close to her is. And that's not usually a good time to ask someone on a date."

Kelly laughed. "I guess not."

"People always want to fix me up though," he said.

"Oh, my god, me too," Kelly said. "Usually it's their brother who just got divorced and is in the middle of custody battle with his psycho ex. Or their cousin that 'never met the right girl' and when you finally go out with him you find out he's really gay and hasn't come out to his family yet."

Halloran laughed. "Both of those sound. . . oddly specific."

Kelly shook her head. "Yeah, I don't want to talk about it." She met his gaze and giggled. "It's just nice to finally meet someone who's normal. So many crazy men out there. So many."

"Oh, you don't have to tell me," Halloran said. "I see them every day."

"Yeah, I guess you do."

"So how long did you tell me you'd been back in Cedar Hill?"

"We moved here in July," she said. "Springfield was just too big. Too impersonal, you know?"

Halloran nodded. "Yeah, I'm a small-town boy my-self."

"I mean, in some ways I liked it. There was always stuff to do. But, I don't know. . . " She took a sip of her wine. "As many opportunities as there were for Trevor there, I just wanted him to grow up in a smaller place. Cedar Hill just seems *safer*. You know?"

Halloran couldn't help but laugh. "An odd conclusion since we've had two murders here in the past week."

Kelly laughed, too. "Yeah, I guess so. But you know what I mean."

"I do," he said. "It's a great place for families. Good community values. No gang activity. And despite recent events, we do have a low crime rate."

"Yeah," she said. "You get it." She leaned back. "I grew up in Tennessee. Tiny little place. After college when Ronnie and I got married, we moved here because his family is here. After Ronnie died I just wanted to see what else was out there. I think I was just tired of small towns. And with Ronnie no longer around, I finally had options."

Halloran looked at her. "'Finally'?"

Kelly looked flustered momentarily. "Well. . . Ronnie and I didn't always see eye to eye on a lot of things. I'd wanted to leave Cedar Hill for a long time, but he refused because he didn't want to leave his family. Especially his mother." She rolled her eyes and giggled. "But that's a completely different story." She pulled a strand of hair behind her ear. "Anyway, after he died I realized I wasn't stuck here anymore. And I thought Trevor and I would both benefit from a fresh start in a place that didn't have so many memories."

"I get it," Halloran said.

"But it just wasn't how I thought it would be. I actually missed Cedar Hill."

"Did you date anyone in Springfield?"

"For a little while," she said. "Nice guy. A car salesman. He had a son in Trevor's class and they got to be friends. But we just kinda fizzled out when I moved back here."

Halloran grunted and took a sip of wine. "So can I ask you something personal? About Trevor?"

Kelly shrugged. "Sure."

"That scar on his face. How'd he get that?"

Kelly took a deep breath. "He was with Ronnie in the accident."

Halloran immediately felt foolish. "Oh. Sorry."

"No, it's okay," she said. "He was hurt really badly.

Spent a week in the hospital. He was lucky he didn't get killed." Her voice trailed off on the last word, and her eyes glistened.

Halloran laid a hand atop hers. "Sorry. We don't have to talk about it. I was just curious."

"No," she said. "Really it's fine. Sometimes it helps to get it out." She focused on the wall behind Halloran's head. "Ronnie and Trevor were on their way to Harper's Lake. They were pulling a boat. The trailer came loose from the truck and Ronnie lost control. They hit an embankment and Ronnie got. . . Ronnie got thrown through the windshield. He never wore his seatbelt. I nagged at him for years, but he would just never put it on."

"And Trevor?"

"Trevor was wearing his," Kelly said, "which was probably what saved him. But his face was all cut up and he broke some ribs. I think it was touch and go with him for a couple of days. He was in a coma, and when he came to I had to tell him his dad was dead."

Halloran shook his head. "Poor kid."

"Yeah. The worst part was that we had to have Ronnie's funeral before Trevor got released from the hospital, so Trevor didn't get to attend. Looking back, I guess I should have waited to have the funeral, but at the time I just wasn't thinking straight. The doctors weren't sure how long he would be in the coma, and I don't know. . . I just wanted it all to be over. I didn't really think about how it would be for Trevor."

"That's tough."

"It is. Kid's been through a lot. So instead of staying in Springfield where neither one of us was really happy, we came back home."

"Well, I'm glad you did," Halloran said. He smiled, and she smiled back, and he felt a sudden rush of warmth spread through him, so strong he had to look away for fear she would see it in his eyes.

"So," she said, leaning forward. "What's your story?"

* * *

The movie was forgettable, some comedy with a few of the cast members from Saturday Night Live. He never kept up with the show anymore, and Kelly had to tell him who they were. He laughed along with her, though, enjoying her company more than the action on the screen, and once came close to reaching for her hand. He held back, though. The night was going well and he didn't want to scare her off by being physical too quickly.

Afterward, they discussed the movie on the ride back through town, agreeing that while it was entertaining it had fallen way short of their expectations. And when he pulled up into her driveway, he felt as though he'd awoken from a beautiful dream and now faced a dull and disappointing reality. He turned off the engine and they sat in the dark for a moment. The anticipation was thick and palpable. "I had a great evening," he said, not looking at her but staring at the cutout ghost hanging on the front door. "I'm glad you came."

"Me, too," she said. She placed her hand on his forearm. "I know it's kinda late, but would you like to come in for a while?"

He glanced at the clock on the dash. 10:40. "It's not that late," he said. His mouth was suddenly dry. He looked at her and she smiled.

"I'm having a good time and I'm not ready for it to end," she said. "I can make some coffee."

He smiled. Something fluttered in his chest. "Coffee's good," he said.

* * *

11:35 PM

Despite the lateness of the hour, downtown traffic was heavy for Cedar Hill, Kris thought. But as she turned off toward the residential areas, the flow thinned out. And by the time she reached the Robertses' street, hers was the only vehicle traveling the roadways.

She drifted past the brick ranch. All the lights were off. The Cable-Com truck sat in the drive. The entire neighborhood was still.

She turned down the next street, then into the alley which ran behind the row of houses, then doused her headlights. The car coasted effortlessly down the narrow street, and she brought it to a stop just behind the Robertses' house, wincing as the brakes gave a protesting squeal. She turned off the engine and sat in the quiet, watching the backs of the houses, searching for signs of activity and seeing none. A dim light burned in one window two doors down from the Robertses'.

She stepped out of the car and eased the door closed. The night was chilly and a breeze cut through her hoodie. The ambient light from the nearby streetlamps illuminated just enough of the area for her to see across the yards to the Roberts house. A dog barked from a neighboring street, echoing through the stillness, and a bolt of panic tore through her as she remembered the encounter with the man early that morning. She couldn't afford to be seen again, as she was sure this time the police would be called about a suspicious prowler.

She had no idea why she was here. She knew she couldn't overpower both Dana Roberts and her husband, especially after seeing his size. But lying restless in her bed, she'd thought through many scenarios, many outcomes. Many possibilities. And after realizing sleep was never going to come, she'd decided to make another visit. To scope things out again, hopefully without encountering any more watchful neighbors. She'd planned only to drive by, cut through the alley, and then make her way back across town to home. Yet here she was standing outside in the dark like a cat burglar. Or a ghost. And she realized she was wearing all black, as if her subconscious had already decided she would not be staying inside the car.

She slipped between the sparse shrubs and moved toward the house, concentrating on keeping her steps slow and light. A thrill coursed through her as she considered the possibility of being spotted prowling through the yard, and her heart pounded a counter beat to her ragged breath. The unseen dog kept up its incessant barking. *He'll wake the neighbors*, she thought, and giggled with giddy hysteria.

The patio was ancient brick but the furniture was practically new. It was a nice, cozy setup, and something within her wilted as she wondered whether something as simple as a backyard patio would ever be within her reach.

The basement door was just to her right down a short flight of cinderblock steps that emanated a dank, musty odor. The stench of wet decay. She tried the knob and wasn't surprised to find it locked, but the door moved easily within the frame. Even in the half-light she could see why. The wood into which the hinges were screwed was rotten and spongy, seemingly held together only by a thin film of old latex paint. She pulled at it and it crumbled in her fingers. In less than five minutes she had loosened the hinges and pulled the door free from the frame. And she had made very little noise in doing it.

Still, she froze for a moment, every sense razor sharp, listening for any slight noise that would indicate someone inside might have heard her. Though what she was listening for she didn't know. Maybe a muffled voice. Or the creak of a floorboard as someone – Joel – got up to investigate the mysterious noise.

Nothing.

She stepped inside the utter blackness of the clammy basement and fumbled in her hoodie pocket for her phone. She pulled it out and hit the flashlight app, surprised at how much the tiny LED illuminated the space. She was in a furnace room. The unit sat directly in front of her, covered in cobwebs and a layer of dust. *They really should get that serviced before winter*, she thought, and again had to stifle a hysterical giggle.

A door to her left led to the rest of the basement, and she threaded her way through cardboard boxes and Christmas decorations, sagging metal shelves piled with junk, and a laundry area which smelled faintly of soap and bleach. An open set of stairs led up into the darkness.

She placed her weight on the first step, and when it didn't squeak or groan in protest, she moved up to the next one, then the next. Only one board creaked, and again she froze, listening intently for any signs of life in the house above. The steady, rhythmic buzz of snoring reached her ears. Deep and masculine. It had to be Joel. No woman, even a pregnant one, could make a noise like that. She reached the door at top of the steps and flicked off the phone's light. She waited for her eyes to adjust to the darkness and eased into the house.

The streetlights outside shone faintly through the windows, and she could see she was in the kitchen. The dining area sat to her right. One chair was pulled out from the table, as if an unseen presence had been waiting for her arrival. She followed the sound of the snoring down a short hallway – sliding close to the wall where the floorboards would be least likely to squeak – past a bathroom and another dark room to the doorway of a bedroom.

The dim light revealed two shapeless lumps on the bed – one very large and one much smaller. The snoring was coming from the larger lump, and Kris wondered how the smaller lump was sleeping through the horrendous noise. She watched them for a moment, a blooming arousal spreading through her. Seeing them like this – unaware, unconscious, vulnerable – stirred something vaguely sexual within her loins. She wondered how the two of them made love, how they looked. How they sounded. How they *smelled.* She gripped the edge of the doorframe and fought the urge to touch herself.

The snoring ceased abruptly and Kris froze, her sexual energy spilling over into panic. Had Joel awoken? Had he seen her lurking in the doorway? The big lump gave off an explosive snort, then resumed its steady snores, though not as loud as before.

The smaller lump stirred. "Dammit, Joel," it said. The covers whipped off and Kris realized with alarm that Dana was struggling to get out of the bed.

There was no time to make it back to the basement. Kris ducked into the nearest doorway and flattened herself against the wall. She listened as Dana shuffled down the hallway and sighed heavily. A light blazed on and spilled a muted glow into the room where Kris had taken refuge. It was a nursery. The walls were a soft yellow, the furniture new and glossy white. A sizeable rocking chair sat in the dead center of the room facing the crib. "SOFIA" was spelled out on one wall in large white letters with purple polka dots. Sofia. What a beautiful name.

Across the hall the toilet seat clattered against the porcelain, followed by a gush of urine against the water. The snoring from the bedroom continued, louder now. "Shit," Dana growled. The toilet flushed and water splashed noisily in the sink. Kris realized Dana was trying to be as loud as possible, and in spite of her panic she felt a smile on her lips. But the snoring continued unabated.

The light snapped off. Footsteps staggered toward the nursery. Horrified, Kris stiffened as Dana slid into the room right past her. Close enough that Kris could smell the soap she had used in the bathroom and underneath it the faint odor of urine.

Dana flopped into the rocker, her back mercifully to Kris, and let out a groan. She rocked slightly, sniffling, and Kris realized she was crying. The snores from the other room hadn't stopped.

Kris remained frozen against the wall. She could do

it now, she thought, if only she'd brought her supplies. Joel would never hear it over his own snoring. And Kris would have had ample time to work. And she and the baby – *Sofia* – could have been on the road before dawn. She cursed her stupidity, her lack of planning. This is what always happened when she didn't stop to think. When she did things on impulse. It was why Maria and the monsignor thought she was not worthy.

She watched Dana for a moment longer before easing out of the room, timing her steps with the rhythm of Joel's snores, afraid to breathe lest the other woman hear her. In seconds she had reached the basement door and pulled out her phone to light her way. The last thing she wanted to do was tumble down the steps or stagger into a teetering pile of boxes.

Outside, she carefully placed the basement door back into position and made her way across the yard toward her car. The dog she'd heard earlier had ceased barking and the neighborhood was deathly quiet. So quiet she could hear the traffic from the center of town.

Back in the car, she sat for a moment as the shakes hit her, as they always did after she'd been pumped so full of adrenaline. She forced several deep breaths until her heart quieted and the panic coursing through her died down. She started the engine and coasted toward the end of the alley to the next street over. Only then did she switch on the headlights.

Instead of turning left toward home, she veered right for one more look at the Robertses'. The house was still dark. She pictured Dana crying in the rocker in the middle of the nursery while Joel snored away in the bedroom. It was pathetic, really. Sofia deserved so much more.

As she slid past the house her gaze was caught by the Cable-Com truck in the drive. Cable-Com. The good looking guy who had installed her cable when she moved to the Network's house had told her he and his brother were the only two servicemen left in Cedar Hill, that they were overworked and on-call practically twenty-four hours a day. Sometimes they were both called out if there was something urgent.

Something urgent.

She sped off down the street, her mind reeling with possibilities.

SATURDAY, OCTOBER 11

5:25 AM

JOEL HAD BEEN AWARE of Dana crawling back into bed around two in the morning, and he had lain awake ever since trying to force himself back to sleep. At one point he had rolled over to spoon with her, but she had pushed his arm off her, mumbling something about being hot before she drifted off again. So he lay on his back, staring at the spinning ceiling fan and hoping the monotonous motion would lure him back down into unconsciousness. But sleep avoided him like a frightened rabbit, darting away the moment he got too close.

The conversation with the detectives played over in his mind. Again and again he saw the fuzzy security photo of the woman in the parking structure. And he wondered whether he should visit the garage to see if he could pick up anything – something the woman might have touched, some free-floating mass of her essence she might have left behind. But he knew that was a longshot. The parking structure was huge, and even if he managed to find anything he was sure it would be contaminated by the dozens of other people who had passed through since then.

He blew out a ragged breath and swung his legs off the bed. He wouldn't be getting any more sleep. It would be dawn soon anyway. Careful to not wake Dana, he eased off the bed and pulled on a pair of sweatpants and a T-shirt, then made his way to the bathroom. He splashed cold water on his face and studied himself in the mirror. God, he looked rough. The dark circles under his eyes were a tattle-tale sign of the sleepless night he'd spent. But right now he needed coffee, and he needed it in the worst way.

He started down the hallway, then stopped. Something felt odd. Out-of-place. Like a tickling on the edge of his brain. A mental whiff of energy he couldn't place. Not his or Dana's. At first he thought maybe it was left over from the detectives' visit yesterday. But it was an elusive entity he couldn't quite focus on. Not masculine, yet not fully feminine. Sexless. Dark. Desperate. He rubbed his eyes. The last vestiges of a dream maybe. The product of a mind that wasn't fully awake and needed a good caffeine jolt.

In the kitchen he started a pot of coffee, and as it brewed he gobbled down three blueberry muffins from the package on the counter. And when he was done, he poured himself a mug of coffee and headed toward the living room. Maybe he could find an old movie or something to watch until Dana woke up.

As he passed the window in the dining room, something on the street caught his attention. A car sliding silently by. A police cruiser. Detective Halloran had said they would step up patrols along the street, and it appeared as though he had kept his promise. A sense of relief settled over him. Maybe things weren't as disturbing as he'd feared. And regardless of what the detectives had told them, he still thought Dana's sense of doom had more to do with her anxiety over the pregnancy than any vision that she or even old Joseph had perceived. In any event, Dana was well protected. She had nothing to fear.

He sipped his coffee and peered out at the lightening sky. They had no plans today. It would be quiet. Maybe later he would get out and do some yard work. The leaves were starting to fall in earnest now, and if he got a head start on them maybe cleaning them up wouldn't be such a huge job.

* * *

8:10 AM

For a moment Halloran didn't know where he was. Unfamiliar smells and textures. But when he moved his leg and brushed against another, he remembered. He was in Kelly's bed.

He'd come in last night for coffee, and while it brewed they sat on the sofa and watched TV, still talking about the movie. They had their coffee. He got up to head home. At the front door he kissed her good night. She tasted of coffee and sugar. He couldn't stop. Her hands traveled up to his head and her fingers entwined with his hair and pulled him closer. His heart hammered in his chest. An erection swelled between his legs. He moved away but her hands grasped his hips and pulled him back against her. His fingertips brushed her breast, and even through her bra he could feel her nipples hardened with need. They stayed locked together for what seemed forever, then wordlessly, her eyes dark and glistening with desire, she led him down a dark hallway to her bedroom. He fumbled with the buttons on his shirt, but she brushed his hands away and unfastened them quickly, her lips never leaving his. How they both ended up naked he couldn't remember. The next thing he could recall was lying on his back while she straddled him, both of them coated in sweat. Both of them crying out with pleasure, then collapsing into a tangled heap on top of the bedspread. At some point they must have crawled beneath the covers and fell asleep.

He looked at her now, her eyes closed and her blonde hair tousled about her face. He felt both aroused and embarrassed. What would she think of him now?

That he was simply a typical sex-driven man? That he'd been unable to control himself?

God, he needed a cigarette, but he'd purposefully left them at home so he wouldn't be tempted. He licked his lips, and they were dry as sandpaper. Maybe he just needed some water.

He carefully slipped off the bed and pulled on his boxers, then padded down the hall to the kitchen. He rummaged through the cabinets until he found a glass, then filled it with tap water and drank it down. Now his thirst was slaked but he still needed a smoke.

He leaned back against the counter and studied the plethora of magnets on the refrigerator. Apparently Kelly and Ronnie had traveled extensively in the past. Key West, San Francisco, D.C., Chicago. . . all were represented. There were also magnets from Disney World, Yosemite, and the Bahamas. All places in North America except one. He reached for it and pulled it off the fridge to study it. It was a molded representation of Big Ben with the word "London" and the British flag beneath it.

"We never made it there," a voice said from behind him. He turned to see Kelly leaning against the doorframe watching him. She was wearing a thin cotton gown, and her breasts were vague shapes beneath the material. "It was always mine and Ronnie's dream trip. Europe. First London, then Paris, Rome and finally Athens. We thought maybe when Trevor was grown and on his own. Or maybe after we retired." She came up to him and placed her arm around his waist. Her hand was warm and soft against his skin. "You ever been to Europe?"

"No," he said, placing the magnet back on the refrigerator. "Never been outside the States."

"Really?"

"Yeah. Never had the time. Or really even the interest."

"Ronnie and I loved traveling. We tried to go somewhere different each time. We took two or three trips a year."

"Did Trevor go with you?"

She pulled away and moved toward the coffeemaker. "Usually." She rinsed out the carafe and filled it with water. "We wanted him to be well-rounded. Ronnie used to say he didn't want Trevor to grow up ignorant of the world like he did." She looked at him. "You want some coffee?"

"Of course I do." He was suddenly aware that he was standing in her kitchen in nothing but his underwear, and the sight of her in the gauzy nighty was stirring him up again. "I'm ah. . . going to grab my clothes," he stammered.

"Sure."

When he returned she was wearing a robe and sitting on the sofa. "I don't have much for breakfast," she said. "Trevor usually sleeps in on the weekends, and I don't really get hungry until close to noon."

"That's fine," he said, sitting down beside her. "I

don't do breakfast usually anyway."

She smiled and looked away. "Hey," she said, "about. . . well, last night. . . "

"I'm so sorry," he blurted out, feeling his face grow hot. "I know I came on a little aggressive. I don't usually do that. I'm usually in better control of myself." She laughed, and he looked at her, puzzled. "What?"

"I'm laughing because I was going to say the same thing."

He chuckled. "Really?"

"This was my first date since we moved back to Cedar Hill. I was really nervous."

"Me, too."

She glanced at him. "You didn't seem nervous."

"Neither did you."

She stared at the stack of magazines on the coffee table. "I'm not in the habit of sleeping with somebody on the first date. But when you kissed me. . . "

"What?"

She looked at him. "It's like all that nervousness went away."

He smiled. "I felt the same way." He laughed. "I really thought you might think I wanted to go on a date just so we could go to bed."

She reached over and placed her hand atop his. He intertwined his fingers with hers. "I didn't think that at all," she said. "I was afraid you'd think I was just easy."

"No," he said.

"Well, I hope I haven't scared you," she said, giggling. "I would like to go out again. I had a really nice time. You're so easy to talk to. Like we've known each other a long time."

"I feel the same way," he said. "I truly thought after I stayed over that you'd think I was just after one thing, that you'd never want to see me again."

"Far from it," she said. She shifted on the sofa so that she was facing him. "You know, you're nothing like what I expected when Diane first talked about introducing us."

"Oh really?"

She laughed. "When she said 'police detective' I pictured some old fat guy with a Wilford Brimley mustache chomping on a cigar. Or a mousy little guy trying to channel his inner Sherlock Holmes."

"Well, I'm trying," he said. "I've put on some pounds, and I do smoke, and up until recently I did have a mustache. But if you want Wilford Brimley, I can change for you."

"Don't you dare."

He laughed and looked at her. Their eyes locked forever. His heart suddenly pounded in his chest, and bolt of heat surged through him.

Something in the kitchen beeped. "Coffee's ready," Kelly said, not shifting her gaze from his.

"In a minute," he said, leaning toward her.

She smiled.

* * *

10:00 AM

Dana was running. Something was behind her. Something awful. Something dark. A voice kept echoing through her head. *You're not worthy! You're not worthy!* She had no idea where she was running to. Vague, indefinite corridors led her farther into a murky maze. Her heart hammered. She clutched her pendulous belly as she ran, and her legs seemed so heavy, as if her shoes were filled with lead. *You're not worthy! You're not worthy!*

She awoke gasping for air, heart pounding and limbs trembling. She rubbed her forehead and her fingers came away slick with sweat. She reached over for Joel and felt the empty bed. The room was bright, and she saw by the bedside clock that it was ten on the dot. She blew out a breath and stared at the ceiling as the last tendrils of the nightmare disappeared. She hadn't slept this late since she was a teenager. From the kitchen she could hear the banging of pots and pans, and the aroma of bacon and coffee drifted in and made her stomach rumble.

She rolled herself out of the bed and made her way to the bathroom, then shuffled down the hall to the kitchen. Joel was at the stove, his back to her. He wore a white T-shirt and baggy gray sweatpants. His hair stuck up at all angles and he was barefoot. A surge of love sparked within her, and she moved up behind him and reached her arms around his middle to pull him close.

He jumped. "Damn!" he cried. "Scared the shit out of me."

She giggled, resting her face against his back. It was warm and his T-shirt smelled of his familiar scent. "You cooking breakfast?"

"Nothing fancy," he said. "Bacon and eggs. Biscuits in the oven."

"Biscuits?"

He glanced at her over his shoulder. "Canned ones."

"Ah."

He turned and wrapped his large arms around her. "Why don't you sit down. I'll get you some coffee."

"That sounds wonderful," she said. Her legs were feeling weak. She managed to make it to the dining table and slumped into a chair, instinctively cradling her belly. Joel set a steaming mug in front of her and she clasped her fingers around its warmth. "Thanks."

He bent down and kissed the top of her head. "You sure slept late."

"Yeah," she said. She thought fleetingly of the nightmare, but already the intensity of it had faded. "I guess I was really tired. I didn't sleep very well. Someone was snoring."

"Sorry."

"I sat in Sofia's room and dozed in the rocker for a while until you got quiet and then I got back into bed."

He nodded and moved back to the stove. "Yeah, I

think I woke up around that time. Never did go back to sleep."

Dana sipped at her coffee. It was hot and sweet. Joel knew exactly how to fix it. She thought back to sitting in the darkened nursery, crying from sheer exhaustion and stifling her sobs. A vague sense of unease floated just beyond her thoughts, a half-remembered feeling of being watched, but she dismissed it as the product of an overtired mind.

Joel forked bacon from the skillet onto a plate covered with a paper towel. "I guess between the two of us maybe we got a good night's sleep."

"Practice for when Sofia gets here," she said. "We'll have to take shifts."

Joel laughed, pulling the pan of biscuits from the oven. "I'll take the early one." He filled two plates with eggs, bacon and two biscuits apiece, then set them on the table.

Dana's stomach growled again, and it was all she could do to keep from wolfing down the food. "This is great, Joel," she said between bites.

"Thanks." He sat down opposite her and dug into his own plate. "It's going to be nice out today," he said. "I'll probably try to get some yard work done. Maybe mulch up the leaves with the mower. You can sit out on the patio and watch me do all the manual labor."

"Yeah," she said. "I'll supervise." She picked up her coffee and jumped as she felt a kick in her abdomen. "Woah, I guess the caffeine's already hit Sofia."

"Oh yeah? Is she kicking?"

"Come feel."

Joel knelt beside her and placed his large hand on her belly just as Sofia gave an especially energetic punt. "Wow!"

She looked at him and placed her hand atop his. "I love you, Mr. Roberts."

His face melted into a smile and he kissed her. "Love you too, Mrs. Roberts."

* * *

4:15 PM

Kris had intended to rest up for a while in the house, then carry out her plan and head out of town. But just at dawn she had awakened with a start on the bare mattress in the bedroom with a feeling of unease. Prowling through the darkened house, she caught sight of a vehicle on the street moving past at a snail's crawl. A black sedan. It came to a stop. Peering through the slats of the blinds, she could see no one behind the vehicle's tinted windows, but she knew they were watching her. She instinctively stepped back just as the car sped off. Someone was casing the house. The Network? She didn't know. And she wasn't about to sit around and find out. She grabbed what few things she still had left in her room and left the house. She drove off through the sleeping neighborhood, zig-zagging between cross streets, watching the rearview mirror for the black sedan, terrified it would suddenly appear behind her from a side alley. But it never did.

She drove blindly through the city for over an hour, past residential streets and industrial parks, finally ending up in the empty parking lot of a movie theater. By then the sun had risen in earnest. She sat shivering behind the wheel, more from panic than cold, wondering what they wanted. What they would have done to her if she hadn't woken up and spotted them. Finally, when her panic was under control, she pulled through a McDonald's parking lot for coffee and a breakfast sandwich. She paid with one of the hundred-dollar bills from the money Maria had given her. The cashier eyed it suspiciously and marked it with a counterfeit-detecting pen before shrugging and handing over her change and her food.

She found a secluded parking spot at the riverfront park and wolfed down the sandwich, then sipped her coffee as the sun climbed higher, wondering when would be the best time to attempt her plan. But even her adrenaline and the caffeine surge couldn't curtail her fatigue, and she found herself growing drowsy as the interior of the car heated with the morning. God, she needed sleep. But a sleeping woman in a parked car would attract attention, and she couldn't afford that. She dug through her belongings until she found an old blanket, then climbed out of the car and headed toward a grove of pin oaks at the far end of the park. The morning was pleasantly warm now, and the park had amassed a few visitors while she had lingered in the parking lot. No one would pay her any attention now. At the edge of the woods she spread her blanket and lay down in the shade. In a few moments she was drifting into a deep doze, and when she awoke it was just after four and the sun was golden with the late afternoon. Her mouth was dry and she coughed at the dusty stench of the fallen leaves about her. The park was crowded now. She gave an anxious scan of the people about her, but saw nothing or no one out of place. Nobody looked at her as she folded her blanket and trudged back up to the car.

On the other side of town she felt a mingled rush of excitement and terror as she turned onto the Robertses' street and the Cable-Com truck came into view. The thrill burned deeper as she neared the house and caught sight of Joel on a riding mower in the front yard. He was mulching leaves, and his gaze never left the ground as she slipped by. Seeing him outside and not vulnerable in bed, she was acutely aware of his size and now her plan to get him away from the house seemed not only smart but defensive as well.

A few minutes on Google Earth had shown her exactly where the cable system's hub station was, just outside the city on a secluded country lane off the main highway. On her way out of town she stopped by Home Depot and picked up a pair of bolt cutters, a sledge-hammer and a crowbar; she hoped she wouldn't need tools more intricate than that.

The entrance to the station was hidden by a bend in the highway, and she nearly passed right by it. It was secured by a feeble gate, and the bolt cutters made quick work of the cheap lock on it. The narrow asphalt road wound up a steep grade surrounded on either side by thick forest; there was no chance anyone could see her from the highway. The car suddenly came to a clearing. The hub station building was a squat white concrete block structure with a gray steel entrance door, no windows, and a flat roof. It sat at the base of a soaring tower that rose up from a cluster of enormous satellite dishes. The entire compound was surrounded by a chain-link fence.

She turned off the engine and surveyed the grounds. No security cameras that she could see. No signs on the fence warning against high voltage. In fact, very little protection at all except for the flimsy fence and that heavy door.

She climbed out of the car. Now that the sun was lower in the sky the air had turned crisp, and a light wind from the north pierced through her hoodie. She grabbed her tools and went straight to the fence. A few nips from the cutters and she was inside.

The door was the next problem. It was an outwardly-opening steel door with a deadbolt. Kicking it in or bashing through it with the sledgehammer would be nearly impossible because it was sure to have a steel-lipped frame behind it for durability.

But the hinges. The hinges were on the outside. And they were rusty.

She nestled the forked crook of the crowbar just behind the bottom hinges, lofted the sledgehammer, and brought it down. The impact was loud, and it reverberated through the open space. But the damage was minimal. She swung again, and this time the hinge twisted a bit. One more hit and it loosened, sending up a dusty puff of brown rust. The last blow sent the hinge flying. The edge of the door had ripped open with the force, and she could see that it wasn't solid metal as she'd thought. It was hollow inside. This might be easier than she thought. She went to work on the second hinge; it wasn't quite as rusty, and it took several more blows to dislodge it. By now she was drained, and her arms were tingling with fatigue, her ears deafened from the clamor. She sat on the ground to catch her breath, dizzy with exhaustion. In spite of the fading light and the chilly breeze, her body was coated with sweat. She took several deep breaths, and when her pulse had returned to normal she grabbed up the crowbar and inserted it into the small gap between the bottom of the door and the metal frame. She threw her weight against it, her shoes slipping on the sparse gravel as they sought resistance, her thighs tensing to the point of bursting with the effort. The corner of the hollow door bent upward with a creak. One more struggle with it and there was a gap large enough to crawl through. She collapsed and fought to catch her breath, peering into the darkness beyond the door.

But there was no time to waste. She grabbed the sledgehammer and slithered through the opening. It was cool and dry inside the building, and dark except for the flickering LED lights on the equipment. Machinery hummed and fans whispered. She felt desperately for a light switch and finally found one.

Racks of equipment stood against the walls and countless cables and lines snaked around the room in an endless circle. She had no idea what anything did, or what was important and what wasn't. What might set off some kind of alarm and what would not. But at this point it didn't matter. She only had to cause some kind of havoc. Something to disrupt the system and get Joel away from the house.

She lofted the sledgehammer and took aim at the nearest shelves.

* * *

4:55 PM

Joel had just made one last round of the back yard on the mower when he spotted Dana on the patio. She was waving her arms frantically and holding the house phone. He cut the engine. "What is it?"

She held out the phone. "It's Betsy. Emergency."

Great. He climbed off the mower and wiped his sweaty face on the tail of his T-shirt. What the hell was this about? He brushed his hands against his jeans and took the phone from Dana. "Hello?"

"Joel, it's Betsy. The intrusion alarm at the hub went off a few minutes ago and the signal is out all over town. I tried calling Wade first, but I couldn't get him."

"Yeah, he's out of town anyway. I can check it out."

"Do you want me to call the police?"

Joel looked at the last remaining strip of un-mulched leaves. "No, it's okay. Probably just some kids messing around. I'll run out there and check."

He disconnected the call and handed the phone back to Dana. "What is it?" she asked.

"Something's wrong with the cable signal," he said, trudging toward the back door. "I've got to go out to the station."

Dana was already punching in a number on the handset. "I'll get Mom to come over."

In the bedroom, Joel grabbed his wallet and keys while Dana followed behind him, trying another number. "Nobody's answering," she said, sinking down onto the bed.

"You try your dad's cell?"

She nodded. "Yeah. Him and that new phone. It's probably ringing in his hand and he can't figure out how to answer it." He looked at her, and she gave a half-smile. "You go on, I'll be all right."

"You sure?"

"Yeah, I'll be fine."

He bent down and kissed her forehead. "I won't be long."

* * *

5:05 PM

Halloran sat outside in the lengthening shadows on the sparse common patio, smoking a cigarette and nursing a tepid cup of coffee. It was only his second smoke of the day, and he was surprised at how well he had done. He'd left Kelly's place a little before noon, grabbed a burger, and headed home. Mel was fussing to be petted when he came through the door, but Halloran made him wait while he sucked down his first cigarette in eighteen hours. Later he'd napped on the couch while a college football game droned on the television, and he'd awakened groggy and disoriented before firing up the Keurig and heading out to enjoy the last couple of hours of sunshine.

Brown and gold leaves littered the back yard behind the apartment building, and from somewhere on another street the scent of smoke drifted on the crisp breeze. He loved this time of year, and now the possibility of sharing it with Kelly sent a rush of excitement through him. They had plans for Sunday brunch tomorrow at the Marriott down by the river. In all his forty-two years he had never been to a brunch, did not even know what "brunch" was or what it entailed. But it didn't matter. He would be with her and that's all he cared about. Maybe next weekend they could go to the downtown Ghost Walk. Maybe Trevor could go with them. The idea swirled through his head, and he wondered if strangers would see them and think they were a family.

But he had to get hold of himself. He had to stop this line of thinking. They'd had one date, one night together. She might not even find him attractive after seeing him naked in the cold light of the morning. But if that were so she never would have suggested brunch for tomorrow. Would she?

He stubbed out the last of his cigarette in the ashtray on the metal table and felt the smile on his lips. He was almost giddy thinking about her. And the fluttering excitement in his belly told him this was more than just mere sexual attraction. They had really connected on a deeper level. He leaned back in his chair and stared up at the blazing colors of the trees in the late afternoon sun. He wondered if she were feeling the same way.

His mind drifted back to work, back to the murders. He'd heard nothing from anyone all day, and he wondered how the Robertses were doing. He knew the department had increased patrols through their neighborhood, but he really didn't know how much good that would do. Or how long it would have to take place. They were no closer to solving the deaths of the two women than they were when they found out Krystine Halpern's name. The woman had simply vanished. No one knew anything about her whereabouts after she had left Dr. Majmadar's office and disappeared from her apartment. But she had to have been close by as late as Tuesday to have been caught by the bank's security camera when she attacked Samantha Jarvis. And now he was almost positive Krystine Halpern was the perp, even if she hadn't been recognizable to the doctor.

He sat up straight. The security footage. The images were burned in his mind. Krystine grabbing Samantha as she towered over her, then rising like a ghoul covered in blood and holding the swaddled infant, her wig slightly askew.

Her wig.

Goddammit, why hadn't he thought of this before?

He leaped from his chair, knocking over the small patio table. The ashtray and his half-empty coffee cup smashed onto the concrete, but he left it all behind.

He had to get to the office.

* * *

5:25 PM

Joel pulled through the open gate and headed up the narrow lane toward the station. He could see the lock had been cut, and his stomach burned with anger. It had to be kids. Or someone on meth hoping to steal some equipment to sell off for drug money. He slowed the truck to a crawl. He had no idea what he would do if someone was still up here. A couple of punk-ass kids was one thing, but even one druggie tweaked out on meth was something else entirely. He wondered if he should go ahead and call the cops, just to be safe. But already the building was coming into view through the trees, and though the security lights hadn't come on yet, he could see the area around the station was empty.

He stopped the truck in the clearing and surveyed the damage. The chain-link fence was cut and separated, and the door to the small building was battered and bent upward from the bottom to create an opening large enough for a kid to squeeze through; maybe even a man. And through the opening he could see the lights were blazing inside. He cut the engine and climbed out into the gathering gloom. The whole complex was eerily quiet. He listened intently for any tell-tale movement either inside the station or the shadows beneath the satellite dishes. Nothing.

He pulled out his phone and dialed 911, spoke to the dispatcher briefly, then hung up. He glanced about the complex. "Hello? Is anybody here?"

Nothing. Not even the rustle of a squirrel in the surrounding woods.

"Cops are on their way," he shouted.

The deafening quiet continued. Either whoever had done this was hiding and unfazed by his presence or they were long gone. He hoped it was the latter. Either way, he wasn't going in until he knew no one was still skulking about.

He called Betsy and told her the news, then hung up and dialed Dana's cell to tell her what he'd found. "I'm going to be later than I thought. I've got to wait for the police," he said. "Did you ever get hold of your mom and dad?"

"No," she told him, "but I'm okay."

"Keep trying them," he said. "I don't know how long I'll have to be out here. I haven't been inside yet so I don't know what kind of mess I'll have to deal with."

He hung up with her, and even though he knew it was futile, he dialed Wade's number and let it ring until his voicemail picked up. He left a brief message, then disconnected the call and leaned back against the front of the truck, listening to the quiet while he waited for the police to arrive.

As he stood there, his gaze lit on the rip in the fence. He stepped closer to it, and held out his hands, letting his trembling fingers trace over the cut wires, wondering if he could pick up some kind of hint of whoever had been here.

A fleeting vision ripped through his mind like an electric current. A sledgehammer. Smashed equipment. Someone – whom he couldn't tell – had squeezed through here on their way out, heading. . . somewhere in town. He didn't get the sense it was a meth-head. Nor did he think it was a juvenile. But whoever it was had certainly left.

Feeling a bit safer now, he unlocked the entry gate

and trudged to the damaged door. Only the top hinge remained intact. The bright fluorescents from inside threw a triangle of light from the hacked opening at the bottom of the door. He unlocked the deadbolt and with considerable effort managed to get the steel door open just enough to squeeze inside.

Joel stood erect and gaped uncomprehendingly at the wreckage about him. Shelves overturned. Cables and wires strung about like the web of some giant frenzied spider. Modulators and switches shattered and strewn about with the other debris. Monitors thrown against the concrete walls, their screens cracked and dark.

He staggered back and leaned against the wall. "Oh, shit."

* * *

5:35 PM

Dusk had settled over the town as Kris made her way through the neighborhood. Here and there, spooky decorations fluttered in front of houses and jack-o-lanterns grinned from front stoops. Kris hated Halloween. Always had. It wasn't so much the ghosts and goblins aspect, or even the bastardized pagan rituals that had evolved into a sort of celebration; it was the costumes. The masks. The dressing up and pretending to be something else. For too long she herself had lived in a costume and had hidden behind a mask of deceit. Her real self was out now, and when she thought of those younger years when she was forced to hide her true face, she mourned the time she had lost.

But now that part of her was dead forever. Tonight would be the start of a new journey. She and the baby. A new life for both of them.

Her pulse quickened as she turned onto Acorn Lane and the Robertses' house appeared. The front blinds were drawn, but lights glowed softly behind them, and the cable truck was gone from the driveway. A smile played across her lips as she imagined Joel rushing out to the substation to find the gift she'd left for him. He would be gone a long, long time, and by the time he returned Kris would be far away with the baby. And Joel would have another mess to clean up.

She made the turn at the end of the street, then wheeled into the back alley, cutting her lights and coasting along until she was directly behind the house. The blinds back here were still open, and through the lighted windows she could see Dana sitting on the edge of the bed with her cell phone in her hand. She looked distressed. And very much alone.

Kris eased out of the car and stepped into the darkness. The breeze had picked up, rustling through the trees and scattering crisp leaves across the pavement. She shivered, wishing she had thought to dig out a heavier jacket. But now there wasn't time.

A voice cried out from somewhere on the next

street, and she was momentarily startled before she realized it was a child somewhere calling out to a friend.
One day Sofia would be that child. And Kris would
open the front door and call her in from the chilly October air, then settle her at the kitchen table with
homemade soup, and they would talk about their day.
And later they would watch TV – the Charlie Brown
Halloween special maybe, because Sofia would like it –
and then it would be time for a quick bath before Kris
would tuck her in bed for the night. The room would
have the letters on the wall – *S-O-F-I-A* – just like now,
and there would be posters of puppies and kittens on the
walls and a big dollhouse in the corner. And Kris would
kiss Sofia's soft cheek that smelled of soap and tooth-
paste and turn out the light. And she would whisper "I
love you" as she closed the bedroom door.

But for now, there was much to be done.

She slipped between the shrubs and trudged lightly
toward the house. Dana was still sitting on the bed. Kris
wondered if Dana could see her in the yard if she so
happened to glance out the windows, and the possibility
sent a delicious shiver through her.

She stepped down to the basement door. It was still
loose, just as she had left it.

She carefully removed it and slipped inside.

* * *

5:55 PM

Dana threw the phone onto the bed. Dammit! Where were they? Not only was she uncomfortable about being home by herself, but now she was starting to worry about Frank and Bonnie. She pictured them huddled up in a booth at Denny's, her dad's phone ringing incessantly and both of them staring at it trying to find a way to either answer it or turn it off. The mental picture made her giggle uneasily.

The TV blazed on the hutch, the picture nothing but a blue screen and the sound muted. She'd kept it on, hoping that when the signal came back she would know Joel was almost finished and would be home soon. But after he called again and told her about the mess in the substation, she feared it would be hours before he was back.

She reached for the remote. She might as well turn it off for now. Maybe she could find something to read. She grabbed Joel's sci-fi novel and read the blurb, allowing herself to again pick up his comforting essence from the cover. Something about a space ship commander and his last voyage…distress signal from a distant planet…mutants running amok. She laid it back on the nightstand. No thanks.

She lay back on the bed and stared at the ceiling fan. She'd turned it off earlier when the house got cooler, but now the air seemed stuffy and she wished she'd left it on. And now she was too lazy to make the monumental effort to roll off the bed and switch it on. She picked up her phone. At least she could pass the time scrolling through Facebook and getting in a few moves on Candy Crush.

She had just logged into the game when she heard a clatter in the basement. Her fingers froze on the screen, every sense now amplified. She strained to listen for any further noise, her mind racing to place what could have made that sound. She knew there was a sweater rack next to the washer. Bonnie had done the laundry this week; maybe she had overloaded it and it had collapsed. She remained still for what seemed like half an hour though it was no more than a couple of minutes, but there was no further noise from downstairs.

"Get ahold of yourself," she said out loud, hoping the sound of a human voice, even if it was her own, would calm her. "Paranoia is not a good look for you."

* * *

6:00 PM

Halloran slipped into his chair behind the desk and fired up his PC. A small part of him hoped he was way off base, but the majority of his mind knew this might be the explanation for why they'd not been able to locate Krystine Halpern.

When his computer booted he logged into the national crime database. He made one last search for "Krystine Halpern" and got nothing. The same for "Kris Halpern."

He cleared the search box and typed in "Christopher Halpern."

He stared at the screen.

Christopher Halpern, age 33. Height: Six foot three. Weight: One seventy-five. The photos showed a pale, gaunt man with wispy blond hair, round eyes, and full lips. Arrested in Palm Springs, California, for prostitution five years ago. Arrested in Kansas City, Missouri, for attempting to lure a five-year-old girl into his car, for which he'd spent a month in jail. Both crimes were committed while he had been dressed as a woman. When confronted by police he'd given his name as "Krystine."

Halloran reached for the phone to call Brooks, but then hesitated. First he should call the Robertses and tell them what he'd found out. He'd told them to watch for a woman. They wouldn't be expecting a man.

He punched the number into the phone, and when Dana answered, the words gushed from his mouth. "Mrs. Roberts, this is Lieutenant Halloran. I've just found out some information I think you should know. I believe the person we're looking for isn't a woman. In fact – "

"Yes," Dana Roberts said, her voice steady. "He's here."

* * *

6:15 PM

Dana disconnected the call and slowly placed the phone back on its cradle, not shifting her gaze from the unkempt scarecrow in front of her. "That was the police," she said. "They're on their way."

The painfully thin figure in front of her smiled, showing overly-large yellow teeth. The sunken eyes were gray and lifeless beneath a matted mop of whitish-blond hair. "It doesn't matter," he said. "You'll be dead by the time they get here." Long, skeletal fingers drew a blade from the front pocket of the black hoodie.

Dana had backed up against the hutch. Her eyes darted to the corners of the bedroom and back to the person in front of her. Though she knew it was a man, he seemed almost sexless. He was blocking her only exit. And there was nothing within reach with which she could defend herself. Her gaze fixed on the knife. "What do you want from me?" she said, her voice cracking.

"I would have thought it was obvious," he said calmly. He pointed at her belly with the blade. "I want what you're carrying."

Dana felt the blood drain from her. Her legs, already weak, threatened to collapse beneath her. Her chest felt impossibly heavy. "No," she breathed. "No!"

The figure advanced a step. "But you seemed so

willing to throw it away. To have it scraped out like an unwanted tumor."

"No," Dana said, her voice little more than a whisper. She felt the hutch tip backwards and bump into the wall. The television wobbled, and for a split second she feared it would fall on top of her. "That was a long time ago. I'd never do anything to harm my baby."

He stepped closer and pointed the blade at Dana's belly, running the tip in a circle across her abdomen. It was almost obscene. Lecherous. "Oh, yes. Little Sofia."

Dana's breath caught in her throat. "How – "

"Honey, it's plastered all over her bedroom wall. I saw it the other night when I was in here. When you and Joel were sleeping. Or…at least Joel was sleeping." He laughed. "God, can that man snore or what?"

Dana's legs collapsed beneath her, and she sank to the floor. As she fell, the tip of the blade grazed her cheek with a sting. Her head swam, her vision grew fuzzy and dark. *I'm going to pass out*, she thought, but the thought was very strong and lucid. She knew she had to stay conscious. Fainting would be death. Warmth trickled down her face to her chin. She reached up with her trembling fingers and they came away red with blood.

"Now look what you made me do," he said.

Frantically, Dana glanced about the room, still searching for a weapon. She fleetingly thought of Joel's desire to keep a handgun and her insistence that they didn't need a firearm with a small child in the house.

Now she was second-guessing herself. But how would she have reached it anyway?

He squatted before her and she peered into his eyes. They were cold as blue steel. He grinned, though it looked more like a painful grimace. His long fingers reached for her belly. His nails were long and polished red, though she could see dirt encrusted beneath them. She could smell him now – a mixture of sweat and stale urine and the cloying odor of cheap perfume. Nausea welled up within her, and she felt vomit gurgling in her stomach. She turned her head away from him, pressing her face against the cold brass handles of the hutch, almost willing herself inside it. Anything to get away from him.

She pressed harder.

The hutch tipped back and bumped the wall again.

The television lurched forward and crashed atop them.

* * *

6:20 PM

Halloran hung up the phone and immediately dialed dispatch. When Camron answered, he didn't bother allowing her to finish her greeting. "Camron, it's Halloran. I'm on my way to 723 Acorn Lane. Possible hostage situation. Send a car over there immediately."

"Yes, sir, Lieutenant."

"Can you call Brooks and have him meet me there?"

"Will do."

* * *

6:25 PM

Joel stood looking at the damage in the station. This was not going to be an easy fix. In fact, it would probably require pulling in some techs from a couple of surrounding franchises to get things back up and running. Dammit. Wade sure picked a fine time to go off the grid.

The dispatcher at the police station had told him it might be a while before she could get someone to come out. Until then he would just hang out and see what might still be salvageable. He'd made a call to Betsy to update her on the situation, and when he'd assured her there was nothing she could help with at the station, she told him she was heading to the office to start PR damage control and speak with the district manager on the best way to proceed. "Probably going to be a long night," she told him.

He disconnected the call to Betsy and dialed Dana to tell her not to wait up. The call went unanswered and then to her voicemail. Puzzled, he disconnected and tried again with the same result. Perhaps she was just in the bathroom. Or had set the phone down out of immediate reach. She would call him back when she saw she'd missed him.

Joel blew out a breath and uprighted one of the racks. A modulator slid from the shelf and crashed to the concrete floor, cracking its plastic front. The LEDs on the readout flickered rapidly and faded out. "Dammit." He grabbed it and unplugged the cables from the back, then set it aside. Probably wouldn't be able to save it.

He turned back to the pile of tangled wires and equipment and spotted something beneath the heap. A wooden handle. He pulled it from the wreckage. It was a sledgehammer.

The vision slammed into him like a concrete wall. The stalking, the planning. The *hunting*. The woman – no, the *man* – they'd been warned about. What he intended to do to Dana.

He dropped the sledgehammer with a clatter and slithered through the door to the outside, running for the truck, fumbling to dial 911 as he did so.

He had to get to Dana.

* * *

6:40 PM

Halloran wheeled onto Acorn Lane, tires screeching, hoping and praying he could get there before Krystine – no, Christopher – harmed Dana. He shot into the drive, climbed out of the car and leaped onto the porch, then banged his fist against the door. "Mrs. Roberts! Dana!" He listened. There was no sound from inside. He banged again. "Dana, it's Lieutenant Halloran!"

He tried the knob, fully expecting the door to be locked. It swung open easily. The house was eerily quiet. He pulled his gun and stepped through the living room. "This is Lieutenant Michael Halloran of the Cedar Hill Police Department," he announced. "Backup is on the way." The kitchen was empty. He followed the diffused light down a hallway, past darkened rooms, to a bedroom.

His first thought was that he was staring at some kind of Halloween tableau, that a display had been set up depicting a filthy cast-off mannequin assaulting a pregnant woman. But he quickly realized the skeletal figure in front of him was Christopher Halpern, and he had Dana Roberts in a chokehold and was holding a very real knife to her throat. Dana's face was smeared with blood and her eyes were glassy with panic. In contrast, Halpern's expression was dead and soulless. His shockingly blond hair, no longer concealed by a wig, was plastered to his skull with sweat and dirt. If not for the full lips and round gray eyes, Halloran might never have known he was staring at the same person as he had just seen in the police photo. A television lay in the floor, its screen smashed and black.

"Mrs. Roberts, are you all right?" Halloran said, his

gaze never leaving Halpern and his gun remaining steadily pointed at Halpern's head.

Dana moved her mouth but whether unsure or unable to speak, she simply nodded.

"Put the knife down," he said to Halpern. "I know who you are, Christopher."

Halpern's face screwed up in a painful grimace. "Don't!"

"We'll get you some help, Christo-"

"*DON'T CALL ME THAT!*" Halpern's eyes remained clenched shut. "It's Krystine. Krystine!"

"I'm sorry. . . Krystine," Halloran said. "Put the knife down, Krystine. Let the lady go."

Halpern's eyes popped open, full of fury. "No!" His gripped tightened around Dana's throat. "She was going to kill her baby! She was going to kill Sofia!" Dana squeezed her eyes shut, and tears slipped down her blood-streaked cheeks.

"Nobody's killing anybody," Halloran said. "She's going to have her baby. Put the knife down and let's get out of here."

Sirens screamed in the distance, getting louder.

"Come on, Krystine. It doesn't have to end like this. Let her go. You can come with me and we'll get you some help."

"You don't understand," Halpern said. His voice was high and reedy, barely a whisper. "They said I wasn't worthy." He looked at Halloran, his cold eyes suddenly welling with tears.

"Who?" Halloran said. "Who said what?"

Halpern continued to weep. "They said I'd never be worthy."

"What are you talking about? Who told you you weren't worthy?"

Halpern's hold around Dana's throat loosened, and Dana gasped, gulping in air. In a flash she slipped from Halpern's grasp and collapsed onto the floor. Halpern remained where he was, his tears washing tracks through the grime on his skeletal face. "All I wanted was a baby," he said between sobs. "Just a baby of my own."

Dana had crawled to a corner on the far side of the room, still gasping for air. The sirens were very close now.

"Come on, Krystine," Halloran said. He lowered his gun and held out his hand. "Come on with me and let's get someone who can help you."

"They'll kill me!" Halpern cried.

"No one's going to hurt you," Halloran said. "I won't let them."

The sirens had reached Acorn Lane. They stopped just outside the house. Flashing red and blue lights bounced through the room from the windows.

"Come on," Halloran said, still holding out his hand.

Halpern's gaze met Halloran's, and for a moment his eyes were clear and calm.

"Where are the other babies, Krystine?" Halloran

said. "What did you do with them?"

"They took them," Halpern whispered, and his lower lip quivered.

"Who did?"

"I was good enough to do their shit work, but not worthy enough for a baby."

Halloran's annoyance with Halpern's vagueness was turning to exasperation. "Who are you talking about?" he said, struggling to keep emotion from his voice. "Who were you working for?"

From the front of the house came shouts and commotion as other officers entered the house. Halpern's panicked eyes darted toward the sound.

"Stay calm," Halloran said evenly. "I promise I won't let them hurt you."

"It's doesn't matter," Halpern said. A single tear crawled down his cheek, leaving a clean streak through the grime. "I'm dead already."

Halpern's hand jerked upward, and the knife he still held plunged into the side of his own throat. He ripped it out and blood gushed from the wound, spraying the walls and floor and showering Halloran. Halpern's round eyes grew large and panicked, and he sank to the floor almost in slow motion, the knife falling from his hand with a clatter.

From the corner, Dana screamed, drawing herself into as close a fetal position as her pregnant belly would allow.

* * *

7:05 PM

As soon as Joel turned onto the street and saw the house surrounded by police cars and flashing lights, his guts turned to jelly. An ambulance was parked in the front yard, its back opened to the front porch. A crowd had gathered along the sidewalk. He recognized Jill Satterley from across the street, and his mind crazily recalled that her husband still had Joel's nail gun.

He pulled the truck to a stop in the street and leaped out, pushing through the crowd and across the yard to the porch.

A burly cop stepped in front of him. "Whoa, whoa, where do you think you're going?"

"I'm Joel Roberts, this is my house!"

The cop's face lit up with recognition. "Oh, sure, go on in."

Joel brushed past him and through the front door. "Dana?"

"Here." Dana lay on the sofa, her arm in a cuff. A chubby EMT with a bushy red mustache was attempting to read her blood pressure.

He rushed to her side and knelt down, elbowing the EMT out of the way. "Oh God, baby, are you all right?" He took her hand in his and kissed it, and through his own panic he sensed her distress, though it was tempered and fuzzy.

"I'm okay."

He caught sight of the smear of blood across her

cheek and stroked it with his thumb. "Your face. . . "

"It's just a cut," she said. "I'm not hurt." She smiled at him. "But if Lieutenant Halloran hadn't shown up when he did. . . "

Joel pressed his cheek against Dana's belly and squeezed her hand. "Don't say anything else," he told her. "Don't say a word."

SATURDAY, DECEMBER 20

4:10 PM

HALLORAN SHIVERED AND pulled his jacket together as he made his way up the walk to Kelly's front door. The sky to the west was dark with dull gray clouds, and snow was in the forecast for the evening. He rang the bell and blew into his hands, trying to warm them against the chill.

Trevor swung the door open and laughed. "You know you can just come in, right? You don't have to ring the doorbell."

Halloran grinned at him and slipped inside. "It's called manners," he said. "You should try them some time."

"I don't need no stinkin' manners," Trevor spat, but the glint in his eyes told Halloran he was in on the joke. "Mom's still getting ready."

Halloran sank onto the couch. "Of course she is."

It felt strange, being this comfortable with Trevor. Over the past couple of months Halloran had spent more and more time with him and Kelly. They'd gone to movies and dinner and football games together, almost like a family. Trevor was a decent kid, and after some of the delinquents he'd dealt with over the years, it gave Halloran hope that there were still genuinely good people inhabiting the earth.

They were still no closer to finding the two missing infants than they were the night Christopher Halpern bled out on the Robertses' bedroom floor. Where he had been living, where he had taken the babies, and who had taken them from him – all was still a mystery. A check of the battered gold Buick abandoned in the alley behind the Robertses' showed it was registered to someone named Maria Furtado at a fake address in Mansfield, Ohio, but a search of records failed to show that anyone named Maria Furtado actually existed. Whatever information Christopher Halpern had on "Maria" or his connection to her had died with him.

As for answers, Halloran had none for either the Richardsons or the Jarvises. The FBI had taken the case from him, and while he felt a guilty sense of relief over that, he continued to grieve with both families over the sense of injustice and lack of closure. J. Daniel Jarvis had already pledged to continue pouring money into his own search, both for his own granddaughter and the Richardson's grandson. "We'll find those babies," he told Halloran during a late-night phone call, and Halloran was sure Jarvis had been drunk. "We'll bring them home if it's the last thing I do, if I have to die trying to find them."

In truth, Halloran wondered if either of the infants would ever be located, alive or dead, and if not how it would continue to haunt everyone involved. Mostly, he kept thinking of Sue Richardson, of how she would probably never get to hold her grandson, or how Bob would never get to take the boy fishing or teach him how to throw a baseball. How J. Daniel Jarvis would probably never watch his granddaughter grow into a young woman. Those were the thoughts that kept him awake at night, that needled at him every time he saw a report of another missing child.

But for now, he was attempting to live in the moment. The Christmas tree sparkled in the front window, and for the first time in years, he felt something other than disdain for the holidays. He'd helped them set it up and decorate it. He hadn't done that in years – not since before he'd moved away from his parents almost twenty years ago. He had to admit, he could get used to this family-man thing. The unresolved aspects of the Halpern case aside, Halloran's whole perspective on life had taken a different but pleasurable slant over the past few weeks. He wasn't sure where all this was headed, but he was damn sure enjoying the ride.

"What are you going to do while we're gone tonight?" he asked Trevor.

Trevor shrugged and pointed to the television where some teen-flavored cartoon blazed across the screen. "You're looking at it. Probably fire up the PlayStation later."

"Fun," Halloran said.

"You should play with me some time," Trevor told him. "It would be cool."

"You'd play with an old man?"

"You would be fun to beat," Trevor said.

"Right."

Kelly swept into the room wearing a cream-colored sweater glittering with gold accents. Her hair softly framed her face, just barely concealing the diamond earrings he'd given her as an early gift. Her eyes met his with warmth "Ready?"

Halloran stood and gave her a quick kiss on the cheek. "You look stunning."

She giggled. "'Stunning'? I think you've been watching too many Christmas movies on the Hallmark Channel." She looked at Trevor. "We'll be at Whiskey Fish with Greg and Diane, but if you need anything, call my cell."

"I'll be all right," Trevor said, his gaze fixed on the TV.

"Keep the doors locked. Don't let anyone in."

Trevor rolled his eyes. "Mom."

Halloran ushered her toward the front door. "He'll be fine, Kelly. The kid's fine. He's practically a man."

He glance back at Trevor and caught his eye. Trevor

smiled and Halloran gave him a wink.

"You guys have fun," Trevor told them.

* * *

5:25 PM

"Let me see that baby!"

Joel and Dana had just stepped into Frank and Bon-nie's house and Bonnie descended on them like a hawk. Joel barely had time to set the carrier on the floor before Bonnie was unbuckling Sofia from it. "How is Grandma's little girl?" she cooed.

Joel and Dana exchanged a glance, and Dana bit her lip to keep from laughing.

"You guys need any help with anything?" Frank said, raising up in the recliner and folding his newspaper.

"Still got the gifts out in the car," Dana told him.

"I'll get them," Frank volunteered.

"They're in the trunk," Joel said. "I'll help."

Outside in the twilight, they made their way down the steps to Dana's car. It was a Honda Pilot, bought to replace the Corolla they'd totaled in October. Joel popped the rear hatch, and Frank laid a hand on his shoulder. "I wanted a chance to talk to you alone," he said.

"Sure," Joel said. "What's up?"

Frank's eyes grew round with concern in the deepening darkness. "How is she?"

"Dana?"

"Yeah. She seems fine, but. . . " Frank looked away. "I'm sure you know how she builds that wall in her head. She doesn't want her mother or me or anyone to see what's really going on in there."

Joel nodded. "Don't I know it." He grabbed two wrapped packages and placed them in Frank's outstretched hands. "She's okay. Keeping busy with the baby has helped."

He was not going to tell Frank that for the two weeks following the incident until Sofia was born Dana woke nearly every night screaming and shaking uncontrollably, no doubt reliving the nightmare in which that demented creature slashed his own throat in front of her. How, even after they'd hired a cleaning team to come in and mop up the blood, after they'd had new carpet installed to cover the dark stains on the hardwood that could never be scrubbed away, Dana refused to sleep in their own bed for a month. How she'd refused to even go into that room until after Sofia came home. There were just some things that Frank didn't need to know.

"Bonnie and I were really worried for a while. You know, she doesn't tell us stuff like she used to before you two got married."

"I know." Joel grabbed the last two packages and slammed the hatch closed.

"Just part of your kid growing up and moving

away." He winked at Joel. "You'll know about it one day."

Joel nodded. "Yeah, I'm sure."

"Anyway," Frank said, "I'm glad she's got you. You know you're my favorite son-in-law."

Joel laughed. "Yes."

He followed Frank back into the house. Dana and Bonnie sat in the living room. Bonnie was still fussing with Sofia, and Sofia stared at her quietly, her expression a mixture of fascination and bewilderment. Joel sank onto the sofa beside Dana, and Dana reached over and took his hand, then rested her head on his shoulder.

For an instant, Dana let him into her thoughts, and he felt her contentment, her overwhelming love, her complete joy in this moment, and then the portal closed and he was left with only the warmth of her beside him, the feel of her hand clasped in his, the scent of her hair and the touch of her forehead against his cheek. But that was enough. Whatever the future held for the three of them, they would be ready.

It was a vision as clear as any he had ever experienced.

ACKNOWLEDGEMENTS

This was a book several years in the making, and was an answer to you many readers who asked for a sequel to *The Killing Vision*. Thanks to you for spurring me to continue the saga of Joel and Dana and Halloran. I'd also like to thank Tracy Overby and Jonathan Lambert for their editing skills and eagle eyes that can spot a misplaced comma, erroneous article, or mistakenly parked car from a mile away. Writing can be a solitary profession, but publishing is never a one-man show, and this one was no exception.

W.D.O.
Owensboro, Kentucky
February 19, 2018

ABOUT THE AUTHOR

Award-winning author and sometime banker Will Overby has spent over thirty years in the boardrooms and glass offices of retail banking. Between dodging mergers and drafting policies he publishes novels.

He lives along the Ohio River in western Kentucky where mysteries still abound and the tradition of story-telling is as strong as ever.

A graduate of Indiana University, Will is an avid Hoosiers football fan.

Connect with him on his website, willoverby.com, on Facebook, or follow him on Twitter (@Will_Overby).